Also by W

The Violet Hour
The first chapter of Harlow's story.

THE
CRIMSON
GATE

THE CRIMSON GATE

Whitney A. Miller

flux
Woodbury, Minnesota

First Edition
First Printing, 2015

Book design by Bob Gaul
Cover design by Lisa Novak
Cover image: 180245288/©Frances Taylor/Getty Images

Flux, an imprint of Llewellyn Worldwide Ltd.

Library of Congress Cataloging-in-Publication Data
Miller, Whitney A.
   The crimson gate/Whitney A. Miller.—First edition.
      pages cm
   Sequel to: The Violet Hour.
   Summary: Harlow Wintergreen, now the new Matriarch of VisionCrest, the powerful religious organization previously led by her father, is trapped inside a Cambodian temple, but she must escape and thwart her double, the evil Isiris, who is masquerading as Harlow in order to bring disease and destruction to the world.
   ISBN 978-0-7387-4204-5
   [1. Cults—Fiction. 2. Visions—Fiction. 3. Supernatural—Fiction. 4. Love—Fiction. 5. Horror stories.] I. Title.
   PZ7.M63913Cr 2015
   [Fic]—dc23

                                                                    2014041552

                                   Flux
                       Llewellyn Worldwide Ltd.
                          2143 Wooddale Drive
                       Woodbury, MN 55125-2989
                            www.fluxnow.com

                  Printed in the United States of America

For Marsha and Lonnie, aka Mom and Dad.
You believe in me, so I believe in myself.

AFTER: CAMBODIAN JUNGLE

Before. After. Before. After.

Before: trapped in the temple. After: escaped from the temple.

Me, the real Harlow Wintergreen, precariously balanced on the razor's edge between before and after.

I ran. Sprinted from the crimson gate into the outstretched arms of the jungle. Red-fire fear burning in my belly. Teeth aching in time with the *pound-pound-pound* of unsteady feet on unsteady bones. Through the barbed-wire brambles and the sticky-hot certainty of what was coming if I didn't, I ran.

It wasn't what I expected freedom to feel like.

I had no idea how much time had passed on the outside since I'd first become trapped in the temple. Just as my eyes had once been Isiris's windows to the world, her eyes had shown me many things, those days and nights in my prison. But not everything. Not enough.

The jungle remained unchanged, the eerie purple-green glow of it just the same as it was during that Violet Hour when Adam and I first entered Isiris's nightmare.

The Violet Hour. It was sacred to devotees of Vision-Crest, the religion my father had created (or so I used to believe). Those violet, pre-dawn moments were supposed to bring us close to the all-knowing, all-seeing Inner Eye. Now that I knew it was real, I also knew it wasn't sacred. It was sinister.

When I look at her, I still see you, he'd said. *There's only one way to end it now. Maybe that will be enough.*

Adam. The boy I'd always loved. The boy I still loved. The boy who'd betrayed me, once upon a time. The thought of him propelled my body and mind forward relentlessly. I felt my way by instinct, hoping that I was rushing toward redemption and not oblivion. Hoping that it wasn't too late for him. Or me.

I ran.

Finally, when the sun was bloated in the sky, a break in the canopy appeared. The clearing. I remembered the last time I stood there, side-by-side with Adam. Back then, I was convinced I could stop Isiris from unleashing a virus meant to purify the world. She'd said my father had failed her as a leader, corrupting her religion by re-interpreting its gospel. Back then, I believed I could stop her. I wished I could tell that version of myself everything that was going to come after—that my misguided actions were going to make things worse, not better. But that version of me, that Harlow, was gone forever.

I broke free of the jungle's last tangled embrace, emerging into open air. I fell, my legs giving way to exhaustion. My hand rose to shield my unfocused eyes from the blaring brightness of the sun. My palm was crusted red-brown with blood from the deep gash across its center. I flexed my fingers, examining them like foreign objects. I was here. Back in the world—*my* world. Isiris hadn't taken that away from me; at least, not yet.

Reality swam out of focus as a wave of nausea swept over me. I clawed my way toward a copse of shaded grass, dry heaving the nonexistent contents of my stomach along the way. My hunger had returned, and my thirst—I needed to find water and something to eat or my escape would be short-lived, literally. I knew where I had to go, but right now I didn't have the strength to take another step. I collapsed, sunlight striping through the leaves overhead.

My mind turned once again to the last words Adam had said to me—the last thing I'd experienced through Isiris's eyes while still trapped in the temple. *It might already be too late*, his words echoed.

A constellation of pinprick stars swam across my vision, and the bright white world went black.

BEFORE:
TRAPPED IN THE TEMPLE

A light blinded me from overhead and the sound of beating wings filled the air. A thousand doors flew open. Wind pulled at my hair.

A high-pitched keening filled my ears; it took me a moment to recognize it as my own voice, screaming my throat raw. Not recognizing the sound of your own voice—that must fulfill at least one of the criteria on the "Have you gone crazy?" checklist.

An eternity seemed to pass. Finally the light went out and the doors slammed shut. Another Violet Hour come and gone.

My memory was murky. I faded in and out of consciousness, my head pounding from the fall I'd taken off the altar in the flurry of my final confrontation with Isiris and her eyeless followers. Every time I lost the thread of consciousness, I saw Adam and Dora and Stubin; I saw VisionCrest headquarters and my family home. It was as if I was seeing home-movies of my life, but through Isiris's eyes. I wasn't sure if what I was seeing was real, or a side-effect of the head injury my throbbing skull said I'd sustained. All the while, the Violet Hour—when the temple doors opened and untethered souls waited to be ferried to new worlds and realities—came and went, came and went.

Finally, my eyes blinked open. For the first time, my surroundings came fully into focus. The throbbing at the back of my skull tamed to a dull ache. My senses felt sharper. I turned my head, my neck rolling against the textured stones beneath me. Everything was still. All around me, lost souls huddled on the periphery of the temple. Their constant murmurs fell silent.

I moaned, my body rocking against the stone floor. I felt like Sleeping Beauty shaking loose the stitches of a thousand-year slumber, my muscles and mind atrophied. Wraiths scattered as I sat up, bunching back together in a quivering heap as far away from me as they could manage.

"I won't ... I won't hurt you," I croaked. *I come in peace* just sounded too cliché, but then again, lost souls probably didn't see a lot of movies.

I was trapped inside the temple. It might have only been one day since Adam had fled the temple with Isiris in tow, thinking she was me, or it might have been twenty.

Sooner or later, I would have to shepherd those wayward spirits through the doors. For better or worse, I was the Guardian of the temple now. If I didn't do it, they would become something fearful—like the eyeless hordes that still lurked here somewhere. It was impossible to know what other consequences there might be.

My head pounded and I reached up, fingers weaving through my matted hair to probe the tender knot. Even though my throat scratched like I'd swallowed the Sahara, I didn't feel ravenous for food or water like I should have; I felt hollow.

Pushing my palms against the floor, I managed to get unsteadily to my feet. A dull ache pulsed along the length of my spine, but somewhere deep inside of me, a tiny spark of will ignited. If there was a way out of here, I was going to find it. I had to—being stuck here was untenable. It made me almost feel sorry for Isiris, or at least empathize with what had made her the way she was. But I wasn't going to let her steal my life; God—or whoever was in charge around here—only knew what she planned to do with it. And I was sure it didn't involve kitten kisses and rainbows.

My eyes swept the room, the familiar details of the temple blinking into focus. Doors, doors, doors, up the cylindrical wall, down the passages. Behind me, the altar. I walked shakily over to its stairs, bending down to crawl up them on my hands and knees, not yet trusting my balance to hold. When I reached the top, I had to bite down on my lip to keep from crying—I couldn't let tears flow, as they might never stop. The altar's surface was covered in blood, dried blackish-brown at the edges and tacky in the center.

So I hadn't been unconscious as long as I'd feared—only a few days must have passed since Adam escaped with Isiris, even if it felt like a hundred. Somehow the thought of Adam being here in this room so recently made everything worse. If I could turn back the clock just the tiniest bit, it would be me out there in the world with Adam while Isiris was trapped in here, where she belonged. Tears came despite my best effort.

If I didn't find a way out, it was worse than a death sentence. There were infinite different worlds beyond the doors of this temple, but Isiris had chosen to enter mine. As the Matriarch of VisionCrest—as *me*—she was going to dismantle my world, piece by piece. Not to mention what she might do to the people I cared about—Adam, Dora, Stubin.

Still, it was the virus that terrified beyond measure. Isiris was going to remake my world in her image.

The last time I'd been up on this altar, Adam was holding a knife held to his own chest, Isiris controlling his actions with her mind. The knife, plunging in. The blood, spilling onto the floor.

I was glad Adam had made it out. It meant he might be okay.

Through my blur of tears I noticed a handprint, pressed into a pool of still-sticky blood. I wiped my cheeks with my tattered cardigan and leaned over to inspect it. It was the exact size of my hand, only mine was clean. I let my hand hover over it—a perfect match. It belonged to Isiris.

Something tugged at the back of my mind, like this detail was important somehow. I had to admit what I already knew to be true—Isiris was on the outside, pretending to be me. Nobody was coming to save me. I had to save myself.

My mind turned to the visions I'd been having when I was unconscious. The glimpses of my life.

———————

Adam's voice murmured in my ear, close yet painfully far away as he held me in his arms. We were in a hospital room—the steady beeping of machines like white noise in the background.

"Isiris is trapped in her house of a thousand doors, exactly where she belongs. And she's never getting out."

The real Harlow—me, the one trapped in the temple, yet also trapped inside of Isiris's mind—wanted to grab him, scream at him, tell him he had it all wrong. But I was paralyzed. Powerless.

"What about the Resistance?" Isiris asked, pretending to be me. She knew that even with me out of the way, she still had to worry about the underground group that had been fighting against her ever since she and her puppet, Sacristan Wang, had begun the process of overthrowing my father.

Adam's jaw clenched. I knew he was thinking about Hayes Cantor, wondering if he still had to compete for my affections with the young leader of the Resistance.

"They sent a delegation to bring Dora and Stubin home," he said. "They're here, ready to meet with you as soon as you're up for it."

Relief blossomed inside me. My best friend and her boyfriend were alive and safe, at least for now.

"Oh, I'm up for it," Isiris answered with false cheer. "I'm looking forward to extending my gratitude for all they did to subvert Isiris."

In the mirror, her pinky and ring finger curved down behind Adam's back, the other three fingers forming the symbol that was her signature. Her cracked lips curled into a sneer. I wondered if it was a message to me. Did she know I was entombed inside her, watching and helpless?

Adam's arms tightened around me. "I was kind of hoping to express my gratitude to you first," he said.

I could practically feel the jealousy radiating off him. Clouding his judgment. Keeping him from realizing that the girl in front of him wasn't me. His lips brushed against the sensitive spot on my neck, just below my ear. A kiss that used to send tingles down my arms.

Now it was Isiris who leaned in to his touch. She tilted her face up to Adam's.

"Oh, don't worry. I'll let you make it up to me."

Adam smiled. He thought he knew what she meant, but he didn't. Trapped inside her, I knew. She was going to hurt him.

A tidal wave of dread washed over me. I tried to make my arms beat against his chest, force my voice to find the words to warn him.

But nothing happened. Adam leaned down and kissed Isiris's waiting lips while hope withered in my chest.

———

They weren't just dreams. They were real. I could almost see and touch every emotion, every sensation ... but not quite. Sleep, it seemed, was a psychic window that let me peer into Isiris's life—*my* life, the one she'd stolen—the way she used to peer into mine. It was maddening, yet at the same time it was like a drug. Sleep tugged, beckoned, and I couldn't help but peep through the window.

Maybe this frustrated existence—always seeing, never being—was what had made Isiris who she was. Ruthless. Insane.

At that moment, though, I didn't really care. All I wanted was to crawl back into my life. I lay down on the altar, next to the pool of blood, curled up, and allowed myself to escape into unconsciousness.

AFTER:
BÊN TRONG MẮT, VIETNAM

The flat-bottom boat hushed through the glassy water, fish guts sloshing over my feet. Great. The fisherman scrutinized my half-covered face, and I pulled the thin fabric I'd stolen from a street vendor in Hoi An tighter. As a convenient bonus, the veil obscured the smell of rotting fish while also protecting me from his curious stare.

My ears strained for any sound, hoping against hope that I might hear the three-toned whistle of the Resistance pierce the crisp morning air. It was a huge risk coming back to Vietnam, back to the Resistance, but it was the only way to discover what came next. Hayes Cantor, de facto leader of the group, was the only person I could trust right now—if he was still alive.

I knew that Hayes had suspected my psychic connection with Isiris, courtesy of Madam Wang, when I was last at the Resistance's island hideaway. Now the Sacristan's wife was dead—hung from the Gate of Heavenly Peace by her husband—and I had no idea what had become of their daughter Mei Mei, who I'd last seen at the Bên Trong Mắt compound before escaping to confront Isiris. Going back to the Resistance outpost was my only chance to find Hayes, or at least get a clue as to where he might have gone.

Thinking of him, my pulse quickened. I could still smell that beach. Remember the way the sun glinted gold in his warm brown eyes. See the shape of his lips and feel their lush warmth against mine. But the intimate moment we'd shared wasn't why I was here; I wasn't living out the fantasy of a schoolgirl crush or imagining I might one day live in the Barbie Dreamhouse. I was fighting for survival—mine, Adam's—and I needed Hayes's help.

I'd gotten this far by begging and stealing my way from Cambodia to Vietnam, plus a generous helping of luck, but the thing about luck is that it always runs out. Fortune was my frenemy. My feet were covered in blisters and I was weak with malnutrition. I'd spent my last stolen coin convincing this fisherman to take me out to Bên Trong Mắt, even though I knew I wouldn't find anyone there. I was chasing ghosts—dreams from the temple—just hoping to find a clue.

Off in the distance, amongst the trees and the mist of the January morning, I got a peek-a-boo glimpse of the compound.

"You can let me off here," I said, motioning to the water's edge. A thin strip of sand edged the jungle. The weathered old man with deeply suspicious eyes frowned, then said a few words; apparently we were still pretending I had a clue what he was saying. For a moment I thought he was going to ignore me and keep going, but then he edged his paddle against the water and steered us into shore.

I wobbled out of the boat and turned to watch him go, keeping my veil tight across my face. I couldn't risk being recognized. He said something unintelligible that sounded like well wishes or some kind of benediction. Then he pushed back from the shore, disappearing into the rising sun on the flat horizon.

I started walking. The thin stretch of beach opened up into a full beachfront, the buildings of the Resistance outpost obscured behind thick jungle foliage, visible only to those who knew how to look for it.

The sun was punishingly hot and it was barely past dawn. I happened upon the last place I'd spoken to Hayes—not that we'd really done that much talking. I thought of his lips, his body pressed against mine; the sound of Adam's sharp intake of breath when he'd discovered us. The memory made me hot with shame.

What was I doing here? Could I really trust what I'd seen through Isiris's eyes to lead me in the right direction? Maybe Isiris was manipulating me again. Tormenting me, same as always.

There was only one way to find out. It wasn't like I had an all-you-can-eat buffet of options.

I hurried my way up the beach, sticking close to the trees and trying to be silent. A few minutes later I was almost to the compound. It was dangerous to be here—if any of the Vision-Crest Watchers were around, or even if any rebels remained, they would shoot first and ask questions later. But I had no choice—the one time I'd seen Hayes through Isiris's eyes, I'd been sure he was telling me to come here. Sure he was hinting that he'd left a clue here as to how I could find him and the Resistance.

Before we'd kissed, that day on this beach, he'd told me that his first mission was to keep me safe. I only hoped he'd been able to do the same for himself, escaping the island before Isiris's orders were carried out.

As I reach the pathway that led to the compound, I saw that someone had drawn a giant eye—closed, with a tear forming at its corner—in the otherwise undisturbed sand. It was crumbled and windblown.

I picked my way up the winding pathway, sand giving way to jungle. The path was overgrown, reclaimed by nature. I ached to know where Dora was—I hadn't seen her since we were last here, except through Isiris's eyes. And that hadn't been pretty. I needed to find her alive and well, and tell her that I was okay.

But I couldn't think about that now. First things first.

The sound of the jungle coming alive—the low hum of insects, mingled with the squawking of eight kinds of birds and the howl of an occasional monkey—obscured the shuffle of my feet. As I rounded a bend in the path, the first building came into view. The wooden shutters were all flung open, as were the doors, and I could see that inside, an electric fan was still rotating at high speed on the ceiling. All was silent—there was no telltale hum of life. Before, the place had been bustling with people coordinating Resistance activities, all hours of the day and night.

I told myself that this was merely confirmation of what I already knew—that the VisionCrest Watchers had attacked this base, on Isiris's orders, and done who-knows-what to the people living here. It meant the clues I'd picked up in my visions could actually be true as well.

That didn't stop the emptiness of the place from hitting me like a suckerpunch. My mind was filled with too much death and destruction already; I wasn't ready for what might lie beyond this threshold.

BEFORE:
TRAPPED IN THE TEMPLE,
DREAMING OF ISIRIS

Hayes entered the office, flanked by four burly-looking guards and a small phalanx of rebels. His face betrayed no emotion. He looked less boyish, more handsome than he had when I'd last seen him standing on the docks in Hoi An as Adam and I made our escape. He had a sidearm strapped to his belt, and his shoulders were broader than I remembered. An air of authority surrounded him, like he'd finally grown into his position as leader of the Resistance. I hoped he still would be after this encounter.

Isiris tapped one finger, over and over, on the massive oak desk. It graced the center of my father's former office in our compound in Twin Falls, Idaho.

Tap-tap-tap-tap-tap.

Adam leaned against the bookcase behind her, his eyes boring into Hayes with hatred. Adam still saw Hayes as a rival instead of what Hayes really was—his only hope for survival.

"It's so good to see you, Harlow," Hayes said, his eyes searching a bit, as if there was something about me that was different but he couldn't quite put his finger on it. He walked nearer, lowering his voice and giving Isiris a meaningful glance. "I'm glad you're okay. I wish I could have been there to help."

Adam cleared his throat uncomfortably, his eyes cutting to me and then back to Hayes, trying to assess the status of our relationship. From the intensity of Hayes's stare at Isiris, it seemed he was too. In fact, it seemed like it was obvious to everyone but Isiris herself that there was something between us.

Irritation pumped through Isiris's veins. The tapping of her finger slowed, then stopped.

"It's Matriarch now, actually. And I didn't need your help," she said, looking over at Adam.

Her words chilled and heartened me at the same time. Isiris sounded nothing like me. Surely someone would notice that.

Hayes's demeanor changed instantly—he stood up straighter and his shoulders squared. Hope thrived within me. Maybe there was one person who knew me well enough to see that Isiris was an imposter. If Dora were here, she would know immediately; I hoped, however, that she was somewhere safely out of Isiris's grasp.

"Matriarch?" Hayes's voice was icy. "You completed the Rites?"

"We initiated ourselves," Adam broke in, stepping forward to hover behind Isiris's shoulder. The gesture clearly communicated what was unspoken—that Adam and Isiris were united against Hayes, the enemy. "The Fellowship needs its leaders."

Hayes ignored Adam, his eyes steady on Isiris's the entire time.

"I've been worried about you, ever since—well, ever since the last time we were together."

He scrutinized Isiris for any reaction. I knew he was thinking about the kiss.

"But," he added, "I'm sure you didn't bring me all this way to talk about that."

"You're here because it's time for you and your fighters to lay down your arms," Isiris answered. She hadn't picked up on the subtext—she couldn't, because she hadn't been hiding inside my mind that day on the beach at Bên Trong Mắt.

"You're not a big fan of boundary crossing, as I recall," Hayes pressed.

"On the contrary," she responded. "I find it's quite effective."

Again, Isiris didn't get the reference—it was something only Hayes and I would know. A spark of something like understanding flashed in Hayes's eyes. His jaw clenched.

I could see what Isiris couldn't—Hayes knew, even if on some subconscious, visceral level. Deep down, he sensed that Isiris wasn't me, and it wouldn't be long before he worked that out in his conscious mind. If I could have jumped for joy in my paralyzed state, I would have thrown a freaking jump-for-joy party.

"We will require time to disband things," he said, a subtle formality creeping into his speech.

Isiris waved her hand. "Of course. But we need you back right away. The Fellowship needs you. I was thinking we might make you Eparch, as well—no reason we should only have one. Right, Adam?" I could feel her lips stretch into what passed for a smile. Adam stiffened in protest but didn't say a word.

"As your second, that would be so fitting, and such an honor," Hayes said.

Every VisionCrest devotee received a spiritual mentor, called a "second," and Hayes was mine. And while every member of the Fellowship knew what a second was, the look on Isiris's face said she did not.

"My second?" she asked, confused.

Hayes's eyes darkened a shade. I wasn't imagining it. He was testing her.

"You never told me that," Adam said.

I'd never told Adam partially because I'd always hoped my second would be Adam, and partially because that bond with Hayes was a secret I wanted to keep for myself.

"I didn't think it was important," Isiris said, not bothering to look at Adam.

But a storm was gathering within her, I could feel it. She'd realized that Hayes's questions weren't as innocent as they seemed. He needed to get out of there before it was too late. If it wasn't already.

"Well, then. I'd better get going, so that I can return as quickly as possible. If it's all right with you of course, Matriarch." Hayes laced the title with irony. The calm expression he'd walked in with was replaced by something manufactured. No one seemed to notice.

Then Hayes winked at Isiris, and I felt a little thrill run through her. Her vanity was her Achilles' heel. I needed to find a way to use it against her.

"I'll expect you back within the week," she said. "Your Rites must be performed as soon as possible and every day is precious, don't you agree?"

"I do." Hayes nodded.

"Adam, do you mind showing Brother Cantor out?" Isiris's voice was syrupy sweet. Adam moved reluctantly to the door and held it open.

Hayes turned to go, his entourage following. He paused at the threshold. "Speaking of precious, I almost forgot." He turned and leveled his gaze at her. "You left the gift I gave you behind. It's at Bên Trong Mắt. Don't worry, I put it in the library for safekeeping—one great deserves another."

This had to be a clue. Hayes hadn't given me a gift when we were together on the island, unless you counted that one glorious kiss. And the meaningful look in his eyes hinted at a message. Did he really know I was in here?

Isiris tossed her hair over her shoulder. I sensed her moment of hesitation as she tried to navigate yet another blind spot. There were so many things she didn't know about being me, so many opportunities to give herself away.

"Of course," she said. "I look forward to having it back."

Hayes's eyebrows fell together almost imperceptibly, and his jaw set. I could see it written plainly in his face—he knew that Isiris wasn't me. He knew.

He looked over Isiris's shoulder at Adam, who just stared back, stone-faced. Then his gaze returned to Isiris. "I'll keep it safe for you. I find that when I feel lost, it's the little things that help me find my way."

Hayes was telling me how to find him. Then he and his phalanx of Resistance fighters swept out the door.

"The little things," Adam scoffed. "That guy is such a pretentious ass. You're not actually planning to make him Eparch, are you?"

He looked so lost. He needed to find his way too, and I couldn't help him.

Isiris looked up at Adam. "You don't have anything to worry about. No one will ever replace you," she said.

He leaned down and kissed her, his warm mouth pressing against hers. A fist of grief lodged in my chest. It was one thing to know the boy you loved was kissing someone else; it was far worse to see him do it. But to actually experience it firsthand? That was being buried alive.

The kiss ended, and something else rose within me as Isiris trailed her fingers down Adam's cheek.

Fury.

I would find a way to crush her. To take back everything that was mine.

"Do me a favor and make sure they get off okay?" Isiris murmured.

Adam's brows knit together, but he nodded reluctantly.

When the door shut behind him, Isiris's voice was glacial. She turned to the nearest Watcher.

"When Hayes Cantor returns to the Resistance base, I want you to exterminate every last one of them."

AFTER:
BÊN TRONG MẮT, VIETNAM

I stepped across the threshold, startling a needle-thin dog.

"Hey! Come back!" I called. His nails scratched across the teak floor as he made his escape.

The building respirated emptiness. My heart ached. Even a mangy stray would do at this point; beggars couldn't be choosers. Objects were strewn about in various states of mid-use, indicating that if the Resistance had evacuated, they'd done it in a hurry.

I thought of what Hayes had said in my vision: *"You left the gift I gave you behind. It's at Bên Trong Mắt. Don't worry, I put it in the library for safekeeping—one great deserves another."*

That statement was my bread crumb, my only hope of finding Hayes. I didn't have anywhere else to go—any other trail to follow. I'd seen a lot of things through Isiris's eyes, but weaving the bits and pieces into something meaningful was challenging. This was the starting point. I hoped.

As I walked farther into the building, I heard classical music filtering through a scratchy intercom system. Despite the torpid head, a chill ran down my arms. I made my way down the hallway. A table was set for a meal that had long-since been carried away by the island's wildlife. Life, interrupted. Everyone had vanished into thin air.

I exited and picked my way through the maze of buildings, searching for the library. At every turn, I expected to encounter the worst—blood, bodies, signs of a struggle. Evidence that Isiris had made good on her promise to exterminate the Resistance. But there was nothing except the eerie sense that the people I'd met here had suddenly dropped everything and gone... somewhere. A tingly foreboding circled my stomach.

Finally I came to the last building—the house where Dora, Stubin, and I had stayed. Not knowing what Isiris had done with my friends was the worst kind of torture. It propelled me forward, even though every fiber of my being told me to turn and run.

Inside, I made my way up a wooden staircase, every creak making my pulse race. There was a thickness to the air in the house that felt different—an odd weight of something lurking just out of reach. It occurred to me that this might be some kind of trap, or maybe a few Watchers had been left behind to gather any stragglers that returned to base. It suddenly seemed colossally stupid to be poking around here unarmed. Not that I had a lot of alternatives. I tiptoed my way up the last few stairs and held my breath at the top.

The silence up here was deafening. I crept down the

hallway, trying not to make a sound, and passed by the room I'd stayed in. I examined myself in the mirror that Isiris had once used to summon me. I tried not to think about how it had felt when she'd invaded my mind—back when she was trapped in the temple and I was just a semi-normal girl. Back when she used to whisper to me and make me see horrible things. I was terrified that she might realize I'd escaped the temple and try to invade me once again, if that was even possible; I hadn't seen anything through Isiris's eyes since escaping the temple.

I moved farther down the hallway, passing the closed door to Dora's room. All I wanted to do was locate the library and get the heck out of here. There was one last door at the end of the hall—it was literally the last possible place in the entire damn compound. It was ajar. I wasn't looking forward to pushing it open; I had no idea what lay on the other side, in the quiet unquiet. I put my hand against it.

Silence.

I pushed gently, and it swung open with a *scriiich*.

When Hayes said "library," he wasn't joking around. Wall-to-wall books towered over me, floor-to-ceiling, with rolling ladders to provide access to the upper shelves. My eyes swept the room, which felt devoid of living things. Then a flutter of wings made me jump as a bird winged its way through the room and out an open window.

I scanned the shelves, looking for anything that seemed out of place. Weirdly, the books were alphabetized by title: A's at the tippy-top, just below the ceiling, Z's on the bottom, lining the floor. *One great deserves another.* Great what? Great kisser? Ha. Great leader? Doubtful.

Because the universe clearly hated me, I figured whatever I was looking for was probably shelved near the top. I grabbed ahold of the nearest ladder and gingerly made my way to the top, rocking unsteadily on the rollers. I moved my way methodically across the shelves, running my fingers across the spines of a thousand books.

My back was aching and my stomach grumbling, sweat dripping down my temples, before I found it. Second shelf from the top, tilted out at an angle as if someone had meant for it to be noticed. Maybe I wasn't crazy; maybe Hayes really wanted me to find this. A flood of warmth filled me—hope. The universe was finally tossing me a bone.

Catherine the Great, the title said when I pulled the thick tome from its snug perch. Yes: *One great deserves another.* There was a delicate drawing of the Winter Palace in St. Petersburg, blanketed in snow, on its cover. I suppressed the urge to break out into ecstatic giggles as I flipped through the pages of the biography, looking for a note or a clue.

My search had me so absorbed that it took me a second to register the rocking of the ladder as it was kicked out from under me. I plummeted to the floor. My attacker pinned me from behind, a knee driving into my back and a hand pressing down so hard on my neck I was already seeing stars.

So much for that bone.

———

"If you so much as blink, I'll drive this knife between your shoulder blades and pin you to the floor," a girl's voice said.

All I could do was lie there, hands spread out on the floor, trying to push back on her weight just a millimeter so I could breathe. Hopefully she wouldn't count that as blinking. I would have felt relieved that she wasn't a Watcher if I didn't suspect that whoever she was, she was just as savage.

"Who are you?" she demanded, grinding her knee deeper into my spine. "What are you doing here?"

"*Gluuurg.*" A strangled choking sound was all I managed. If she didn't ease up soon, this was going to be a very short conversation.

I felt the tip of what I could only assume was the knife poke against the skin just behind my ear.

"Answer me or I drive this into your skull," she threatened.

I managed to turn my head far enough that my trachea wasn't being smashed into the floor, then eked out "Harlow."

"How do you know about this place?" she asked.

"Hayes," I wheezed. "Hayes Cantor."

She jumped off me as if I'd turned into a bed of hot coals. I writhed on the floor, coughing and trying to catch my breath.

"Oh my god. It's you," she said, gaping at me from above. An intimidating kitchen knife hung from her now-limp hand. "You're Harlow Wintergreen."

The relief in her voice told me she wasn't my enemy. I put my hands up to signal that I wasn't a threat. "And you are ... ?"

She just stared at me.

I was now getting a good look at my assailant, from the ground up. She was barefoot. Flamingo-legged. Scabby-kneed. Dirty. In tattered shorts, with ripped tights and a Ramones T-shirt (awesome). Big black headphones looped around her neck, the cord dangling inexplicably toward the floor. She was my age, maybe younger. Blue-eyed. Hazel-eyed (one of each? weird). Blond-haired. Ponytailed.

In other words, definitely not from around here. And except for the assault and battery thing, probably my kind of girl.

"Your T-shirt kicks ass," I said, wary that any moment she might remember the knife and decide to use it.

"You were here before," she said, refusing to be taken in by my compliment. "Last year."

Last *year*? I'd marked the days inside the temple by scratching tick marks against the wall with a jagged-edged stone. When I escaped, there were thirty-two, not counting the who-knows-how-long I was gone when I went through the not-mine doors and—I suppressed a shudder. I didn't want to think about one of those gates.

"Well? It's you, right? Her Majesty, Queen of Vision-Crest?" the girl demanded.

I nodded. Her multi-colored eyes sparkled with glee, liked she'd just cracked the code to Ancient Sumerian instead of identified one of the most well-known figures in the modern world.

"What are you doing creeping around here?" she continued. "Shouldn't you be running your evil empire?" Her fingers flexed around the handle of the knife. I could see the wheels turning behind her eyes as she tried to make it all add up.

This "getting to know you" moment didn't seem ripe for an evil twin sob story. I'd save that for later, assuming she didn't turn me into skewers à la Wintergreen first.

"I came back to find Hayes," I said. "Do you know where he is?"

Her chin tilted up. "If I did, I wouldn't tell anyone. Especially not you."

"How long have you been out here on your own?" I asked, changing the subject.

She shrugged, the bony points of her shoulders visible through her baggy shirt. Her pursed lips were her only answer.

"Are you keeping watch for him or something?" I asked, even though it was absurd to think Hayes would leave this scrawny hellion in charge of anything. No, she looked more like something accidentally forgotten. Left behind.

"Stop asking questions. You don't ask the questions," she said, annoyed. I'd apparently found her big red button, but now wasn't the time to keep pressing it.

"I'm going to stand up now. I don't have any weapons, but you're welcome to check for yourself."

The girl backed up a step but didn't protest. I got to my feet, my eyes cutting to *Catherine the Great* splayed out on the floor across the room. Her freaky eyes flickered over to it, following mine.

"If you're here to find Hayes, what are you doing poking around in the library?" she asked. "And don't tell me it's because you were low on reading material."

I laughed a little, despite the situation. Even though she had a much tougher edge, something about this girl's moxie made me think of Dora. Those two would definitely hit it off. My heart squeezed, thinking of my best friend.

The girl's eyes narrowed and she lifted the knife out in front of her. I noticed that her arm was shaking. I took in her snarled ponytail and the hollow bruises of sleeplessness ringing her eyes. I recognized the signs because I'd so recently lived them. She'd obviously been hiding out in the jungle, and she was afraid.

"I was looking for *Catherine the Great*," I said, hoping she might miraculously understand the code.

She raised the knife a little higher—not the reaction I was looking for. But I saw a glimmer of recognition in her eye.

"I need your help," I continued. "And it looks to me like you could maybe use mine. I need to find Hayes and the Resistance. Based on the looks of you, I'm guessing you do too." It was a gamble.

"You don't know anything about what I need," she said. But there was a shimmer of something else—hope.

"I may have a clue about where to find them," I said. "But I need you to stop pointing that at me—being menaced by cutlery isn't when I do my best thinking."

The girl seemed to perk up at the idea of finding Hayes. She hesitated for a moment, then reached up to swat a mosquito off her neck. I could have rushed her and knocked the knife out of her hand, but it would be dangerous to underestimate her. Getting stabbed wasn't at the top of my to-do list.

"Okay," she agreed, lowering her arm back to her side.

"But if you so much as breathe too fast, I'll have no problem pinning your heart to the wall."

"I definitely prefer that you not do that. It would be great if you could do me a favor instead," I said, trying to sound calm.

She tilted her head. "A favor?"

"I'd really like to take a shower. I haven't had one in ... well, a year."

Her nose wrinkled.

"You smell."

"Thanks," I said.

"Your hair is a mess. You may just want to cut it off— those tangles aren't going to go quietly."

I smiled. "I don't want to cut it." I couldn't say why. Although the threat of being recognized was my greatest vulnerability, it felt consummately important that my identity remain intact.

The girl contemplated me for a moment, then lowered the knife.

"I'm Parker," she said, holding out her non-knife hand.

I shook it; the firmness of her grip was reassuring. "Nice to meet you, Parker."

"So how about that clue you mentioned?" she asked.

"Show me to the spa and I'll tell you all about it," I said. "Mind if I bring my reading material along?"

Her eyes went back to the book lying on the floor. She walked over and picked it up, tucking it into the baggy waist of her shorts. The girl knew how to maintain an advantage, I had to give her that.

"You first." She motioned out the door.

I tried not to dwell too much on Parker's knife at my back as we walked out the door.

BEFORE:
TRAPPED IN THE TEMPLE

The temple doors flew open. I was splayed out on the altar, the artificial sun beaming down from above and blinding me. Blurs of color streaked above my head as souls filled the air, the displacement of air sounding like the release of a thousand doves. I knew that I needed to ferry them—I'd been silently promising myself that I would start, but I couldn't yet bring myself to do it. All I wanted to do was sleep.

Next time, I kept thinking. Presiding over the Violet Hour would feel like I was entertaining the idea that I might stay here. Possibly forever. That realization made me feel hollow; a despair deeper and blacker than the most infinite abyss. It was worse than sadness—it was emptiness. And that was the first step to becoming as undone as Isiris.

When I'd first seen Isiris impersonating me in the hospital, she'd wrapped her arms around Adam like he was something to be possessed. But that vision didn't tell me anything useful, other than the fact that Isiris was impersonating me and I had grossly underestimated her. But this last vision—Isiris impersonating me in the General's office at VisionCrest headquarters—was something else entirely. It seemed Hayes was telling me something. Giving me a clue that I could use to find him if—scratch that, *when*—I got out.

Now that my fury had given way to purpose, I wanted to make Isiris wring her own neck. If I could learn how to channel my anger, maybe I could control her. I could make her give herself away, so Adam would realize the mistake he'd made and come back to release me. Maybe I could make her come and release me herself. At the least, maybe I could find a way to get myself out of here.

Maybe I was the queen of wishful thinking. Maybe this was my freaking ivory tower and not my prison. Right.

I thought of Hayes and the other Resistance members in Bên Trong Mắt. Hayes, whose soulful eyes might have actually been sending me a message. A message in a bottle.

Maybe maybe maybe.

Regardless, Hayes was probably under attack by Isiris's henchmen right at this very moment, or just about to be, and there wasn't anything I could do about it. I got to my feet and paced. Suddenly, I understood what people meant when they said they wanted to tear their hair out. I walked to the stone wall and pounded my arms against it, screaming until my throat was raw. The only answer was silence.

At my wit's end, I beelined down the altar stairs and headed for the nearest soul. I had to take some kind of action, and at the moment there was only one thing I could control. I'd seen Isiris shepherd the souls to their doorways once before, and I'd even helped one along myself, but I wasn't entirely sure how the whole thing worked. But I was so immersed in rage and frustration that I didn't stop to overanalyze it; I just knew what I was supposed to do. There wasn't much time left before the Violet Hour would be over. I needed to assert a tiny ounce of control over my life.

I motioned for the wraith to follow and headed up the ramp that spiraled around the inner cylinder of the temple, lined all the way with doors. Adam and I had ascended this ramp once before, when we'd finally met Isiris in the flesh. Back then, she was the one with souls huddled at her feet, flicking her three-fingered symbol toward different doorways, sending souls from this limbo into whatever life awaited them next. I forged up the ramp, examining each open doorway as I passed.

In my peripheral vision, I could see that the newer souls had drawn close, seeming to sense my fresh resolve. I worried that I'd neglected this so long, some of the older ones wouldn't be able to pass through, doomed to join Isiris's zombie followers who, I knew, must still be lurking somewhere in the deep, dark recesses of the temple. The only thing worse than no company was having an army of whatever-they-weres surrounding me.

I neared a doorway and felt a pull deep down inside of me, a little instinct that told me that this was the right door for the soul I'd chosen. On the other side of the door was a listless sky and weather-beaten buildings as far as the eye could see. Not exactly a cheery tableau, but I knew this was where this particular soul belonged. I hoped this place would treat it well, whatever became of it once it crossed over.

As dreary as the destination appeared, it had to be better than this nothing in-between. I made the three-fingered sign with my hand and took a deep breath. Then I flicked my wrist and the soul passed through the door, disappearing like vapor. I wondered if somewhere in that world, a baby was taking its first breath. The thought gave me comfort, and at the same time struck a chord of dread in my heart.

What would happen if I escaped and no one was here to shepherd souls?

There was some higher force at work within these walls. Bigger than Isiris and bigger than me. A balance that should not be disrupted. Surely there would be consequences, in my world and others, if it was.

I surveyed the trail of souls still shadowing behind me.

There would be time to contemplate all that later. Probably an eternity. Right now I had work to do.

AFTER:
BÊN TRONG MẮT, VIETNAM

"We have some serious work to do." Parker shoved a hand mirror up to my face with an artistic flourish. "There's probably a family of swallows living in that monstrosity."

I squirmed, and the uneven-legged chair wobbled beneath me. I patted the sides of my newly clean hair as if it were some sort of foreign object. Parker was right, it was a snarled mess. We might have to resort to scissors after all.

At least the kitchen knife was now stuffed in the back pocket of Parker's cutoffs, although the point of the blade poked through a hole in the bottom as if to taunt me.

I blinked at my reflection, both strange and familiar. I couldn't help but see glimpses of Isiris. But I was changed, too. The girl in the mirror wasn't the same Harlow who'd entered the temple.

"Ready for the grand finale?" Parker asked, bouncing gleefully as she snatched the mirror away.

"As ready as I'll ever be," I said.

"Tip your head back and woman up. This is gonna hurt."

I tilted my neck back and saw Parker's purse-lipped grin hovering over me. Maybe it was the social deprivation, but she was enjoying this little project way too much. An economy-size hairbrush swung into view.

"I can't be held responsible for lost or damaged hair follicles," Parker warned.

I winced as she tore into the first clump; my hair felt like it was being pulled out by the roots.

I tugged at the hem of the ratty T-shirt I'd found in one of the bedroom dressers, bracing against the pain. I was pretty sure the room I'd showered in had belonged to Hayes. It wasn't just the lacrosse stick propped casually against the wall (my father had told me Hayes was a Junior Olympian), or the floral-print boardshorts I recognized slung over the leather recliner in the corner. It was the way the T-shirt smelled when I held it to my face. Sunshine and salt water. It was Hayes's smell, and it made me want and miss him in a way I hadn't really expected.

At the same time, it recalled the poisonous cocktail of confusion, guilt, and anger I'd experienced when Adam caught us making out. Confusion over how I could possibly feel drawn toward Hayes but still be deeply in love with Adam, guilt at betraying Adam, and anger at Adam for making me feel either love *or* guilt after he'd hurt me so irreparably.

Thinking about Adam renewed my sense of urgency—the clock was ticking, and if it wound down to zero ... well,

I couldn't bear to even think about that. Failure was not an option. I had to reach him before time ran out.

Parker was tugging away, the brush finally starting to move a little more smoothly through my hair. A few clumps drifted to the floor and she shrugged apologetically.

"You won't be hair modeling any time soon," she said.

Her tough-girl edge seemed to be fading the tiniest bit. I sensed my opening.

"Were you here when everyone left?" I asked.

She screwed up her mouth, chewing on the inside of her cheek. Finally she said, "You were the one who was supposed to be telling me things, not the other way around."

I considered her for a moment. "And understanding what happened here will help me make sense of what I know, which isn't a whole hell of a lot."

She whipped the Catherine the Great biography out of her waistband and held it up in front of her face. "What's the story with this?'

I could see she wasn't going to give an inch until I offered something first. "I think it's a clue to where Hayes went, assuming he wasn't taken or killed by..."

The sentence had no ending. What did I say—Assuming he wasn't killed by VisionCrest? By an evil pseudo-deity pretending to be Harlow Wintergreen, Matriarch of Vision-Crest? I had no idea how much Parker knew, but I supposed it probably wasn't much. And explaining that your deranged doppelgänger was on the loose and may have kidnapped her compatriots was a bit of a non-starter.

Parker's eyebrows rose impatiently.

"Someone," I finished. "Listen, some very bad people have taken control of VisionCrest. And they don't have the best of intentions for Hayes or you or me, if you know what I mean."

"And you think this library book is the key to turning that ship around? No offense, but I think you might be sniffing glue. It's not going to tell you where my friends went." She wrinkled her nose in dismissal.

"So you're part of the Resistance, then. Why aren't you with the others?"

Her gaze darkened; she was clearly not pleased about giving away this little sliver of information, no matter how necessary it was.

"If Harlow Wintergreen was lurking around your abandoned Resistance compound asking to play beauty parlor, would you answer her questions?" she countered. "Because I wouldn't. I would think it was pretty freaking suspect. Like she might be lying. Like she shouldn't be trusted."

Her hand moved to the handle of the knife in her back pocket. I was supposed to be earning her trust, and this was headed in exactly the opposite direction. I took a deep breath, hoping that a vague sort-of-truth would do the trick.

"I was kidnapped and held prisoner by the same people you and Hayes are fighting against—people who are bent on corrupting VisionCrest's power. When I escaped, I couldn't go back to the Fellowship; there are powerful people there who want to see me dead. Hayes is my only hope for survival."

Parker's hard look softened at the mention of Hayes.

"Hayes is a lot of people's only hope for survival. At least he used to be."

She looked off into the dense tangle of the jungle. Night was beginning to creep across the sky, the sound of the crickets off in the distance a symphony tuning its instruments. There was clearly more to that story.

I swallowed past the lump in my throat. "Did something happen to him?"

Parker shrugged, then looked back at me. "Dunno. I went out into the jungle to get some space—camp out by myself for a few nights. Let's say I was upset about something. When I came back, everyone was gone. Poof! They just disappeared into thin air and left it all behind. Left me behind."

So Parker didn't know anything more than I did; less, even, since I at least knew that Isiris sent the Watchers here with orders to exterminate. If only I knew everything Isiris knew, I'd be able to tell Parker exactly what had transpired. But I only knew what I'd seen in the visions, which was both not enough and way too much.

"And you've been lurking in the forest, waiting to see if they come back?" I asked. It seemed like an odd thing to do.

Parker huffed. "Maybe I was waiting for whoever scared everyone away to come back, so I could eviscerate them and hang their intestines from the rafters." She scuffled her feet against the patio and cast a sidelong glance at a battered backpack stowed in the corner.

I was betting it was her survival pack, holding what she needed to make it in the jungle. It occurred to me that it might come in handy for my own escape.

"I see. That would take some serious guts," I said with a sly smile.

Parker's mouth quirked as she tried to suppress a smile. "Very funny."

"So you really have no idea what happened to them?" I asked her.

"Not a clue. I think you're done," she said, putting down the brush.

"You guys didn't have like, a meet-up spot or other secondary locations?" I pressed.

She turned around, pointing the brush at me. "Of course there are secondary locations. But I wasn't exactly in the circle of trust."

My stomach turned over. Parker seemed a little wild, but I assumed she was just the victim of bad timing. Maybe there was more going on here than met the eye.

"Exactly how far outside the circle were you?" I asked, hoping I still sounded playful.

"What's with the book?" Parker countered, evading my question.

"Hayes once mentioned it to me," I said vaguely. "At the time, I thought I was just imagining things, but later I thought maybe he was handing me a clue about where he might go if he ever had to make a run for it."

Parker seemed to stand up a little straighter. She whipped the book out and peered at the cover, then flipped through the pages. "Seriously? You think there's a clue in here?"

"I'm certain there is," I answered.

"Do you think it's, like, in a secret code or hidden compartment or something?" she asked.

I shrugged. "I guess so, yeah. Now I just have to figure out what it is."

Actually, that was exactly what I'd thought at first, but there wasn't anything special about the book. Now it seemed pretty clear to me that the clue to what I needed to do next was right there on the cover: go to St. Petersburg, Russia. Specifically, the Winter Palace, long-ago home to Catherine the Great. It was a long shot, but it was the only shot I had.

I wasn't exactly sure I should trust Parker with this information, though. It was a little weird that she'd been out doing a walkabout alone in the Vietnamese wilderness at the exact moment everyone cleared out. Maybe it was just bad timing, but something about her didn't sit right with me. Possibly it was the butcher knife.

"Want me to help you?" she asked.

I nodded and lied again. "Sure."

There was no room in my plans for a stranger, especially not an untrustworthy one. As good as it felt not to be alone, there was no other choice. I had to find a way to ditch Parker and get out of here. And I had to do it quickly

———————

Parker insisted that we sleep in the same room, which threw a wrench into my escape plan. I'd decided to bust out of there in the middle of the night, but, since I needed provisions, I'd hidden Parker's backpack under the bed in one of the guest rooms. A quick glance inside her pack had confirmed it held enough food and essentials to last me a few days. I'd shoved *Catherine the Great* in on top of that, just in case my hunch was way off base and it held some other clues.

Unfortunately, while Parker was many things, stupid wasn't one of them. When I tried to retire to my room, she set her jaw, got a suspicious glint in her eyes, and insisted we sleep in the guest room together. Of course, she chose the bed that held the backpack underneath. There was no way I could dislodge it without waking her.

"What's the story with the headphones?" I asked her as we were settling down to sleep, nodding to the giant earphones perpetually strung around her neck. She never put them on.

"No story. They're my headphones," she answered.

"Yeah, obviously. But like, what are you listening to?" I asked.

"Nothing." She shrugged. "I lost my music player a thousand years ago."

"So they're, like, your safety blanket?"

"They were my brother's," she said, in a tone that said she didn't want to talk about it.

"You like punk?" I asked, trying a new angle. She was still wearing the Ramones T-shirt.

"I like things that are loud," she said.

She was so weird, but it was an endearing weird.

My plan B went like this: be extra quiet sneaking out of the room, then hope to rustle up a new pack, some loose change, and a few day's worth of food in the surrounding buildings. But first I needed Parker to go the eff to sleep. I could feel her owl eyes watching me in the darkness from the twin bed next to me.

"Now it's your turn to tell *me* a story," she said.

"What, like a bedtime story? Once upon a time, happily ever after, the end," I said.

She propped herself up on one elbow. "A real story. Tell me the one about Harlow Wintergreen, Matriarch of Vision-Crest, and what she's doing sneaking around Bên Trong Mắt instead of sitting on her throne of lies." Her voice was soft.

The darkness of the room, the remoteness of this place, the uncertainty of the future. They invited confession. I sighed.

"There's another queen on that throne," I said. "Someone pretending to be me."

"Pretending? That must be one hell of a disguise," Parker said.

"This isn't a Shakespearean play. No costumes or mistaken identities. It's more like a fairy tale—Grimm version."

"Like an evil witch type of thing?" Parker asked. She sounded curious, not dubious.

"Something like that. But more like an evil spirit … or deity or something. I'm not sure. She escaped from her world and wants to destroy mine."

"So you're telling me that a supernatural doppelgänger took over VisionCrest and is trying to trigger the apocalypse?"

"Unless I stop her."

"Unless *we* stop her," she corrected.

She should be treating me like an insane person right now, not signing up for my army. "Why aren't you freaking out?" I asked.

I could see the outline of her shrug. "I always knew VisionCrest was some spooky shit. This just confirms it."

"I don't want to drag you into this," I said.

"I was in it before you showed up," she answered.

"Being with me will get you killed," I said.

"Staying here will too. It's a draw," she answered.

I rolled onto my back, blinking up at the ceiling. Her chances were better here, despite everything. I was a walking death sentence.

"Good night, Parker," I said.

"Good night, real Harlow."

As we were drifting off to sleep a few minutes later, Parker whispered one more thing into the dark. "Just for the record ... I believe you."

———

My eyes opened in the darkened room, and at first I wasn't sure if I'd been asleep or had simply blinked my way into this moment. My newly dreamless sleep was like a foreign object to me—inside the temple, sleep had been a conduit into Isiris's life and was about as relaxing as a kick to the shins. Now I was routinely dragged into a blank abyss, unable to see anything that might help me accomplish what I had very little time to accomplish. I could almost hear the seconds ticking down. Or maybe they'd already run out, and it was over before I'd barely begun.

Adam. Just the word filled my chest with a knotty tangle of hope and despair. I let my mind bring forth an image of him the way I liked to remember him: standing at the top of the skate ramp behind the Blue House, T-shirt cast aside, blue eyes squinting into the sun to evaluate the angle of a particularly difficult trick. Before the abduction, before the tattoos, before Isiris.

I shook my head, banishing the image from my mind. It was too much to bear.

Parker breathed in and out with an airy wheeze. She moaned in her sleep, her head thrashing to the side like she was re-experiencing some subconscious trauma. If Isiris's minions hadn't killed the Resistance fighters here, they might have captured them and put them in their virus testing labs, or worse. Who knew if the rebels would ever be coming back. And I knew that as tough as Parker tried to act, she wouldn't last much longer alone in the jungle, and she didn't stand a chance fighting on her own.

Maybe somewhere out in the world, someone was contemplating whether or not to help my best friend, and my deciding to bring Parker with me would tip the scales in Dora's favor. Balance restored.

If only the universe were that equitable.

As if to punctuate that thought, I heard a barely discernible but still unmistakable rumble of male voices carrying across the humid night air, floating through the slats of the shuttered window. My entire body stiffened. Maybe it was just fisherman, or traders rowing from some nearby island. My ears pricked, listening for the rounded vowel sounds and bell-like resonance of the Vietnamese language.

The voices came again. And they weren't speaking Vietnamese.

"Parker," I whispered, reaching across to her bed and poking her on the shoulder.

Moan. Thrash.

"Parker," I said in a low, insistent voice.

She snorted awake, sitting bolt upright and putting her arms in front of her face as if to shield herself from a blow.

"Wha? What? What?" she said, way too loud, looking at me and then at the window and the door with wide-eyed alarm. She reached under her pillow and whipped out her best friend the butcher knife. If she got any closer to that thing she might have to marry it; a fact for which I was suddenly very grateful.

I put a finger to my lips, then pointed out the window. The rumbles came again, this time much closer. The swishing sound of someone moving through the jungle nearby made my heart leap double-time against my rib cage.

"I hid your backpack under this bed," I whispered to her. "We need to grab it and go."

A wrinkle formed between her eyebrows as she puzzled this out, but there wasn't time now for her to unlock it. That would come later. Assuming we made it out of here before whoever was coming caught up with us.

The sounds grew closer and Parker threw off the thin sheet covering her and slipped into the weather-beaten Vans she'd left by her bed. I burrowed under the bed, grabbing the bag and slinging it over my shoulder as I stood up. Parker jerked her head *no* and practically knocked me to the floor, pulling the pack away from me. I put my palms up, then motioned between us—we were a team. She scowled at me and put on the pack, grabbing a flashlight from the nightstand and motioning for me to follow her. Like I said, she was no dummy.

We tiptoed into the hallway and down the stairs, Parker leading the way. It occurred to me as I followed her soft footsteps that this might be a setup—maybe Parker was the bait, waiting just in case I ever made it here, meant to keep me here long enough for the Watchers to come collect me. If so, I was already doomed.

A whistle, low and hollow, sailed across the night. They were very, very close now. I had two choices: trust Parker or knock her down the stairs and run alone into the jungle. I looked at her ponytail and the headphones dangling around her neck.

As much as I preferred to go it alone, I now knew that I could never do this to Parker. My heart told me she was legit.

We made it downstairs and padded across the wood floors. The beam of a flashlight swept across the building next to us, cutting through my midsection like a samurai sword. I froze, understanding for the first time what was meant by the phrase "deer in the headlights."

"Target! Target!" a deep voice cried out. An army of red dots like an ant swarm swung wildly across the darkened walls of the house.

Target. Those were gun sights.

Parker's arm shot out and grabbed my T-shirt. She pulled

me toward the door and flung it open, abandoning the pretense of quiet.

"Run your ass off and don't lose sight of me," she hissed, then took off sprinting across the small slice of lawn that separated the house from the surrounding jungle. She was really growing on me.

Parker was a blur of pale arms and legs. For someone so scrawny, she was seriously fast. I ran hard after her, the knee-high grass at the back of the compound swishing past my legs at what felt like ear-splitting decibels. Blood pumped loudly in my ears and every breath felt like a beacon.

Parker darted between the first thicket of trees, disappearing inside. I was steps away from following when a single bullet glanced off the tree next to me. Instinctually I veered away, still charging headlong into the jungle but on a different path. A spray of bullets followed, kicking up the dirt behind me. As soon as I crossed the threshold of the jungle, the darkness was immense, as if someone had pulled the shades down on an already black night.

I kept running as fast as I could, the only thought in my mind out-maneuvering the red dot army. Bullets swished through the bushes around me, and every second I expected to feel the biting sting of a gunshot wound or the sound of a voice right behind me telling me to freeze or die.

But after a few minutes of sprinting, somehow dodging the trees and undergrowth by instinct alone, a horrible realization settled over me. Parker was nowhere in sight. In my flight for survival, I hadn't managed to follow her like I was supposed to. Now I was alone, without supplies, in an unfamiliar jungle. Basically a nightmare sundae with a crazed assassins cherry on top. Great.

Dodging behind a tangle of trees, I stopped and held my breath. My lungs were like two white-hot balloons waiting to burst, but I stopped them up so I could listen for a moment.

Silence.

I let the air out slowly, forcing myself to inhale-exhale in a silent, controlled way. I could hear the men shouting in the distance. It sounded like they were spreading out. Maybe the silver lining to Parker and I getting split up was that those bozos wouldn't know which way to go. Thin the Darwinian herd.

I wondered how they'd feel, reporting back to Isiris in the morning and telling her they'd been outfoxed by a couple of unarmed girls. She'd probably make their livers into an omelet. *Take that, asshats.*

I looked around, the irrational hope that Parker was somehow nearby suffusing me. If the universe wanted me to prevail, Parker would magically appear. It was amazing how quickly I'd gone from trying to ditch her to wishing nothing had come between us.

"Psssst."

The sound came from just to the right of me. Not possible.

"This way, dummy," Parker whispered through the night. "Before you get both of us killed."

She materialized out of nowhere. I never thought I'd be so excited to see cut-off jean shorts.

"Relax, I'm coming," I said.

Secretly, I high-fived the universe. We had a long way to go, but this was not such an inauspicious start after all. It was nice to have a friend again.

BEFORE:
TRAPPED IN THE TEMPLE,
DREAMING OF ISIRIS

Isiris was standing in the rectory on the second floor of the Hall of the All Knowing. She was in the General's private chambers within the Twin Falls temple, the largest and lushest building on the sprawling grounds of the VisionCrest compound. The sun was setting over the rows of post-modern buildings and manicured mansions that belonged to the VisionCrest elite— even more of whom had gone missing in the months following the return of "Harlow" from the Cambodian jungle.

Isiris came completely into focus as I inhabited the moment. She was smiling at her reflection in the floor-to-ceiling windows, long and slow like a crocodile contemplating its prey.

A door opened and shut behind her. The hop-skip of carefree footsteps that could only belong to one person sounded across the marble floors.

"What's your story, morning glory? I thought you, quote, loathed this place."

Isiris turned. Dora pushed her glasses up the bridge of her nose. Her smile was eighty-percent teeth and twenty percent eyebrows, and I one hundred percent loved her. Every cell within me ached to throw my arms around her and sob with relief. But couldn't. I wasn't here, not really. I was stuck, helpless, behind Isiris's eyes.

"I don't know what you mean," Isiris responded, trying to mimic Dora's playfulness but unable to disguise the edge of irritation sliding beneath it. Even if she impersonated me for a million years, she would never understand the way Dora and I communicated. It was a members-only club, party of two.

Dora scrunched her nose up, which she always did when confronted with something she needed to puzzle out. "Is this dramatic contemplation, or are you just admiring your minions from afar?" she asked, slinging her arm around Isiris's shoulder.

Isiris stiffened in response. "What?"

A flutter of panic rose within me. I wanted to warn Dora, tell her to drop it and go away, send her some signal from the beyond. But I was bound, captive within the straitjacket of Isiris's mind.

Dora dropped her arm and grabbed Isiris by both shoulders. "Earth to best friend, please come in."

Isiris blinked at her. The way Dora talked was an unbreakable code to Isiris—it wasn't in her playbook. I could feel the confusion writhing around in her mind, like a school of piranhas darting first one way and then the next. Reactive, afraid. Dangerous.

I could also feel something else—her confusion giving way to anger. Stop, Dora. Stop.

"I was just watching the sunset," Isiris said, turning back to the view. Dora moved a few inches away, as if sensing her closest friend was now a stranger.

"Do you want to ditch the solo scene and, like, have a sleepover and braid each other's hair? You've been knee-deep in Adamland. I'm sure he's an amazing suckface and all, but I've barely seen you the past few weeks."

"I don't want to talk about Adam," Isiris said.

"Okay, okay. I get it. Young love, keep it to yourself. But you're going to have to give up the goods eventually, Wintergreen."

Isiris looked at Dora, narrowing her eyes to bring her into focus as if she were some exotic creature.

"I've been feeling a little overwhelmed," Isiris said unexpectedly. "Not quite myself."

Dora frowned, then pulled her close for a hug. Isiris had to physically fight the urge to recoil.

I noticed that I was beginning to experience Isiris's emotions more strongly, as if by osmosis. I wondered if the visions I used to have were Isiris doing the same thing in reverse, forcing me to experience her thoughts and feelings. Maybe I could learn to use those same tactics against her.

"It's probably like a post-traumatic-thingamajobber," Dora said. "I mean, thanks to Kooky McCrazyPants, you've basically been through the equivalent of a war."

Isiris pulled back, knocking Dora's arms away. I felt the anger rise up in her like mercury with the rising sun. "You should be careful who you call crazy," she snapped. She did everything but bare her teeth. No. Oh, god.

Dora shrank back. "I wasn't calling you crazy, Crazy. But the way you're acting lately, maybe I should."

There was something dangerous in Dora's eyes—a new inquisitiveness, like some sleeping part of her subconscious was waking up to the fact that maybe Harlow wasn't Harlow after all. I wished she would just shut up. Just turn around and leave. I rattled against the cage of my subconscious, but nothing happened.

"What are you doing here anyway?" Isiris asked. Her voice was cold.

"I just wanted to check up on you. You've been acting weird ever since you came out of the coma. I'm worried about you." Dora sounded wounded. I tried to reach the tenuous tendrils of my consciousness out to her, to let her know I was here, buried deep inside the evil of what was standing next to her.

Isiris contemplated the vista, unresponsive. Then her voice grew sly. "Did you hear about the people in New York? The ones who died?"

"No." Dora's eyes grew wide with panic. "It isn't the virus, is it?"

Isiris knew she hadn't heard the news—I could feel her certainty. In all likelihood she'd seen to it that only certain information made it into the compound. The citizens of VisionCrest's various bases around the world were likely living in a censored state, as was most of the world. Civilization would fall down around them and they wouldn't know it until it was already gone.

"Hard to say," Isiris answered. "I did hear that their flesh melted right off their bones. So who knows."

"Holy Hera, that's horrific," Dora said, wringing the hem of her VisionCrest uniform inside her fist.

"I thought it was sort of poetic," Isiris said.

"Poetic? Seriously, Lo, that's not even funny. I thought Wang was in prison—is there a chance he could have let the virus out before you had him arrested?"

"His laboratories were empty. Who knows what could have happened?" Isiris shrugged.

"You're being awfully casual about this. Shouldn't we be freaking out?"

Isiris grabbed Dora's hand. "One of us should be."

Their twin reflections turned violet as the sun set over the compound my father built. If he'd known that he was laying the foundation for Isiris's vengeful return, I wondered if he'd still have done it all anyway. Power is a potent cocktail and the flesh is weak; something I knew better than anyone.

Dora slid her hand out of Isiris's grasp. "You're kind of freaking me out. You're not acting like yourself."

Isiris turned and looked at her. I could feel the jagged edges of her glare cutting through to the core of my friend.

"You should stay out of my way. If you don't, something bad might happen," she said.

Dora's expression re-arranged itself from one of worry to one of fear. "What do you mean, 'something bad'?" she asked, her voice shaking.

"I'm sure I'll think of something," Isiris answered.

Dora backed away, bumping into a limestone pedestal that

held a bust of the General. It fell to the floor and shattered into a thousand pieces. Dora turned and ran.

I'd never seen Dora run away from anything before in her life. Dread washed over me. My best friend's naiveté had been her shield, but now she was in mortal danger and there was nothing I could do to help her.

Isiris turned back to the view, purple with foreboding. She chuckled softly under her breath. I felt as if I would explode.

Isiris removed something from her pocket. A little silver bell. She rang it, and a young woman appeared from a side door. She was wearing a drab gray gown with the VisionCrest symbol branded across the front, as if she were a piece of property. Flaxen hair hung in limp strands around her face, obscuring it from view.

So Isiris was taking servants now—perhaps slaves. Nothing she did should shock me, but this unbinding of basic humanity pierced my heart with dread.

"Matriarch?" the girl asked, her voice barely audible.

"Have the Watchers call for Adam," Isiris ordered. "I want to see him in my private quarters."

No, I thought.

"Yes, Matriarch," the girl said, her gaze slipping up for a moment. Long enough for me to get a look at her face. One half was transcendently beautiful, and the other was horribly mottled and pink with scars—a gift from Isiris. A shock wave of recognition to run through me.

It was Mercy.

Devoid of liberty and drained of hope, but it was her. Isiris's slave, hidden away. It was almost more than I could believe or bear. On the one hand, Mercy was alive—last I'd seen her, she was attached to a flurry of tubes and encased in plastic, a twisted experiment in Isiris and Sacristan Wang's basement lab of horrors. On the other hand, she was a hollowed-out shell of her former self. I used to think I hated her, considered her my enemy. It would be laughable if it weren't so heartbreaking.

This couldn't be happening.

Isiris had everyone I loved by the throat, and by all appearances she planned to tear them out. She winked at her reflection.

I had the creeping feeling she was talking to me when she said, "Darling, this is just the beginning."

AFTER: BEIJING, CHINA

I surveyed the crowded Beijing street. Parker had a blue bandana wrapped around her face; I was back in my veil from Vietnam, fearful that someone might recognize me and cause a scene. The longer I went without Isiris knowing I was free, the better chance I had at stopping her.

Making our way to China had been nail-biting. At least we'd found a Resistance rowboat anchored on the far side of the island, which saved us an epic swim, and then Parker had stolen a moped from a ramshackle farm on the outskirts of Hoi An. She'd been standoffish ever since the hidden backpack incident, yet despite my urging her to go her own way, she inexplicably refused to leave my side.

I regretted ever thinking of leaving her behind, but I hadn't yet found the words to tell her how sorry I was.

We rode only at night until we'd made it a safe distance from the city. Luckily the border agents were too consumed with panic about the increasing pockets of viral outbreaks to scrutinize us. Instead they focused on putting us through an elaborate series of motor tests and Breathalyzers aimed at confirming we weren't infected with anything mysterious and deadly. Parker's backpack contained enough money for us to scrape by, apparently collected from various hiding spots within the compound.

As we traveled, I filled Parker in on the details about Isiris, Adam, and the whole sordid mess. She took the story in stride with a characteristic shrug and flick of her ponytail. "I've heard worse," was all she said.

On the streets of Beijing, everyone wore hospital masks and looked through us like we were invisible. Immaterial. Non-existent. They had their own lives to worry about, literally. The threat of random virus outbreaks had everyone duly terrified and absorbed in their own little bubbles. I had built up resistance to the virus thanks to the tattoos Isiris had forced onto Adam, which made him an inoculated carrier. But Parker was still vulnerable. If I lost her, I would be back on my own. My palms got clammy and my breathing shallow just thinking about it. I couldn't let that happen.

Of course, Isiris might have mutated the virus further. Maybe no one was safe.

"You're being weird. Act natural," Parker instructed me as we walked through a crowded alleyway, threading our way via back streets to the Beijing Railway Station.

"Natural?" I asked. I'd been raised inside a multi-national corporate cult and recently escaped captivity from a supernatural limbo formerly inhabited by my evil twin. What the eff did I know about natural?

"Yeah. Like, pretend I'm your friend and we're just out for a stroll instead of being some paranoid schizo. You must have a best friend, right? Or do you treat everyone like an object of your convenience?" she asked.

I thought of Dora. All the things she'd gone through because of me, and then because of Isiris. If I only accomplished one thing with my freedom, it had to be to make things okay for her. That is, if my best friend still existed after everything I'd seen. The thought made my stomach lurch.

"Wait," I said, putting my hand on Parker's arm.

She let out a frustrated groan. "What now?"

"I just want to tell you how grateful I am that you're here. And how stupid I was to ever contemplate doing this without you."

Her ponytail twitched. "Don't get all sappy on me," she said. "Come on, let's go."

But I could tell I'd earned a little more of her trust.

Despite the population's paranoia, China had been largely spared from the virus, as far as I could tell. VisionCrest now seemed to be in control of the media—every shop we passed on the streets of Beijing had a television broadcasting an endless stream of robotically sunny weather reports and feel-good stories of the Fellowship from around the world, all delivered in front of an unchanging backdrop of the VisionCrest Inner Eye symbol. It was the only thing on any channel, and if it wasn't mandated that every public place tune in, then people were doing it strictly out of fear. Either option was chilling.

More than that, there was a striking absence of cell phones, and Internet cafes sat empty and dark. From what we could tell, Isiris's regime had taken over and locked down all communication channels. Word of mouth was the only source of information now, but news still spread like wildfire. From what little we could gather, even this was a tainted mix of hysteria and fear. It was impossible to know truth from fiction. Isiris probably had a hand in that too. The thought filled me with a foreboding so strong I felt it in my molars.

VisionCrest flags hung from every pole lining the streets and every spare inch of unclaimed real estate. Every one of them had Isiris's face—*my* face—emblazoned on it, looking triumphant and vaguely dictatorial.

The alleyway opened up into a market. A cacophony of umbrellas and wooden produce carts created a patch-work of color and life. Shoppers and vendors mingled in the between spaces, a little slice of normal life amidst the weirdness and chaos.

Out of nowhere, a siren pierced the air. It wailed louder, then receded, then wailed again in rhythmic waves. Every-one in the square froze for a moment, then dropped to their knees on the cobblestone. VisionCrest Watchers flooded the area, pouring like cockroaches from the dark seams and alleys around us. Parker and I looked at each other in alarm, unsure what was going on.

"Get down," she hissed. We knelt like everyone else.

The Watchers prowled through the knots of stunned citizens, cradling semi-automatics like precious children. An elderly man looked up as a Watcher paused in front of him, a few hundred feet in front of us. The Watcher slammed the butt of his gun into the man's face; teeth and blood exploded onto the ground as he slumped over.

I drew in a sharp breath. Parker grabbed my arm to keep me from running to help.

A young woman, probably the man's daughter, bent over him and tugged at his shirt. She sobbed, keening as the Watcher grabbed her by the back of her dress and jerked her to her feet. She was pregnant. The square was silent but for the siren's wail, everyone on their knees with downcast eyes. The Watcher pointed his gun at the old man and fired, and the girl keened louder. He grabbed a fistful of her hair and dragged her away into a side alley. Others were being plucked from the crowd, seemingly at random, by the flood of Watchers and dragged toward the same place.

I couldn't just let this happen; I moved to get up.

"Don't do anything stupid," Parker warned.

The indifferent click of heels against the stone a few inches to my left turned my bones to ice. A Watcher. My movement had drawn his attention. I froze, unsure what to do next. I couldn't let the girl get taken away without trying to help, but I didn't want to endanger Parker either.

Black combat boots came into view. They paused right in front of me, polished so high I could see my reflection. I could hear the Watcher breathing, imagine his soulless eyes as he evaluated me and Parker. Choosing us.

"Who is the one true leader?" His gravelly voice was menacingly soft. There was no doubt the question was addressed to me.

"The Matriarch, Harlow Wintergreen," I said.

The tip of his rifle poked into the underside of my chin, through my veil, forcing me to look up and meet his glare. He had dull brown hair the color of tree bark, and his black eyes were as empty as I'd imagined they would be. He swung the barrel of his gun so it pointed at Parker's temple, next to me.

"Death to unbelievers," he said.

For a horrifying moment I was sure he was going to shoot her in the head. The *rat-a-tat* of gunfire sounded from the alley. Someone was dying.

I stood up, drawing his aim back to me. His eyes widened in surprise; my stare never left his.

"Death to the Matriarch," I hissed.

Parker's body tensed next to me, and I heard a soft gasp roll through the crowd behind me.

The Watcher grabbed me by the back of the neck, his fingers a vise. He dragged me through the crowd so fast I couldn't keep my feet; my knees banged against the stone as the terrified eyes of kneelers blurred past me. The staccato of more gunfire.

We rounded into the alleyway in time to see the pregnant girl and a handful of others lined up against the wall, a line of Watchers pointing rifles at them in a firing squad formation. A pile of bodies already lay at their feet, wine-red blood pooling in the crevices between the stones.

The Watcher pushed me against the wall, lining me up next to the others. There was shuddering and sniffling and the smell of urine.

"Ready!" he yelled.

Every gun was raised. The pregnant girl was sobbing softly. I couldn't let her and her unborn baby die.

There was only one option.

I ripped the veil off my head.

"I command you to stop!" I bellowed with authority, raising my palm flat in front of me.

I tried to push down a memory of something that had happened to me inside the temple: the unshakable image of a red-drenched altar and a still-beating heart. *You're surviving*, I told myself. But I wasn't sure I believed it.

The rifles wavered, but did not lower.

"I said stop!" I gritted my teeth. The coldness in my voice surprised even me.

Several of the Watchers faltered, jaws dropping and weapons drooping. They recognized me, but couldn't fully process what they were seeing. A few of them remained at the ready, looking sidelong at my Watcher, who was apparently the one in charge.

His eyes narrowed as he took me in. Unmasked, there could be no doubt about my identity. He knew something wasn't right, but he couldn't reconcile it with the person who stood before him.

"Matriarch, I—" he began. The lack of certainty in his voice gave me an opening.

"On your knees!" I commanded.

This time, they listened. Every Watcher and prisoner dropped to the ground. The man next to me convulsed in fear. If the Watchers had frightened them, the sight of

Harlow Wintergreen was worse. The damage Isiris had done was greater than I feared.

"Drop your weapons," I said.

Every Watcher but the one who'd dragged me to the alley complied. I walked over to him. He looked straight ahead, but held tight to his weapon.

"Why are you here?" His eyes dragged upward, meeting mine. Then he added, as an afterthought, "Matriarch."

"A test," I lied. "And you have failed. Miserably."

His gaze held mine, a war going on behind his eyes. The troops were watching this exchange, horrified but sensing something wasn't quite right. I couldn't afford to have them think too much.

"Put down your weapon or I will put you down."

I kicked him hard in the ribs, the exclamation point at the end of my sentence. He doubled over, dropping his gun. I picked it up.

"Now, I will kill these unbelievers myself, and you"— I nodded at the cadre of Watchers—"will crawl on your hands and knees to the Tiananmen temple, contemplating with every inch how you have failed your Matriarch."

The Watchers looked confused yet contrite, uncertain as to exactly how they had failed but certain that they had. Their leader looked up at me, suspicion in his eyes. If I let him go, he would pass the information along to his superiors. If I killed him, which I couldn't even fathom, his team would be forced to explain what had happened. Either way, Isiris would eventually discover that I was free.

Our best hope now was making it out of Beijing before

that happened. I had no idea how far Tiananmen Square was from here, but I hoped it was really damn far.

I pointed the gun at the head Watcher. "Start crawling."

Their leader began crawling, the rest of them falling in behind him.

I waited until they'd made it around the corner, the leader looking back one time with accusatory eyes. As if he felt disappointed to not kill the innocent bystanders himself. My only comfort was that Isiris would probably execute him for letting me go, finishing the job that I could not.

When the Watchers were finally out of sight, I surveyed the trembling prisoners. They expected their fate at my hands to be worse than with the Watchers. My throat tightened. Isiris had made Harlow Wintergreen a monster.

I looked over my shoulder. Parker stood at the mouth of the alley—behind her, the entire square remained on its knees.

"We gotta go," Parker hissed.

I nodded, setting the gun down.

The pregnant girl hazarded a glance, looking at me with a question in her eyes.

"Don't give up hope," I said to her. I wished I could speak Mandarin.

She just stared at me, terrified. Silent tears ran down her face.

Parker and I hurried out of the alley. We had to make it to the train before it was too late. It was only a matter of time before Isiris discovered us. There was no turning back now.

We hustled back to the station in complete silence. My left eyelid had developed a twitch that wouldn't go away, and Parker wore her empty headphones like a suit of armor, impossible to penetrate. Darting through the throngs of travelers on the crowded platform, we approached the train that would transport us from China to St. Petersburg, certain that at any moment we would be recognized and detained. There were people teeming across the concrete and flooding onto the rickety trains, most with luggage and packs that weighed them down. We were conspicuous with our one lonely backpack. My pulse quickened.

If we made it out of Beijing, the journey would take us across China and into Mongolia. Once we made it past that point, it would be just a hop, skip, and continent to reach St. Petersburg. So many things could go wrong. I hoped we weren't circumnavigating the globe on a fool's errand—there was no room for more mistakes.

A tired-looking woman stood at the train door, scrutinizing tickets. My hands shook as I handed her ours. She paused for a moment, then looked up with bored eyes and waved us in. Beyond her, a couple of assault-rifle-clad Watchers swaggered down the platform. One of them met my eye, and my pulse pounded a staccato in my ears. His eyes slid away, disinterested. I was just one of the crowd.

For now. I wondered what would happen when we got to Europe. Once Isiris sounded the alert, all bets were off. I couldn't imagine anything worse than getting close to our destination and having things ripped away once again.

Once inside the train, we bustled our way down the aisle clogged with low-rent travelers on their way to or from the hinterlands. Groups of traders hauled wares into the crowded cabins that housed four travelers at a time. Since Parker and I had to ration our funds, we'd decided there was no way we could afford a cabin to ourselves—we'd have to chance the week-plus journey with a cast of strangers, as dangerous as that was. I tried not to break into a cold sweat at the thought.

Parker halted in front of the cabin marked with a symbol resembling the symbol on our tickets and slid the door open aggressively. Pretty much the way she did everything.

"*Ni hao*," she said to the two men sitting together on the bottom berth in our cabin. There was a makeshift table in the middle of the tiny space, surrounded on both sides by bunk beds. Cozy.

They blinked at her; clearly they weren't Chinese. I guessed they were Mongolian, probably traders who made the journey back and forth—the Trans-Siberian route was famous as an import-export pipeline connecting the interior of the Asian continent with its metropolitan outliers.

One of the men uttered something to the other as Parker shoved her way in and swung her pack onto a top bunk, then monkeyed her way up the iron sides. She put her headphones over her ears and plunked herself horizontal on the bed.

I knew the silent treatment when I saw it. The incident in the square had frightened us both, but Parker was also angry.

I could feel it radiating off of her. I'd pretty much decimated the bit of trust we'd been building.

I nodded at the two men, who were silently staring, and sat down on the other bottom bunk. I cursed Parker for leaving me alone and attempted a wan smile, then shrugged. The men looked at each other, then back at me, then at each other again. They picked up their conversation where it left off. I was, for all intents and purposes, alone.

The train began its slow chug out of the station, its *sway-sway-clack-clack* oddly soothing. A burst of metallic-smelling air came through the seam in the window. I lay back on my thin pillow and tried to force myself to relax for the first time since we'd fled Vietnam. Against impossible odds, we had somehow made it here.

I gazed out the window as the built-up metropolis of Beijing gave way first to the destitute rubble of suburbia, then to the lush, rolling green hills of the Chinese countryside. I thought about the day Adam and I had spent at the Great Wall, before Mercy became infected and the Wangs revealed their betrayal. Basically, before everything went completely to shit.

Now the clock was ticking, every moment potentially Adam's last, and I was on this ancient freaking hunk of metal lumbering way-too-slowly in what I hoped was ultimately his direction. *If* Hayes was able to help me find him. If I could even find Hayes.

Adam and Hayes. Hayes and Adam. Their images tumbled and tangled. Love. Loyalty. Loss. Love. Loss. Loyalty.

I didn't know what I felt for either of them, only that it was different. I wondered if any of us would live to find out.

AFTER:
SOMEWHERE IN MONGOLIA

Parker didn't speak a word to me until the traders got off in Mongolia thirty hours later, but I had felt her stewing above me the entire way.

The traders bustled out, weighed down with a strange assortment of trinkets and blankets, casting Parker and me sidelong glances under furrowed brows, rumbling to one another about how strange the two of us were. Or so I assumed—to be fair, my grasp on the Mongolian language was tenuous to nonexistent. I kind of wanted to go with them. A yurt in the Mongolian tundra was probably a pretty safe place for a hideout, if you could tolerate fermented yak's milk.

Parker wasn't the only one who couldn't stop thinking about the incident in the square. It had been dangerous and stupid of me to reveal myself like that, even if I'd had no other choice. Between that and the escape from Bên Trong

Mắt, Isiris may have already been alerted to my escape from the temple. The entire world could be on high alert for all I knew. Every security camera, every Watcher, every dutiful VisionCrest devotee we encountered could be a new opportunity for me to be found out. It was no longer just the situation I was running toward that was a ticking time bomb; I was just as explosive.

The moment the last trader left, sliding the sleeper car door shut behind him, Parker's skinny legs swung down from the top bunk and she jumped off, landing on both feet right in front of me like she was freaking Catwoman or something. She turned to face me, hands on hips. Bitch-face, locked and loaded.

"What the hell was that stunt in Beijing?" she demanded.

"I couldn't just let them murder innocent people," I said softly.

Her hazel eye looked more brown, as if it darkened with her mood. "And what about everyone else?" she snapped. "What about us? If Isiris finds you now, what happens then?"

"Every life is worth saving," I said.

Her chin trembled. "I know that."

"This just reinforces what I first thought," I added. "I should do this alone. Being with me puts people in danger. Everyone I care about is either dead or … or getting close. As you experienced in Beijing."

My stomach did a sick little twist as I thought of Adam. What were the chances that Adam could hold out? We could be a million miles away from him for all I knew.

"I make my own decisions," Parker spat. "I have my own reasons for being here."

This was an angle I hadn't considered—that Parker was here out of more than just the goodness of her spunky little heart. "Would you tell me about them?" I asked.

For some reason, Hayes's face popped to mind. My stomach did a revolting lurch for entirely different reasons. Had Parker been Hayes's girlfriend?

"What's the story with you and Hayes?" I asked, trying not to sound too interested.

She raised her head and gave me a look that would wilt the sunniest of sunflowers. "You think I like him. Gross—not even."

I tried not to think too much about why I felt so relieved. "Do you want me to tell you what my story is with him?" I asked.

She gave me a *whatever* flip of the ponytail, but I could tell she wanted me to tell her.

"I met him briefly when I was twelve, but it was years before I saw him again. It was in Tokyo last year on my birthday, when my dad decided to initiate me to the first Rite. Before everything went to shit. Hayes was my second," I told her.

Parker sat forward, her sour grapes momentarily forgotten.

"What does that mean, your second?" There was an edge of anxiety in her voice.

I looked at her, perplexed for a moment. Then it dawned on me—Parker wasn't a VisionCrest cast-off. She'd never been part of the Fellowship at all. Every VisionCrest devotee knew that a second was someone who was one step ahead of you in the Rites of Initiation, the ten-step journey that would supposedly lead the chosen few into the secret center of the Inner Eye.

I considered explaining it to her, but then stopped. Maybe what seemed obvious to me would sound ludicrous to someone outside the fold. I'd never really questioned it before—it was just the way it was.

"It's kind of like a spiritual guide," I answered finally.

Parker bit at the ragged edge of her thumbnail. "So, like a friend, then?"

"More like a mentor," I said. "Strictly professional."

It wasn't technically a lie. What came after, between Hayes and me, was neither friendly nor professional. Still, until I knew for sure what the relationship was between Hayes and Parker, I wasn't willing to divulge. It was impossible to discern what was hiding behind her kaleidoscope eyes, but I hoped it wasn't love.

"Now you. How do you know Hayes?" I asked.

She sighed hard, then looked out the window. For a minute I thought she was just going to ignore me and slip back into the silent treatment, but at last she started talking.

"My older brother Aaron joined VisionCrest when he went off to college. They drew him in with one of those creepy campus recruiting houses." She gave me a side-eye.

I knew exactly what she was referring to—fancy mansions the Fellowship purchased on the peripheries of affluent university campuses. They were a safe haven to kids away from home for the first time, especially those who felt set adrift by the new experience of adulthood. Or a lure. I'd always thought they were slightly creepy too. My father, on the other hand, thought they were a stroke of marketing genius; the million-convert brainchild of Sacristan Mayer, Mercy's mother.

"Yeah, I know the ones," I said. Trying to explain to her that I didn't support them would fall flat, so I didn't bother.

"At first Aaron tried to convince my parents to join Vision-Crest, which they of course refused, because they weren't sniffing glue," she said bitterly. "After a few months, he stopped calling home. He didn't show up for the holidays. Then he just disappeared altogether, like he'd dropped off the damn face of the earth. He was part of the cult, and if we wouldn't follow him, then he had to cut off all contact with us."

"It's not a cult," I said reflexively.

Her blue eye was icier than a winter pond. "You're kidding, right?"

"It's called severing," I mumbled, chastened. The extent of my indoctrination surprised and embarrassed me.

"Well, that's the freaking perfect word for it," she said.

"So is that what led you to the Resistance?" There had to be more to her story.

"I got a letter from Aaron about six months later. He said he'd volunteered to be part of some kind of experiment the Fellowship was doing, and how it was this big important honor. He said he had a feeling he wasn't coming back. That he was moving on to some higher plane of existence or some bullcrap like that."

The side of VisionCrest that preyed on vulnerable would-be converts was something I'd always been sheltered from, even though on one level I must have known it was happening. For my father and me to be royalty, a million others must be made slaves. I thought of Wang's underground lab, wondering if Parker's brother was behind one of those antiseptic white doors lurking under Wang's palatial home. Bile rose in my throat. I was complicit.

"Did he tell you where he was going?" I asked.

Parker shook her head. "Aaron wanted me to get his journal from his room at home—our parents kept it for him like this pathetic shrine. He asked me to burn it. At first I figured he didn't want my mom and dad to read about how he'd peeped on the neighbor lady back in junior high or something, but it turns out it had all these extra pages inserted. Between his sappy junior high poetry there were names and places and, like, some kind of cryptic code for the insane. He must have left it there the last time VisionCrest let him visit home."

"That's awful," I said. I wanted to ask Parker if I could see the journal, but I'd learned the only way to get to her: slowly, as if I were melting a glacier with a hair dryer.

Parker's eyes hardened. "Awful? Want to know awful? Awful is that he was right. He never came home. I tried to track him down—even went all the way to the VisionCrest compound in good old Beijing, China, the first location on his precious list. I was bringing his damn journal to him so he could burn the stupid thing himself. Or maybe wake up and smell the brainwashing and remember who he really was."

"You went to Beijing? Holy crap. What happened?" I asked, blown away by her bravery.

"Yep. Went right up to the intercom and told them they better produce my brother or I was going to expose them for the kidnapping, lab-rat freaks that they were," she said. Her hands curled into fists.

I didn't want to think about what that must have been like for Parker. How many other families must have tried the same to save their loved ones. Families torn apart a million times over, in the name of a religion that, for all I knew, Isiris had created to amuse herself.

"What happened then?" I asked.

"Chinese military police came and carted me off to jail. Big bad VisionCrest was actually so threatened by a fifteen-year-old girl that they had to call in an entire platoon. They threw me in jail. Trust me, Chinese jail is not a place you want to ever be."

Parker was even tougher than I'd thought. The fact that she'd survived alone in the jungle—probably for months—didn't seem so far-fetched now. Nor did the idea that she might actually know her way around a butcher knife and not have any qualms about using it.

"I was pretty sure I was going to land in a hangman's noose, but two nights later one of the jailers came to my cell in the middle of the night. He unlocked my cell, plucked me from the human knot of my cellmates, and hurried me through the building and out a side door. There was this boy waiting in the shadows of the alley, which was completely dark. It was Hayes. He took me to Vietnam that night, and I never looked back. I owe him my life," she said.

It was no wonder she idolized Hayes.

"So did you burn it?" I asked.

"What do you think? It was the last thing I had from Aaron—my only clue to rescuing him from the effed-up mess he'd gotten into," she said.

Curiosity burned like a white-hot flame in my chest. I wanted more than anything to see that journal. Maybe it contained other names and places that could be useful. But the hard look in Parker's eyes made me hold back.

"I'm so sorry that happened to you and your family," I said.

She looked me square in the eyes. "Sorry enough to help me find my brother and make those VisionCrest assholes pay?"

"I know you don't have much reason to believe me, but I promise—that is exactly what I'm trying to do," I answered. A lot of people needed saving from the destruction VisionCrest had wrought.

Parker nodded at me, the severe set of her jaw softening just a little. She looked out the window once again as the sun dipped low on the flat plane of the horizon. Somewhere out there, I hoped Adam was still alive to see it too.

BEFORE:
TRAPPED IN THE TEMPLE

No matter how hard I searched, I couldn't find the stupid door. I'd been wandering the labyrinthine halls of the temple for about a million hours, determined to find the door that led back to my world. Even though I didn't have a way to cross through it, this was the first step. I would worry about what came next once I found the damn thing.

According to the marks I scratched into the wall of the temple, it had been twenty-six days since I'd regained consciousness. Twenty-six days of the same fruitless searching down the seemingly infinite corridors within this stupid temple. Twenty-six days without so much as a single drop of water or a flipping Go-Gurt, but no sensation of thirst or hunger. Twenty-six days of ferrying souls, but not having a clue how to ferry myself. Twenty-six days of pseudo-sleep filled with visions of Isiris taking over my life and plotting to undo my world atom by atom.

Yet each time I took a turn down yet another non-descript, door-lined hallway and squeezed a drop of blood from the pinprick puncture wound at the tip of my finger to mark my path, I felt a surge of hope. Maybe this would be the turn that led me to my door. I'd used a safety pin from the waistband of my skirt—I never thought I'd be so grateful that our VisionCrest uniforms were so ill-fitting, but there was a first time for everything. The blood droplets weren't exactly a high-tech navigation system, but while I was stuck in here I might as well work on that VisionCrest Violets merit badge for ingenuity.

"Hello!" my voice echoed down the hall. Was talking to yourself just to hear the sound of someone's voice a sign of impending insanity, or evidence that it had already arrived?

I began my painstaking trip down the hallway, looking through each door as I passed. My mind wandered to my father talking to me about "the quilted universe"—a scientific theory he held in religious regard. It posited that true existence was made up of infinite variations on reality. If it was true, then right now in some parallel universe my father was still alive, aggravating me like he always had.

The scenes on the other sides of the doors I passed were almost always strange, but the first door I looked through was up there on the top-ten weirdness charts. The landscape looked like the surface of the moon—a gray, lava-rock surface, barren of any sign of life, surrounded by a midnight sky twinkling with stars, and a fiery red planet burning in the distance.

Even though I'd tested this door a hundred times and my rational mind knew that I couldn't cross over to the other side, I still felt the same creeping anxiety I experienced whenever I stood on the balcony of the penthouse my father had kept in New York City. It was on the eightieth floor, and the demonic wind whipped around it. Even though it made my stomach feel like a bag of angry cats, I couldn't help but step up to the edge of the railing and peek over. The people on the street below looked like ants that I could smush beneath me. Even though I was terrified, my mind always wandered to the image of me stepping up on the thin railing, then free-falling forward until the ants were smushed and so was I. The bizarre thought tugged at me until I had to break free from it and go back inside—there was almost nothing more frightening than experiencing the razor-thin restraint that protected us from our own worst instincts.

I put my toes right up to the edge of the door. I could imagine what it would feel like if I could cross over. There would be a sucking sensation before I was pulled into outer darkness, floated endlessly in that night sky, then withered and died. Actually, I would probably die in, like, thirty seconds from lack of oxygen, but that fantasy was much less poetic.

I leaned forward, my face meeting the invisible resistance that kept me separate from the worlds behind every door I'd opened. I put my finger up, touching it against a distant pulsing star, feeling its imaginary gravitational pull.

My finger lurched forward, and suddenly it felt as if the skin of my fingertip might leap off my flesh. I wasn't imagining this pull. It was really happening.

I jerked my hand back and jumped away, stumbling

backward as a surge of adrenaline rushed my body. I had nearly been sucked across the threshold.

Maybe my mind was playing tricks on me. The tenuous thread between sanity and insanity was wearing so thin that it barely existed anymore. Then again, maybe it didn't.

Either way, it was all I could take for one day. I scrambled back the way I'd come, following a trail of my own blood back to the center of my tiny, grim little universe.

———————

Four more Violet Hours came and went before it finally clicked. I was pacing around the altar, trying to decide which serpentine hallway to squander my time in; not that it really mattered, considering time was the only thing I had in spades. I hadn't allowed myself to return to the doorway with the starry black horizon; the one that seemed to draw me over its threshold. The prospect of the same thing happening again was terrifying. Yet the prospect of it not happening was even worse. If I operated under the questionable assumption that I wasn't crazy—an assumption that grew thinner by the moment—then what had happened in that doorway suggested there might actually be a way out of here. Not that escaping into an airless void would do me much good.

I stood, staring down at the altar but not really seeing it. The pool of blood from our battle against Isiris had long since dried completely, flakes of it curling up from the crusted edges. Isiris's handprint was dead in its center, a perfectly outlined *screw you* courtesy of my mortal enemy. I stared at it, not really seeing it at first.

"Eeny meeny miny moe, I spy a clue for my girl Lo."
Dora's voice reverberated off the walls.

I whipped around, my mind fogged with affection. There
was a little tug in my subconscious that said it couldn't be
real. But what I saw was Dora, perched on the edge the altar
swinging her rainbow-striped legs. Nothing had ever seemed
more real in my entire life. Maybe she'd come to get me.

"Dora?" I asked, afraid it was some kind of trick.

She pulled at her gum, straining a long pink serpent from
her mouth and then letting it dangle from her mouth.

"Want to take a picture?" she grinned, and then winked
playfully. "It'll last longer."

There were a million questions running through my
mind. Was I crazy? Was she really here? How did she get here?
Why was she sitting there acting so nonchalant about it all?

"What are you doing here?" I finally managed.

She jumped down off the altar, and I hurried down
after her.

"Well. It seemed like you could use some help. Am I
wrong, Donkey Kong?"

As fast I scrambled to keep up with her, I could never
entirely catch up. All I wanted was to touch her skin, look her
in the eye. I'd been alone so long. I craved human touch, my
best friend more than anyone.

"No, you're not—Dora, stop," I said, pleading.

She had her back to me. Her curly hair puffed in eighty-
two directions, just like it always did. Her uniform was a
disheveled mess, just like it normally was. It was flawless Dora.

"Isn't there something you're missing, Harlow?" she asked, turning around.

"Am I?" I asked.

She raised her eyebrows in impatience.

A spark ignited in my brain, setting my entire body on fire. *Blood.* Isiris's hand must have been smeared with blood as she escaped from the temple with Adam. I thought of my father's VisionCrest origin story—how he had carried me from the temple as a newborn, blood streaming from his empty eye socket. I saw my pinpricked finger drawn through a portal to the mysterious other place that existed in a billion different parallel realities outside this horrible temple.

That was it. Blood was the variable that made the difference between staying trapped in the temple and getting to the outside. More was contained within that ruby-red mystery than we even realized.

"Correlation does not imply causation," Dora said, rematerializing next to me. "Remember how Brother Howard used to say that? When he wasn't *totally lusting for your loins*," she said, one furry eyebrow raised in jest.

"Don't say lusting. Or loins. It makes me barfy," I said, almost forgetting that my best friend wasn't real.

But hallucinatory Dora was right. All along, Isiris had thought the key thing was that one of us remain inside the temple to be the Guardian. But if my suspicions were right, that didn't matter—at least, not to anyone but the poor souls who would wander aimlessly in the Violet Hour without a Guardian to shepherd them. If I knew Isiris—and unfortunately I did—she had simply assumed that she couldn't pass through the doorways until I was safely ensconced inside the temple.

Correlation does not imply causation. I did remember Brother Howard teaching us that, now that pseudo-Dora mentioned it. It was a well-known principle of science, arguing that it was dangerous to presume that just because you can create a link between two things it's a foregone conclusion that one actually *causes* the other.

"*A logical fallacy,* he called it," Dora said. "Which, incidentally, would make a pretty kickass name for a band."

"You're flipping right!" I said, trying to throw my arms around imaginary Dora and give her a big, crazy kiss.

I was losing it.

But maybe I was also right, and if so, then I needed to find the door back to my world. Like, *yesterday.* My fists clenched in frustration. I had no clue where the right doorway was—and who knew how long it would take me to find it. Adam had told me that when he'd been held captive inside the temple, he was gone only days while months passed in the outside world. If that was true, it might already be too late to prevent Isiris from destroying everything. Every moment that passed was like a death sentence for the people I loved.

Action was my antidote to insanity.

There was only one way to test the theory. If I couldn't find my the doorway into my world, I would have to go through a different one. If it worked, I would know I was on the right track. Assuming I was able to find my way back in here.

"You'll find your way back, tiny dancer. I know you will," not-Dora said.

She dissolved into the ether, leaving the same blank stone walls that surrounded me before.

AFTER:
ST. PETERSBURG,
MOSKOVSKY STATION

By the time the train rolled into St. Petersburg seven days later, Parker and I were both about to crawl out of our skin. We pressed our noses up against the cold glass of the window and squinted out at one of the most famous and historically significant cities of the world, blanketed under a thick winter snow.

An eerie silence filled the urban sprawl on the outskirts. Although this was the city where the Tsars of Russia ruled in decadence for centuries, until the Russian Revolution, now it looked deserted. Either that or all its residents had gone underground. There were bonfires of trash burning in the empty street, casting noxious black smoke into the robin's egg air. Little flecks of ash lodged themselves against the windowpane. I couldn't tell what time it was; this far north, the lazy winter sun didn't rise until nearly mid-day.

Neither Parker nor I would say it, but we were terrified of what came next. Not only were we entirely ill-equipped for the elements, but not knowing what our next move was pressed down on us with a bone-crushing weight.

Whispers among the scant passengers remaining on the train suggested that all westward transportation had been halted. A quarantine was in effect—you could enter the city, but you couldn't leave. Parker had overheard two terrified backpackers from Australia in the dining car, one girl sniveling against the other's shoulder as they relayed their story to another equally terrified traveler. They'd been supposed to meet up with a friend in Beijing, who never showed. They'd been showing her photo to anyone they encountered, and the day before, someone had finally recognized her. That person had seen her get rounded up into some kind of military caravan that was rumored to be headed to a labor camp. The person who saw it happen had barely escaped the same fate.

Similar stories ran up and down the train car. Almost everyone else had disembarked in Moscow, hoping the beating heart of this most democratic nation in the world would protect them from whatever truth lay behind the rumors. The crushing sense of dread in my chest made it hard to breathe. I was partially responsible for this situation, but there was nothing I could do to help. At least, not yet.

Now, as the gears ground to a halt in Moskovsky Station, Parker and I looked at each other. We both wore medical masks with the VisionCrest emblem on them, which Parker had somehow charmed from the steward while I was sleeping.

I hoped they would help us go unnoticed into whatever hell was awaiting.

Unlikely. We were two suspicious-looking girls, wearing clothes appropriate for a tropical climate, who had desperate gleams in our eyes. In other words, we were screwed.

I stood up, reaching my hand out to Parker. "Come on."

I took her hand and squeezed it. For a moment we stood shoulder to shoulder. The train jolted to a stop. I let go, took a deep breath, and marched down the corridor with Parker's footsteps right behind me.

The light of the thin winter sun blinded me as I stepped through the open car door onto the platform. It was quickly followed by the wasp's sting of biting cold. Parker and I were going to be human Popsicles if we didn't get some winter gear ASAP. I held my hand up to my forehead, blinking the nearly abandoned platform into focus as Parker stumbled out behind me. The few remaining passengers wandered out of other cars, snaking out to our left and right. Two girls with Australian flags on their backpacks clutched each other and looked around the empty platform, wild-eyed.

"Where is everyone else?" Parker asked, noting the odd desolation. It was like riding a train into the aftermath of the apocalypse. Literally.

"I don't know," I said.

But even as I said the words, an ear-splitting siren sounded overhead.

All of the passengers covered their ears, instinctually doubling over into a protective stance. I knew that siren, and it wasn't the welcome wagon. The sound was debilitating, but I forced myself to focus. I expected to see some kind of Watcher offensive filtering out of the main terminal, just like we'd seen in the market in Beijing, but there was nothing.

"We've gotta go!" I yelled, turning to grab Parker's shirt. She had her hands firmly clamped over her ears, bent in half.

I tugged at her shirt and the two of us took off sprinting down the platform toward the main building, the only direction we could go until we got off the platform. We passed the other passengers, who were paralyzed by the deafening noise. The Australian girls were crumpled into each other, just the way Parker had described them in the dining car. A pang of dread shot through my heart—I feared the worst was yet to come for them. Maybe for us, too.

As we neared the end of the platform, I veered hard left on instinct, avoiding the main doors of the train terminal. Despite the high-pitched keening, I could still hear the comforting echo of Parker's flimsy shoes echoing against the concrete. The moment solidified things between us—it was me and her against the world.

For a shining moment, I thought we were in the clear.

Not so much.

Right in front of us, a frenzy of black-suited Watchers wearing gas masks that made them look like an alien swarm marched out of the central terminal in organized columns. It was impossible to miss the VisionCrest emblem emblazoned on their lapels. They were no longer just the Ministry security force; they were Isiris's soldiers.

On second thought, they were technically *my* soldiers.

For one crazy second I considered commanding them, the way I'd done in Beijing.

"Don't do anything stupid," Parker whisper-hissed, as if she'd heard my thoughts.

I made eye contact with the lead Watcher in the phalanx. His eyebrows rose, as if in surprise. For one twisted moment, I thought he recognized me. Then his brow collapsed into a V, and I realized it was only the shock of seeing someone actually daring to resist. His was jaw set in grim determination, his internal systems set to "contain or destroy."

We'd reached a dead end, which came to a pinpoint around the pounding of blood in my ears and searing-hot rush of air into my lungs. I slowed to a stop. There was no use running. If we'd made a break thirty seconds earlier, we might have avoided the Watchers; instead, we were headed right into their arms. By now Isiris might have gotten wind of my stunt in Beijing—if there was a moment to reveal my identity, I had to be sure it was absolutely my only card to play. This wasn't that moment.

The soldier intercepted us, wrangling me from Parker's grip as a knot of Watchers descended on us. Parker's words echoed in my mind. Even though I was furious and wanted to wrench myself away in anger, I forced myself to feign confusion. I let my body go slack beneath the soldier's grip, allowing him haul me across the platform while desperately craning my neck to confirm that Parker was still behind me. He grumbled something in guttural Russian. His nonverbal cues told me it wasn't *Welcome to St. Petersburg.*

The soldier dragging Parker ripped the backpack off her

shoulders and casually tossed it into a makeshift mountain of luggage and rucksacks stripped from other unlucky travelers. Parker and I exchanged a look—the good news was that they hadn't searched it and identified us as atypical; the bad news was that the only possession we had in this entire world-gone-to-hell had just been tossed into the discard pile. Shit.

We were shoved through the doors into the main terminal building, a soldier on each arm. For a moment I was grateful for the heated air, until a sticky-sweet wave of human stench hit me full-on. My eyes watered, flitting across the roiling mass of people spread across the terminal floor. They were divided into sections by what appeared to be age. Every group was closely guarded by Watchers toting assault rifles.

The iconic terminal, with its egg-crate ceiling and giant train system map etched into marble along one side of the interior, had been turned into some sort of refugee camp. People from all walks of life were spread out across the floor. Their limp, smudgy clothes told me that many of the detainees had been there a while, and their defeated postures said they weren't particularly enthusiastic about their final destination. It was a place devoid of hope.

Parker gave me a heavy glance as the Watchers hustled us past the sallow-faced captives and shuttered terminal shops. The smell was overwhelming—sweet and sour notes, like rank trash and excrement. The whole operation was excessive. None of the captives had the strength to stand up, much less put up a fight.

Even though we hadn't had much choice about coming to St. Petersburg—it was our only hope of finding Hayes and the Resistance right now—I wondered if it had been the wrong decision.

The soldier man-handling my arm hustled me toward an empty cordoned-off area. There were a few raggedy blankets strewn across the small square of space, giving it the sense of having been recently vacated. An involuntary shudder ran through me as I wondered what happened to the people who had been here before.

The Watcher lifted the rope and shoved me into what was essentially a holding pen, Parker right behind me. He said something gruff in Russian and I tried my best not to spit at him. I tried to maintain the *who me* innocent look that said I was harmless, but Parker's pinched expression said I wasn't getting an A+ on this exam. We needed to find a way out of here, and drawing more scrutiny than we already had wasn't the way to do it.

"What now?" Parker whispered to me.

My eyes searched the perimeter of the terminal building. Every exit, every inch, was crawling with Watchers. I wove my arm into hers, half-expecting her to shrug me off. Instead, she pulled me tighter.

"All I know is we've made it this far," I said.

"And we're not failing at the finish line," she replied.

I nodded.

A string of guttural yells came from the far end of the terminal as more Watchers burst in, dragging the other passengers from our train with them.

"We need a signal," I whispered frantically.

"What?" Parker asked, dazed.

"A signal. So we know when to bolt if we need to. They're going to throw the other passengers in here with us, and we can't trust people not to recognize me and rat us out. The survival instinct is strong—trust me," I said.

"The whistle. The Resistance one. Do you know it?" Parker asked.

I remembered skimming across the darkened water to Bên Trong Mắt, Hayes's three-toned whistle piercing through the night.

"Yeah. I know it," I said.

The Watchers were only feet away, dragging the Australian backpackers and others by the arm. It was like they had lost all empathy—as if the people suffering around them were nothing more than inconvenient scenery. I was suddenly very afraid of the society I'd returned to; it was beyond terrifying that one evil person could propagate so much of herself into the world in such a short time. Why didn't people refuse to become the monsters she demanded them to be?

"We should take turns keeping watch. They have to let their guard down eventually," Parker said.

As they shoved the remaining passengers from our train into the little square we now called home, Parker and I huddled against each other.

"I sure as hell hope so," I said.

———

My stomach growled so loudly it seemed to echo off the walls of the station.

We'd been captives for less than twelve hours, and according to the institutional clock hanging from the wall opposite our makeshift pen, it was nine in the morning. But it had to be the middle of the night. Nothing here made sense.

Parker was leaning heavily against me, asleep, making it impossible to get comfortable on the hard floor. All around me, the rhythmic quiet of slumber filled the air. Still, I could feel others like me. Those that stared into the darkness of the terminal, unable or unwilling to escape into dreams.

Just before sunset, the Watchers had rounded up a square of captives, forced them to their feet, and marched them out of the building. They'd all started crying piteously—too worn down to protest but begging for mercy. They were shepherded out of the building, rifles poking into their backs, into what appeared to be giant military convoy trucks idling outside. I could feel the frigid bite of winter threading in through the open doors and smell the crisp freshness of the snow on the ground. I could also smell the burnt-hair stench of fear. Wherever those people were being taken, it wasn't anywhere good. I'd closed my eyes and let my mind wander in search of a happier place.

A gooey slice of pizza, fresh out of the oven. The smell of jasmine on the trellis of my bedroom window, in a Twin Falls so far away it might as well be Oz. The crash of waves against the sand. The beach. Hayes. His golden hair catching the sunlight; his warm eyes hinting of a secret something more.

My mind reached out to him, trying to imagine that sunny boy in this frigid city, huddled up for warmth someplace close by. I couldn't conjure the image. For me he was warmth and light, and this place was nothing but darkness upon darkness.

Dark places, dark things. My thoughts turned to Adam. Where was he right now? What was he doing? It was almost too much to bear, thinking of him. After everything I'd seen. After all I'd seen him do. Was I already too late?

A viscous-sounding cough at the catty-corner end of the terminal brought me back to reality. It was swiftly followed by another, this time more like a rough hacking sound. It had been a while, but I recognized a certain quality in it. It reminded me of one of the worst moments of my life—seeing Mercy burst into the Wangs' dining room and vomit blood all over the floor before collapsing into a nearly lifeless pile of flesh and bone.

No. No way.

I jostled Parker awake and she snorted in objection, then sat bolt upright. To her credit, she didn't make a peep.

Whoever was responsible for the coughing staggered to their feet, a shadow outlined against the dim gray light filtering out of some distant recess of the terminal. From what I could discern, it was a boy, not much older than Parker and me. He lurched toward the nearest Watcher, trampling over the other prisoners underfoot. The Watcher seemed unsure what to do, gaping at him and shrinking back in fear.

Finally springing into motion, the Watcher yelled something and then blew on a whistle that was hooked to his utility belt. The boy crashed into him, his arms wrapping around the soldier as he began to vomit a stream of blood. The soldier stumbled back, trying unsuccessfully to get away as the boy's hacking got worse, droplets of blood spraying shadows through the stale air.

Parker and I both sprang to our feet, our fellow train passengers still sleeping unawares around us.

In the same catty-corner square, another person rose, coughing. Watchers clattered from all corners of the sleeping terminal as the postage-stamp of prisoners at the far corner sprang to life, two of them coughing, then vomiting and convulsing. Looking around, I could see the wide-eyed look of other captives. They shrank back from the scene, arms slung across their faces as if that might protect them from the virus that was most certainly hurtling through the air.

The Watchers seemed unsure exactly how to proceed, pointing their guns at the coughing prisoners who were now stumbling across the barriers. They careened toward the Watchers, arms outstretched in pleas for help.

"This is it," I said.

Parker nodded toward the door near the back of the terminal, where we'd come in from the train platform. One of the Watchers who'd rushed in to inspect the commotion had left it ajar. Everything else was still locked down tight.

"If we go around the back, they might not notice us," Parker whispered.

One of the Australian girls looked up at us, fear shining in her eyes. I held a finger to my lips. I wanted to take her with us—I wanted to take them all with us. I nudged Parker and motioned to the girl. She shook her head sharply: *no.* We couldn't take anyone with us, not without sabotaging our only chance of getting out of here.

That's what I told myself. What I'd told myself when I almost left Parker, and now I couldn't imagine doing this without her. Was this girl a part of our cosmic equation too?

Every life is worth saving. My own words haunted me. I couldn't save them all.

Parker jerked me away from our group, her mismatched eyes unable to meet mine. I told myself it was for the greater good. But I didn't believe it. Parker slid under the ropes as the chaos continued to grow, and I followed behind her. I was grateful we both still had our hospital masks on—even though I was supposedly immune to Isiris's virus, thanks to Adam's tattoos, Parker wasn't. Besides, there was no telling what mutations Isiris may have come up with since my imprisonment in the temple. All bets were off in this horrible new world.

We slid like shadows along the walls, holding our breath and hoping no one noticed two girls slipping quietly across the terminal while death erupted inside it. We made it all the way to the open door, where the suitcases and backpacks sat unguarded. Parker jutted her chin at the pile, and we each reached down and grabbed the closest bag available. They were sure to contain something useful—I only hoped there was at least a jacket, or we would be dead from hypothermia before the sun came up.

A Watcher shouted, and more boots tramped into the terminal. I froze for a moment, sure we were caught. Then floodlights bathed the main floor of the station in a garish glare and I turned to see the gruesome scene playing out, as if on a cruel stage. It was Isiris's new reality.

The group of coughing prisoners who'd stumbled past the ropes of their holding pen were surrounded. Watchers were gathered in a semi-circle around them, assault weapons raised, far enough away to avoid the backsplash but close enough to keep the prisoners from progressing any farther. On the periphery, other captives were beginning to cry, everyone shrinking back from the terror playing out in front of them. The infected were staggering in wild circles, crashing into one another as blood began to seep from their eyes and stream down their faces in rivulets of red. One of them—a young girl, her hair in two ragged braids—began to vomit violently, a viscous black mass. Her eyes flew wide in panic and she careened toward one of the Watchers, her arms outstretched in a plea for help. Just like Mercy.

The flat crack of a rifle echoed off the walls, followed by a cacophony of others. The smell of sulfur filled the air. The girl was blown backward off her feet, blooms of red spreading across her tattered clothing like some kind of terrible tie-dye. The Watchers turned their guns on the other two. The horrible thought that nobody but the Watchers would make it out of this terminal alive gripped me, rooting my feet in place.

"Harlow, we have to go," Parker said, tugging at my arm.

"They're going to kill them all," I said, my lips trembling.

"This is our only chance. If we stay, we die," she said.

"We don't leave people behind," I said, my voice firming with conviction.

More shots rang out—all three of the infected prisoners were prostrate on the floor now, pools of red seeping out from beneath them. The Watchers were still pumping them full of bullets, but some of them were beginning to snap out of their murderous haze and look around. We only had minutes—maybe seconds—before they turned their attention to everyone else. I was so afraid of what would happen then.

Parker's eyebrows fell into a scowl, but my words had met their mark. "Fine, you win. Hey assholes! Over here!" she yelled, waving her arms.

The Watchers lifted their heads and looked in our direction. Parker waved her hands wildly.

"What—" I started, feeling all the color drain from my face. Every head in the terminal turned our way, and I realized what she was doing.

"Everyone run!" I yelled, joining in.

There was a frozen moment where it seemed no one in the entire building moved or even breathed. Then, chaos. A bullet whistled past my head and exploded a piece of marble in the wall behind me. I barely felt Parker grab me by the collar and pull me hard in the opposite direction. It felt like I was moving in slow motion, swimming in a dream. Then the collar of my T-shirt tightened around my neck like a noose and pulled me up short; my feet skidded against the ground. I turned sharply in the direction of the tug and ran full speed out the door and onto the platform.

Parker was in front of me, sprinting faster than I thought those matchstick legs could carry her, vaulting herself off the platform and onto the tracks. The night was so bitter cold it was like a physical barrier, turning my muscles to solid blocks of ice. I imagined a ghostlike graze of fingers at the back of my neck as I followed her off the platform, needles of pain shooting through my feet as I landed hard. I realized it wasn't fingers I'd felt; it was another bullet.

Parker volleyed between the metal ties of the tracks, kicking up gravel that pelted me in the shins as I ran after her. I didn't dare glance behind us. Every step forward felt like it was bringing me back, closer and closer and closer to the beasts that pursued us.

We broke clear of the canopy of the station, and the single thread of track branched into a many-veined network. We dodged between parked train cars, jumping over axles. Blackened snow drifted out from the sides of the rusty metal tracks and seeped into my tennis shoes, numbing my feet but not slowing my escape. The air was so cold it felt like ice crystals were forming inside my lungs, causing a pain so caustic I feared I might never breathe again.

Parker chose a random track and broke free alongside it, obscured behind the camouflage of an abandoned train. I felt no more fingers on my neck, so I chanced a glance over my shoulder. There were Watchers on the platform, but none in pursuit. They were too busy trying to manage the stream of escapees pouring through the doors. The intermittent crack of their rifles made my stomach turn.

We had escaped, for now. But not everyone would be so lucky. I thought of the poor girl with the braids lying in a pool of her own blood, and I ran twice as hard as tears stung my eyes.

BEFORE: TRAPPED IN THE TEMPLE, DREAMING OF ISIRIS

"Remember the first time we listened to the Descendants together?" Adam said, brushing a strand of Isiris's hair back from her face.

He was so close. The familiar smell of him—musky and minty—made my chest ache with sadness. I could feel the warmth of him along the length of Isiris's body; knees touching, hands woven together. His eyes looked into mine. I could see the little flecks of silver around his irises, which were so blue they sometimes almost looked purple.

I loved Adam's eyes. I loved Adam.

He and Isiris were lying down on a large, sumptuous bed in a room I didn't recognize. Everything was black—the bedspread, the pillows, the furniture, the walls. There were punk rock posters on one wall and a collection of skateboards propped against another. This must be Adam's room. Other than for his things, *it wasn't how I'd imagined a room of his would look. And I had imagined his rooms—first at his parents' house, and later at the Blue House—many times. Adam may have been into dark things, but I'd always pictured his rooms as filled with light— books strewn everywhere, little pieces of writing on random pieces of paper, discarded record sleeves littering the space. No. This room didn't fit him. It seemed like a room someone would create if they presumed to know him but didn't understand his heart.*

I had a pretty good feeling who that someone was.

"Yes, I remember. But I want to hear you tell me," Isiris lied. "I never get tired of hearing that story."

She didn't know that story from a hole in the wall. For a second I imagined what might happen if Adam recognized her counterplay for what it was—a liar's bargain. But instead he broke into a lazy smile, flashing his straight white teeth and the adorable dimple that would make any hetero girl in her right mind lose it. He leaned in a millimeter closer.

Part of me was horrified, yet still I felt myself straining toward him. Willing him to make contact. Even if it wasn't me he was kissing, I would give almost anything to feel the warmth of his lips on mine.

Just before contact was made, he began to recount the story I knew so well.

"We were rummaging around in the storage locker we'd found in the basement of your house. The General was away on some kind of errand, and we'd spent all day eating cheese puffs and soda I'd pilfered from outside the compound. I dared you to take a swig from the little bottle of whiskey one of the delinquents down at the Blue House had given me, and we were feeling

invincible. It was a week after the first time I kissed you, out back against the carriage house, and I was really hoping it was going to happen again."

Adam paused, making a humming sound in the back in his throat that vibrated in my soul. The thought of that time in our lives—the excitement, the hesitance, the feeling that we were about to discover something we'd always known but couldn't uncover until just that moment—made me want to make that sound too.

He closed the gap between us, his lips pressing against Isiris's. But it felt as if they pressed against mine.

The warmth of his lips made me burn. Made her burn. The way his entire body flexed, as if he could barely restrain himself from all the other things he longed to do with me. With her. The quickening of his breath as he responded to the feel of me—of her—against him. It was so sweet and right and good that I could almost forget it was happening to Isiris, not to me. But almost doesn't count.

It was as bitter as it was sweet.

I couldn't forget. Just like I couldn't press myself against him to let him know I felt all those things too, or hold him tighter to me, or kiss him back so passionately that he would know I was trapped inside Isiris and dying to get out. And when I thought of it that way, it started to feel more like a betrayal. It started to feel so unbearably awful that everything within me rebelled, a tide welling up inside me and rejecting this tender moment that was so finely wrought with pain.

Isiris jerked her head back. Adam's eyes flew wide.

"What? What is it?" he asked, his hand running up her arm in reassurance.

Isiris's mind was a flood of confusion. It took me a moment to realize it, so caught up in my own drama, but Isiris's own actions had taken her by surprise. Something deep within me perked up. Maybe she hadn't expected to pull away—maybe I made that happen.

"Nothing. I just—tell me the rest of the story," Isiris said, *her silky response belying the turmoil I felt shaking in her very bones. I'd lived a lifetime getting used to the feeling of someone inhabiting me, taking over my body; for her, it was entirely new. If that's what had happened at all. There was really only one way to find out.*

A wrinkle of concern appeared between Adam's eyebrows, but he obliged. His eyes watched Isiris's carefully.

"We were wading through all those moldy boxes. They came up practically to your neck, you're such a teeny-tiny. Remember that?" he asked.

"I'm not tiny except in stature," Isiris said. *I could feel the offense settling into her soul, as if it were the worst thing someone could say about her.*

"There's no doubt about that," Adam said, smiling his signature smile. "So here we are, tramping through those boxes, frantically looking for more records, and you trip over something and fall face-first into a gold mine."

I could feel Isiris bristling at the idea of her being so clumsy or comical, but I remembered it another way. I recalled how I saw that record sitting in an open box like a sign from the universe. So excited at the prospect that I'd found something that Adam was most certainly going to love. So much so that in my haste to grab it, I tripped and fell on my face.

But far from remembering my embarrassment, what I remembered was the way he rushed over to pull me up. The way his hands felt on me as he ran them up and down my sides, making sure I was okay. How he'd picked me up and half-spun me when he saw what it was that I'd face-planted over. And how, when he set me down and leaned over, I was sure he was going to kiss me. How crushed I was when instead he reached past me, plucked the record from the box, and held it high over his head in victory.

"I thought you were going to kiss me that day. It crushed me when you didn't."

I was so caught up in my own intense feelings at the memory that Isiris's words took a moment to register.

There was no way she could have known that. No way, unless she guessed, or... my feelings flowed two ways. If I could feel her emotions, maybe even control her—then maybe she could feel me. And it would only be a matter of time before she realized I was lurking in her head. Maybe she already knew.

I felt Adam's hand slip beneath the hem of Isiris's shirt, his palm warm against her stomach. He moved it higher and whispered against her mouth. "Let me make it up to you."

I wanted to scream. I wanted to rage. But I was too afraid. I couldn't afford for Isiris to feel me there. So instead I smothered my feelings until they couldn't breathe, and retreated somewhere deep within. Somewhere I didn't have to experience all the glorious things Adam was making Isiris feel.

AFTER:
ST. PETERSBURG, RUSSIA

Parker and I stuck to darkened alleyways, our footsteps muffled by the snow. The makeshift outfits we pillaged from our stolen backpacks made us look like escapees from some kind of demented carnival. We only had one pair of fingerless gloves, so we each took one. My fingertips were so cold it felt like there were ten individual snake bites throbbing at the end of my arm. I had on a giant army parka, and Parker wore a lime-green ski-bunny jacket, complete with a rainbow striped scarf that reminded me of the socks Dora used to wear to add flair to her uniform. I missed Dora. I wanted to go home—home to a time and place that didn't even exist anymore. At least, not in this world.

"The sun's going to be coming up soon," Parker said.

"It's almost the Violet Hour," I said, watching the words form crystalline clouds in the freezing air.

Parker rolled her eyes. "I'm not in the mood for religious mumbo-jumbo right now."

I looked at her and blinked. Her caustic comment caused a flare of anger in me for reasons that were not entirely rational. Psychological conditioning, of course. But also it made me think of Adam and Isiris; it made me wonder if they were together now, sharing this Violet Hour as they had others.

"I'm not really in the mood for it either," I said. "In fact, I wouldn't mind never seeing one again."

"Just keep watching the walls. If the Resistance is here, they'll have left a sign somewhere," Parker said.

A moment after she spoke, a hulking shadow merged into view. It towered over us in the shape of an inverted triangle—the VisionCrest calling card. There were more shadows of a similar shape coming into focus behind it. My blood ran colder than the icicles glimmering from the rooftop eaves.

"What the—" Parker began.

The blurry outline came into clearer view.

It was an old man, hung upside down on a cross. His legs were splayed and nailed horizontally, his head pinned to the planks by two stakes driven straight through his eyes. His arms dangled toward the ground as if he were still reaching out for help. The upside-down posture had caused blood to pool in his head, and it was purple and distended like an overripe plum. Behind him a row of similar bodies hung, nailed in a posture meant to imitate the VisionCrest logo. As my eyes adjusted and I stifled the urge to gag behind my hand, the cross behind the old man came into view—it was a little girl, no more than eight.

I leaned over and vomited into a snow drift, Parker's hand on my back.

There was no doubt that this was Isiris's doing—her and her Watchers. There was writing scrawled on the cross in Cyrillic. I knew it must say something along the lines of "traitor." In St. Petersburg, this was what happened to anyone who defied the new authority. I wanted to fall to my knees and weep.

I will even this score, I vowed to the silent victims.

"We can't be out here when the sun comes up. They'll spot us in a second," I said. The nights of Arctic winter were long, but maybe not long enough.

Patrols had been rolling through the deserted city streets all night, police boats cruising the canals that veined the city and sweeping spotlights across the snowy landscape. St. Petersburg looked like the dessert case at an abandoned bakery: row upon row of aging pastel mansions in baby blues, precious pinks, and canary yellows, finished with swirling white ornamentation. Bare-branched trees frosted with snow-like icing, chunks of ice floating like miniature glaciers in the canals. It was sweetness smothered in rot, just like everything Isiris touched. Looking more closely at the houses, I saw for the first time that some had VisionCrest symbols graffitied on them with red spray-paint—a sign of either friend or foe, I couldn't be sure which. The only thing I knew for certain was that either the haves or the have-nots had met an unfortunate end.

"Just keep watching the walls," Parker repeated, willfully ignoring the horror. "We'll find what we're looking for."

We came to the end of yet another alley. Every time we reached a crossroad, my stomach tied in knots. We had to scurry along the sidewalk in full view to get to the next alley over, and eventually we were going to run out of alleys and have to cross one of the canal bridges. If a patrol came along at the right time, we might as well be wearing giant neon arrows over our heads. Trying to find the Resistance was like trying to find a needle in a haystack, only the haystack was filled with jerks who wanted to shoot you.

"Do you think anyone's still living in these buildings?" I asked, huffing for breath as we hustled past the doorstep of yet another hulking cupcake. There were no lights on anywhere—the whole place was like a ghost town, haunted by the crucified innocents.

"If they are, they don't want anyone to know it," Parker said.

We were almost to the entrance of the next alley when a spotlight swept around the corner. Parker put her arm out to stop me. We both froze, the only sound in the snow-blanketed dimness the heavy in-and-out of our breathing. There was a knot of four Watchers coming around the corner on the next block, just past the alley. They paused at the corner, chattering among themselves. Two of them lit cigarettes, the tips glowing red under the rapidly lightening canopy of the Arctic sky. If we moved, we risked them seeing us; if we didn't, we risked the same.

I looked ahead to the next alley, trying to judge the distance. My eye caught on a symbol nestled among a riot of other graffiti. I'd seen it drawn in the sand on the beach at

Bên Trong Mắt when I'd returned to the Resistance compound—a closed eye with a teardrop coming from its corner. At the time, I thought it was just something a contemplative artist had done with idle hands. But as soon as I saw it on that wall, I knew it for what it really was.

Hope.

"Parker, look," I whispered, so quietly it barely counted as a sound. She shot daggers in my direction, but then her gaze followed to where I was pointing and her face lit up. She nodded vigorously, her hand gripping my arm.

At that moment, one of the patrolmen looked up from his cig. I saw him squint a little against the lightly falling snow. Parker's lime-green jacket was pretty hard to miss, even in the midst of a full-on blizzard.

"Oh, shit. Run!" Parker said, barreling ahead. I took off after her, trying to catch up.

For a few crazy seconds, we were headed right for the pack of Watchers. They just stared at us, cigarettes dangling from lips and puffs of air forming like comic-book *WTF* thought-bubbles over their heads. As we skidded hard-left into the alley, they sprang to life, pulling their guns and charging toward us. I could hear their CBs squawking as someone in their posse sounded the alarm. Maybe they recognized us. If so, they were alerting the authorities that they'd hooked some very big fish, and we were very likely what is commonly known as screwed.

Up ahead of us the alley was like a black hole. There were no lights, so I couldn't see farther than a few feet ahead. We could be about to run into a brick wall and I wouldn't know it. Parker was such a fast runner that I couldn't even try to keep up with her—in another life, the girl would have been some kind of track and field champion—but we were both faster than the dudes chasing after us. Barely.

I had no idea how she did it while busting out a dead-on sprint, but Parker whistled the three-toned whistle I'd heard Hayes sound at Bên Trong Mắt. Unbelievably, off in the distance, someone else's whistle mirrored her call.

"Keep going, don't let up!" she huffed.

I felt like my lungs might explode. The familiar whizz-sting of bullets pierced the air. Being shot at was becoming, like, my job or something. A piece of pavement exploded at my feet as an amorphous blackness opened up at the end of the alley. There was an enormous boulevard up ahead, lit up with streetlights on either side. It might as well be target practice, we were so exposed. The whistle sounded again, closer this time.

We broke past the end of the alley and Parker careened right. The whistle sounded again, this time directly overhead.

Incredibly, there was a rope ladder dangling from a third story window, a feral-looking boy peering over its edge. Parker grabbed ahold and scrambled up a few rungs, me on her heels. I could hear the Watchers scrambling behind us, almost to the end of the alley.

As we clawed our way up the rungs, a crew of unseen people heaved the ladder up the side of the building, pulling it up from inside. Our pursuers came out into the light of the street just as I was hoisted the last few inches over the edge of the window.

I fell into the strange house and landed on top of Parker, but not before catching a glimpse of the Watchers below looking left-right-left in confusion. The street was silent—there was no sign of either Parker or me. We'd disappeared into thin air. None of them thought to look up.

Parker wriggled out from under me. There was a pale half-moon of curious faces leaning over us.

"Park? Is that seriously you?" the boy who'd dangled the rope ladder asked. If it were possible, he was even scrawnier than Parker and looked to be just as scrappy.

Parker sprang to her feet and barreled into him, nearly knocking him out with the force of her hug. "Yes, it's me! Didn't think you could get rid of me that easily, did you?"

Feral boy didn't seem as excited to see her. He untangled himself from her arms long enough to point at me, still sitting on the floor.

"Who's she?" he asked.

The others shifted nervously, looking first at each other, then at me, then at Parker, then back at me. If I didn't know better, I'd say they seemed a little hostile. I searched the faces for any sign of familiarity, but there was nothing. If these were the same people who'd lived at Bên Trong Mắt, they must have been hiding then. This tattered group looked nothing like the people I remembered from the compound—there were no adults, for starters, and these kids looked hungry and haunted.

"*I* am the reason you're going to take us to Hayes," I said to the boy.

Just saying Hayes's name made my heart leap, and it also

spawned a reaction. The half-moon closed in a little tighter, leaning in even closer to scrutinize me. Apparently these were the right people after all. I recoiled a bit and rose shakily to my feet. The afterglow of adrenaline had faded, leaving in its place a brave but shivering uncertainty.

Feral boy squinted at me, no discernible glint of recognition in his eyes. His condescending smile revealed a set of braces missing half its brackets, glinting in the glow of the moonlight. He looked from me back to Parker.

"Hayes isn't going to let you back just because you bring some random girl to him," he said to her. "You're just like this cat I used to have—Bootsie—kept killing rats and leaving them on my doorstep like I was supposed to throw him a frickin' parade."

Parker's self-satisfied smile fell from her face.

I took a step forward. "I'm not a rat, and you can quit talking about me like I'm not standing right here," I said. What was this kid, like, twelve?

I was about to demand to be taken to Hayes immediately when bellows pierced the night. Down on the street, the Watchers were still looking for us. Even from here, we could see the flashing of blue and red lights that meant they'd called in reinforcements—after what happened at the train station, the Watchers were probably planning to cordon off the neighborhood.

With the window standing wide open, it was only a matter of time before someone took note of that incongruous detail—it wasn't exactly common practice to leave your window open to enjoy a refreshing winter breeze when you lived on Siberia's doorstep. It might seem like the entire city was abandoned, but every window was shut tighter than a drum. People were hiding.

"Truman, we've gotta go. They're going to be up our asses any second now," a bedraggled girl with a gnarly nest of hair said.

Everyone looked to feral boy, myself and Parker included. Like it or not, he was clearly the tiny lieutenant of this ragtag outfit.

"Let's get up to the roof," he said, cocking his head toward the interior of the house. "Priority number one is keeping this one safe." He jutted his chin at me and broke into a sly smile that told me he'd known who I was all along. He was just tormenting Parker. "Hayes will have our asses if we let anything happen to the real Harlow Wintergreen."

BEFORE:
TRAPPED IN THE TEMPLE

I knew how to escape—at least I thought I did. But no matter how hard I looked, in a house of infinite doors it was impossible to find the one that was my ticket out. The one that was *mine*—where *my* world, *my* life was waiting. So I'd decided to test my theory on another door, risking the chance that I would be stuck somewhere and never get back. Doing nothing was no longer option—I had to act or I would die.

I peered through the door I'd chosen. The world beyond it seemed innocuous enough. A sweeping vista of emerald trees stretched across the horizon, a tiered series of bone-white steps folding out in front, dropping off at a steep angle that prevented me from seeing what was beyond but provided a clear landmark so I could find my way back into the temple if this experiment worked. I'd watched this door for ten consecutive Violet Hours and nothing had moved, save an occasional swallow winging its way across the sky. Everything looked tranquil and empty. So long as I was gambling with my existence, this seemed as good a place as any to put my chips on the table.

The negative pressure of beating wings and empty space filled my head—the Violet Hour beginning again. I looked to my right; a sharp outcropping of stone jutted out beside me. I slashed my hand brutally against it. Garnet blood flowed between the creases of my palm. I held my breath and pressed my hand against the waiting doorway.

A sucking sensation. The chaos of disorientation. And then there I was, standing on those white-tiered steps at the top of some kind of pyramid. I closed my eyes and breathed in. The crisp air was so different from the stifling stillness of Isiris's temple. A faint, rhythmic sound filled my mind, then my limbs. It was like a lullaby. At first I thought it was the euphoria of freedom, but then I realized it wasn't coming from inside of me. It was coming from all around me. From below me. This world was like wearing someone else's skin.

Here there was no Harlow.

My eyes opened. Somewhere far below me, at the base of the pyramid, a sea of bodies swayed as if in a trance. I was too far away to discern individuals, only noticed they were dressed in white to match the limestone steps.

I moved forward, straining to peer over the steep-angled steps. The din rose a decibel, as if in acknowledgement.

My eyes trailed down the tiered incline. Brilliant slashes of red stained the path at odd intervals. The *drip-drip-drip* of blood, falling like teardrops from my palm, dotted the ground beneath me. I looked at those dots, then back at the steps.

Though a shade darker, and dried and baked under the constant sun, there was no mistaking that these marks were the same. Blood.

I put my hand up to shield my eyes from the sun, straining to get a better look at the people below. Why was there blood on the steps?

My feet carried me forward, despite the tug-pull inside me that told me to turn back. The crowd chanted, louder than before. Voices carried on the wind, up-up-up to the highest heights. Though I didn't want to see what was below me, an inexorable force inside me pulled me on.

A procession began, inching its way up the incline toward me in two even columns. It would take a long time for them to ascend, but the Violet Hour was far away. Fear knotted in my stomach.

I looked to my left and right. There was only warm wind and open air and a very long fall to the scrub-brush ground below. Behind me was what appeared to be some kind of pyre, just taller than my head. Carved within it was a symbol of the Inner Eye, the place from which I must have emerged. Sooty ash flew from it, minuscule flakes of charcoal-gray fluttering in the air like snow every time a new gust blasted the pyramid, knocking me off balance.

I turned back to the revelers, who were still marching their way up the steps. They suddenly looked closer. Close enough that I could make out the crimson sashes of the two people at the head of each column and the apparently heavy lump of something that they held between them, also shrouded in crimson. They were carrying something that had an unmistakably body-like outline, visible even from this high vantage point. It seemed to be writhing a bit in their arms. Something about the movement made my knees go weak.

I sat down on the top step. The group was closer still, their incessant chant louder by the second. The sun arced across the sky as I watched them. Waiting. Time slowed down, time sped up. There was nothing I could do. Nowhere I could run.

I watched and watched. They got closer, their chanting louder. The crimson lump rippled with movement on occasion, but mostly it was still. When the sky purpled, the climbers lit torches they produced from hidden places. The flames exploded at the front of the line, and the fire was passed down farther than my eye could follow. It seemed that the ant-like column stretched miles, all the way to the ground.

I looked behind me, at the hulking pyre that cast one last shadow over my head. I knew now what this was.

An altar.

Something inside me made me rise to my feet. The din of voices rose another decibel, as if frenzied to ecstasy by my mere act of standing. The thing writhed beneath its crimson cloak. In my gut I knew this was something terrible, and I was going to have no choice but to face it. This wasn't a game of Truth or Dare. The unthinking masses would leave me no alternative.

Well if this was an altar, then the only way I could survive was as a god.

The world was reborn, fresh and gleaming. The little wounds of the pilgrims who came to me with their twisted offering no longer mattered. I would destroy them before they could destroy me. I was a god. I watched and waited, waited and watched, past the setting of the sun and through the night.

The dark was almost overtaken by dawn when they finally reached the last step. We were face-to-face at last.

A man and a woman, robed in white and carrying the crimson-cloaked figure, stared unblinking into my eyes. Each of them had a necklace with what appeared to be a human eye on it. I should have felt revulsion, but I couldn't remember how to. The chanting rose up behind them like a thunder-cloud, scrambling my synapses.

I should have been all sweaty palms and quivering bones. Instead, I was a balloon about to take flight.

I opened my arms to them, as if I could pull aside the curtain of myself and swallow them whole. The chanting thundered its obedience. Power sang through my veins, the deadliest of drugs.

The white ones lifted their crimson offering; the chanting was smothered by silence. The sky tinged purple in response— the Violet Hour announcing its presence. I wanted to stop the seconds from growing into minutes. Maybe I could. This world made me immortal.

One corner of the scarlet shroud ruffled in the breeze. An invitation. I caressed it between my fingers. The man and woman stared, unblinking. It slid away like silk over satin.

Beneath it lay the secret to my power. The beating heart of the heart. The truth of me.

It was a young girl, with angel-white hair that grew in

dream-like tendrils from her head and two crimson hollows for eyes. She turned her neck in my direction. It was her eyes that dangled from the necklaces around the man and woman's necks. The girl's chest was flayed open, her ribs shining in the waning darkness. Within them, her caged heart was beating, beating, beating.

Beckoning. Inviting the newly born part of me to hold its power in my palm.

It wouldn't beat much longer, no matter what I did. But somehow I knew that if I were the one to stop it, I would become something that could never be undone.

It was never a choice.

My hand reached out for it, reaching between the jailer's bars and closing over the slippery surface. *Beat, beat, beat.* It transferred a piece of its power to me, promising so much more.

The pilgrims dropped to their knees as I plucked the sacrificial heart from its perch like the first apple from the Tree of Life.

A gush of crimson splashed over the stairs, rivulets of red slipping down the staircase. Believers anointed themselves in it and were forgiven. I raised the heart up to the sky, beating its last. *Beat, beat…*

With every faint throb, I felt the pieces of me that were still human slipping further away. The pilgrims were frenzied now, swaying and chanting on their knees before me, rubbing themselves in blood. I saw one follower bite a chunk of flesh out of another's arm, the others swarming like piranhas to get a taste of flesh. A Bacchanalia of brutality.

There was a sensation of gravity changing, the space behind me unfolding into an origami of emptiness. It was the temple door, re-opening.

The followers snapped to attention, bright-eyed and rabid. With one last pulse, the heart ceased to beat. The last thread of my humanity nearly slipped through my fingers. Nearly. In my mind's eye, I caught it and held on for dear life.

I didn't want to be a god; or rather, I wanted it very badly, but knew it was something I should not have. Something no one should have.

I looked over my shoulder. A thousand rays beamed against the temple door. They pulsed, brighter and brighter. Blinding. I turned to run.

The believers scrabbled after me, their moans of rhythmic ecstasy turning to anger. The white-robed man grabbed my ankle, his fingers curling around it stronger than any vise. I lost my balance, falling hard on one knee with a lightning flash of pain I felt in my teeth. I kicked violently, bone connecting with bone. The man lost his balance and was shoved over the side by the advancing swarm, but it was too late. The believers were over, above, and around me. They lifted me up, holding my arms and legs immobile, the heart still lukewarm and spongy in my hand. Over my head, the pyre roared to life above the gate. The chanting voices merged to one, called to purpose by the flames. I wasn't sure if it was the heart, or me, or both that they meant to burn. But I couldn't afford to find out.

We were a stone's throw from the door to the temple, its brilliant lights fading as the Violet Hour neared its end. I had to get through it—I wouldn't survive in this world, with these people. And if I did, I would never escape. They had no intention of letting their god go free. With a flick of my wrist, I said a prayer to whatever twisted god really was in charge in this infinitely crazy universe and tossed the heart through the gate to the temple.

A cry of anguish rose up from the believers. Momentarily distracted, they loosened their grip on me. I wrenched my way free and tumbled to the ground. I jumped up as one of the believers put her hand through the gate. Testing it.

No. I couldn't allow them into the temple. Being trapped in the temple was one thing; being trapped with these worshippers was another.

"Stop!" I bellowed.

The believers froze, heads swiveling from me to the door and back again.

"Move. Now! Move!" I yelled, commanding them.

I could tell they didn't know the words I was saying. But they understood it was a command. The crowd parted before me.

It was time to perform a miracle.

All eyes were on me. It was clear they were deciding whether to obey, or to recommence carrying me to the pyre. Without the heart, it seemed no one knew quite what to do. I was a god, but I was misbehaving.

I kept eye contact with as many of the followers as I could, willing myself to look confident instead of what I really was. Ashamed. Horrified. Afraid.

I was just a foot from the gate when it began to close, the

clear view of the temple on the opposite side becoming cloudier at the edges. My feet wanted to run, but I knew that any sudden move could cause the believers to collapse in on me.

Calmly, calmly.

"Stay there," I said.

I turned my back to the gate, my palms faced out to them to underscore my meaning. I backed up, feeling my foot catch on the edge of the temple door.

One of the believers shouted something unintelligible, and they sprang into motion. I launched myself backward, desperate to make it. I was halfway into the temple when I felt a hand close around my wrist, then another. They pulled me back toward their world as the gate closed in around me. Teeth bit into the taut line of my Achilles tendon, but I kicked my way free. I was going to be torn in half.

I thrashed wildly, smashing my arm against the door's side. The hand was knocked loose, my fingers pulling back just as the door closed around me. A slicing sensation whispered across the tip of my finger. I fell back onto the temple floor, hyperventilating.

My leg throbbed where the worshippers had bitten through my flesh. Blood dripped onto the floor from the missing tip of my finger. It mingled with the blood from something else. My eyes fixed on the innocent heart. It gave one last twitch before falling completely still.

Something inside me had come to life—something dark and frightening. Another part of me had died. Maybe being trapped in here was a punishment I deserved.

AFTER:
ST. PETERSBURG, RUSSIA

Truman rolled back a section of the chain-link fence surrounding the Winter Palace. The former home of Catherine the Great still retained its imposing grandeur; a hulking teal sentinel, it was lined with white colonnades and gold leaf accents as far as the eye could see. The Neva River thrummed unseen behind it, the icy waters rushing to the Gulf of Finland.

It was the absolute most conspicuous place in the city, which made it the best possible hiding place.

"Age before beauty," Truman said, motioning for me to climb through the gap. His braces winked at me.

We'd jumped from ice-slicked rooftop to ice-slicked rooftop like a pack of mongrel cats, shimmying down a fire escape only when we were well outside the search radius. We'd traveled in silence, listening to the growl of engines as caravans gunned through the streets on their way to join the search party. Every Watcher in the city seemed to have been called in, which wasn't good. Hopefully no one had connected the dots between what I'd done in Beijing and the shitstorm that erupted in the train station. My stomach flipped.

Parker had stayed by my side the entire escape, helping me across gaps and steadying me as I slid across the slick snow. Gnawing doubt about why she hadn't been welcomed with open arms by Truman and his gang needled at me. What if I couldn't trust her? Worse still, what if she wasn't one of the good guys?

It was too late now. All I could do now was hope my instincts could still be trusted and I hadn't led the wrong person right to the Resistance's doorstep.

I ducked and went through the gap in the fence, Parker and Truman following behind. Truman made some kind of hand motion and the rest of the gang dispersed, disappearing like smoke into the blue velvet sky.

"They'll keep watch, just in case the goon squad decides to catch a clue," he said.

I nodded, not wanting to think about it. After so long on the run, all I wanted was a moment of security. Somewhere behind the thousands of windows that covered every inch of the palace exterior, Hayes was waiting. Right now, he was my safety. I was nervous and exhilarated all at once.

We slipped across the abandoned plaza and into the dark shadows along the edge of the palace. Truman moved stealthily along the side of the building until he stopped beneath a seemingly random window.

"Give me a boost," he said to Parker. She laced her hands

together, and he stepped up into them like they'd done it a million times before. Then he tapped out a rhythmic signal on the glass, which felt as if it was blaring through a loud-speaker that could be heard across the entire city. I held my breath.

A moment later, the entire pane of glass was lifted out from the inside and a girl stuck her head out. "What took you so lo—" She halted when she saw Parker and me, then softly swore in German. "*Scheisse*."

"Well, what are you waiting for?" Truman demanded. "Get us a lift."

The girl ducked her head inside and whistled softly. A moment later she was replaced by a teen who looked like he spent all day every day hitting the weights. He leaned out the window and pulled Truman inside. Parker held her threaded hands out to me and I stepped up, grabbing the burly guy's hand.

Just like that, I was inside the Winter Palace.

I used to spend a lot of time reading up on women who ruled empires—not wanting to admit it to myself, but looking for clues in the unlikely hope that one day I might be called upon to rule one myself. If I got what I wanted—another wish in the string of unlikely hopes that defined my life—that calling might actually come true. In a weird way, stepping onto Catherine's hallowed ground felt like I'd stepped across a line. It reminded me of the few brief moments I'd spent as the worshipped deity of an unknown land. Completely intoxicating, in all the worst ways.

If I was going to be a ruler, I was going to have to start acting like one.

"Hey!" Parker called from outside. "Don't forget me."

Truman leaned his head out. "I didn't forget. You're not coming."

Parker's face contorted and her eyes went wild. "What? You can't leave me out here!" she hissed.

"You're a traitor. We don't help traitors," he said.

A lump formed in my throat. If I didn't put myself on the line for Parker, she might not survive. If I did and I was wrong, the rest of us might not. Parker looked up at me, her mismatched eyes wounded yet hopeful. I saw a little bit of Dora in those eyes. I didn't know how, but I knew she was one of the good ones.

"We're not leaving her," I said.

Truman glared at me. "Stay out of it."

"Parker's the only reason I'm here right now, so get your friend to lean out that freaking window and help her inside," I said, the flint in my voice causing Truman to take a small step back.

"Fine. Whatever," he said, nodding at his friend. "But you're the one who can explain it to Hayes."

"My pleasure," I said, raising my eyebrows for emphasis.

The bigger kid leaned farther out the window and Parker jumped up to catch his hands. He pulled her in and she made a sour face at Truman as she came through. He made one back, but not until her back was turned. Not so tough after all.

Truman moved across the room without saying a word

and we followed at a distance, turning into a cavernous hall-way lined with doors on either side.

"Is Truman somebody important?" I whispered to her.

"He wishes," she scoffed, but I could hear the hurt in her voice.

"Why did he call you a traitor?"

"My side of the story or theirs?" she asked.

"The truth," I said.

"There's no such thing. Just my side and theirs." Parker slipped her headphones on, clearly signaling her unwillingness to discuss it any further.

I wondered what exactly I was walking into. With Parker in tow, Hayes might not be so excited to see me after all.

Truman turned and whistled at us, a low, urgent sound that demanded we catch up. Turning a corner, we emerged from the hallway into a cavernous hall. Sweeping staircases spilled down either side of the room like a white marble waterfall, and the frescoed ceiling was held up by massive baroque columns several stories high. Every inch of the place was carved and filigreed with enough gold to fill Ali Baba's cave three times over. My breath came out in chilly puffs. It was like being inside the world's most ostentatious meat locker. Truman was waiting there, his arms crossed and impatience creasing his forehead.

"This way," he said, not bothering to turn around as he began marching up the staircase, which seemed to go on forever.

I was short of breath in no time as I focused on putting one foot in front of the other. It wasn't until we were nearly to the top that I noticed something move in the shadows of the landing above. I squinted into the darkness. The person moved into a sliver of moonlight filtering in through one of the windows. I stopped dead, rooted in place by an overwhelming mix of emotion. Parker stopped at my side, her entire body tensing.

It was Hayes.

His hair was dyed a dark black and his cheeks looked hollow, but the golden-brown glow of his eyes was exactly the same as I remembered. He had a gun strapped to his side and he was more muscular than the last time I'd seen him. He looked like a warrior. Hayes wasn't my boy of sunshine and light anymore. Still, he took my breath away.

"Hayes," I said.

He regarded me with suspicion. Of course. I was lucky he hadn't killed me on sight—he had no way of knowing I wasn't Isiris pretending to be the real me. Things were getting very meta.

"What did I bring you to eat the day we went to the beach?" he asked.

For a moment I just stared at him, confused. Then I remembered.

"A banana," I said, feeling completely ridiculous. Who knew that stupid piece of fruit was going to save my ass.

"I knew it wasn't you in the General's office that day," he said, the corners of his mouth turning up into a smile. "Harlow."

His voice was raspy yet ebullient, and the sound of him saying my name sent delicious shivers up my arms. All the tension I'd been holding inside flowed out of me. Hayes knew me for who I really was. Thank god. It took every ounce of my self-restraint not to go running right into his arms.

"Fancy meeting you here," I said, attempting a wan smile.

We took the last few steps toward each other. I resisted the urge to touch him, make sure he was real. He had that same hungry look that Truman's gang all had.

"I see you brought a friend." He nodded at Parker. She reached up and pulled her headphones off, her hands trembling slightly.

"I tried to leave her outside but she wouldn't let me," Truman broke in. Hayes gave him an inscrutable look.

"Parker's the reason I made it here. She stays," I said.

Parker stood in silence at my side, holding her breath. Desperation radiated off of her.

Hayes considered Parker for a moment, then nodded. "Well then, I guess we all have a lot to talk about. I've got it from here, Truman. Why don't you and the crew get some rest."

Truman gave Parker and me an irritated glance, but he didn't protest. Hayes was clearly in charge. Truman bounded down the stairs, every pounding footfall conveying his unspoken displeasure. Hayes entrusting that petulant brat with a leadership role meant things for the Resistance must be worse than I'd thought.

"This way," Hayes said, touching my arm lightly. I saw Parker's eyes flit to his fingers, then back again. She knew there was more between us than the shared objective to bring down VisionCrest. I pulled away, feeling guilty. Hayes's eyes flickered to mine, but other than that he didn't react. Still, I could tell I'd hurt him.

We curved down several dark hallways, Hayes navigating the darkened palace like he'd lived there his entire life. I wondered how long they'd been hiding out here—it must have been a while. Finally, he pushed open a set of colossal double doors that led into a tall, narrow room. The entire space—walls, ceiling, edging—was painted baby blue. There was a fire roaring in a massive marble fireplace. Plush velvet furniture was arranged in front of it, and there was an assortment of canned food set out on a fancy dining table.

"Step into my parlor," he said. "What do you think?"

The intensity of his eyes made me feel Jello-y.

"I think you have expensive taste for a fugitive on the run," I said.

"Well, you know. I was hoping that VisionCrest royalty might drop by, so I wanted to be prepared."

He smiled. Straight white teeth and playful grin. Sinewy muscles flexing under his thin cotton shirt. If Parker hadn't been standing there, I might have pushed him down on one of those imperial settees and had my way with him—my craving for safety and escape in human contact was that overwhelming. Keeping my distance from him was nothing short of torture, but I needed to sort things out first.

I picked up a strange but delicate crystal replica of the VisionCrest symbol, which was sitting on the mantle over the fire. I'd never seen one like it before.

"The Fellowship is giving these out. 'Believers' are supposed to display them in their homes as a symbol of their devotion and fidelity to VisionCrest. Everyone is rabid to put them in their windows, hoping it will protect them from persecution," Hayes said.

I turned the crystal over, examining it in the light. The eye had a small amount of red liquid in the iris that sent prisms over the wall. It was strangely beautiful.

"What do you think it really is?" I asked, wondering what its true purpose was.

"Propaganda." Hayes shrugged. "Psychological warfare, maybe."

"Hmm." I set it down. It seemed to watch me as I moved around the room.

"Hayes, I was hoping we could talk in private," Parker said. Her voice was meeker than I'd ever thought possible.

He looked at her, the light in his eyes going black as coal. "Anything you have to say to me can be said in front of Harlow. We don't have any secrets."

Parker squared her shoulders, trying to look like she didn't care but wearing the burden of her unhappiness as clearly as if it were strapped to her back. She was suffering under the burden of being cast out—it was obvious to me that Parker simply wanted to belong.

"No, it's okay," I said, giving Hayes a meaningful look. "We're all on the same side here."

I needed them to just get past whatever wedge was between them. She couldn't have done something so terrible that Hayes would ostracize her forever, or else we wouldn't be standing here having a polite conversation. Casting her out for a small offense would make the Resistance no different than the Fellowship, and Hayes was better than that. I knew he was.

Hayes paused for a moment, running a hand through his messy hair and looking unsure. I could see he didn't really want to be alone with Parker, but he finally relented.

"Okay, fine. But then you and I are going to speak privately," he said to me.

Despite my best efforts to ward against it, his words sent a thrill through my body. I wasn't sure if I could restrain myself with him behind closed doors, and I was even less sure that I wanted to. Every cell in my body ached to be touched and held by him. He was the closest thing to home I had, and after the ordeal I'd been through, a little piece of home sounded like nirvana.

Hayes might the one person who could help me find he strength to save Adam and defeat Isiris. I needed him. *Viscerally* needed him. And I could see in his eyes that he needed me, too. It was going to be hard to hold that back—for Adam's sake, for mine, for anyone's.

BEFORE:
TRAPPED IN THE TEMPLE,
DREAMING OF ISIRIS

Isiris stood over Adam, watching him sleep. He lay on his side in the center of the bed, one sinewy arm crooked beneath his head, lashes like spider legs. His chest was fragile in its arrhythmic rise and fall, tattoos stretching and retracting with every breath. A fortress of pillows surrounded him.

A light breeze ruffled through the open windows into the palatial room. It traipsed across the thin sheet covering him, leaving just enough to the imagination. I didn't recognize the room, but I knew one thing for sure—they weren't in Twin Falls anymore. In fact, it seemed like they were inside some kind of castle. Ceilings several stories high. Elaborate carvings, Renaissance art and museum-like tapestries clinging to the walls. The vista outside the floor-to-ceiling glass was a sea of brownish buildings tumbled together like stones cast up from the ocean. The room looked down on it all from on high. I couldn't place the city, but it was vast. Just like this new place Isiris had claimed as home.

Isiris's dark thoughts coursed through my veins. She remembered how it felt to touch him—her tongue tracing spirals across the ink, the salvation and damnation of his beautifully branded skin. She imagined what it would be like to discard her dress and slip beneath the sheets next to him; to press the length of her cold body against the full measure of his warm one. He was always so hot, like there was a fever boiling just beneath his skin. Which, in a way, there was.

Isiris's eyes darted to the half-empty glass, cloudy with narcotics, on the nightstand next to Adam's sleeping form. A vase bloated with star-gazer lilies drooped over it; the cloying scent of flowers and rot hung like a fog in the air. The sense of smell was something new. Like I'd somehow poked a hole in Isiris's world so a little more of it could seep through.

Drugged. The word whispered through my mind.

It took me a moment to realize that this thought was not my own—it was Isiris's. I wasn't sure if something had changed or if I was getting used to being on the other side of the looking glass, but this time I wasn't just a bystander. I was, at least in some small way, a participant. If I was getting stronger— the same way that Isiris had when she was the invader in my mind—then I was doing it much faster than she had. I could no longer feel the ache of my bitten ankle or missing fingertip— Isiris's body was my body, whole and unblemished. Maybe I had more power than I realized.

Helpless. Another word zigzagged across my subconscious.

I stopped marveling at my new awareness and took notice

of the sinister direction of Isiris's thoughts. Her eyes cut to the cloudy glass again as she slipped her hand into the pocket of her dress. She pressed her fingertip against the sharp corner of something small and square. Metal pricked her skin, a shiver of anticipation tickling down her spine.

She'd drugged Adam, for reasons I had no hope of understanding. Isiris was a psychopath. It might have been for nothing more than the enjoyment of toying with him. And now he was lying here, completely at her mercy. Which wasn't exactly something she had to spare.

Her twitchy finger ran along the length of the razorblade, as if testing its ability to wound. She was going to cut Adam. And I had enough experience to know what Isiris was most fond of cutting—or cutting out.

No. *My mind's eyes willed her to stop.*

Isiris's finger stilled. She cocked her neck as if searching out the source of a sudden sound. I recoiled, curling my consciousness deeper within her. Had she actually heard me? Had I been the reason her finger had stilled on the blade? I strained to hear her thoughts, but there was only silence.

Isiris returned to her fixation, taking two deliberate steps toward Adam. She pinched the razorblade between her fingers and withdrew it from her pocket, the rough silk of her dress whispering across the back of her hand. Adam was utterly still, but for breathing. Isiris raised her hand, tilting the blade so she could see the thin-sliced reflection of her eye in its surface. She blinked; for a moment, I swore I could see myself trapped within the pitch-black pupil of her evil eye.

*A protest formed in my mind, but this time nothing hap-
pened. A flutter of panic beat inside me. I wasn't in control of
this—not at all.*

*Isiris pounced, cat-like, onto the bed. She pulled the sheet off
Adam's sleeping form. I wanted to shut my eyes, to turn away
from the sight of him as I'd imagined him a million times but
never seen him until now. He was so beautiful. Perfect. His tattoos made him look like a warrior from ancient Sparta, except
he wasn't a warrior. Against Isiris he was utterly defenseless. We
all were. I couldn't close my eyes. My only option was to retreat
within, but that would mean leaving the love of my life alone
with Isiris and her razorblade. I wouldn't do that to him.*

*She crawled up next to him, sitting back on her heels and
pushing him gently so he rolled onto his back. He murmured in
his sleep. The sound of his voice vibrated in my bones. It made me
nearly insane—my desire to help him tugging against the ties that
bound me motionless, a hostage buried so deep inside Isiris that I
would never get out.*

*Frustration and fury boiled inside me. I imagined it spilling
over the edges of my subconscious and into Isiris—scalding her,
scarring her.*

Don't touch him! *I screamed.*

*Isiris's arm flew back, twisting behind her body in a light-
ning storm of pain before it dropped back to her side.*

*It took us both a second to recover. For a fleeting moment,
I felt victorious. I had done it! Controlled her!*

*I focused every thread of my consciousness on putting her
hands to her throat, imagining the life being choked out of her by*

her own traitorous fingers. Her hands rose, floating through the air as if pulled by some unseen puppeteer. It was working.

The sun moved briefly from behind the clouds, and a stray band of dim sunlight glanced off the razorblade still clutched in her hand. All I had to do was hang on—let the bright edge of the blade slash its way across her neck and be done with it once and for all. I would gladly stay inside the temple for all eternity if I could do this one thing for the people I loved.

The blade met flesh, quivering.

Push, I thought.

I felt the bite of the blade as it separated cell from cell, burrowing toward the beating lifesource that tethered Isiris to this world. I was really doing it.

"Aaarghhh." Adam's head thrashed, as if he were dreaming of pain.

Instinctually, my thoughts turned to him. Ensuring he was okay. The moment's distraction was all Isiris needed to regain control. Her hands dropped from her throat, still pinching the razorblade.

She turned her head and looked directly into a mirror that hung on the wall. It was round, with an elaborately gilded gold frame. Her lips curved up, a smile splitting her face. There was no longer any doubt. Isiris knew I was there with her. And she didn't seem the least bit afraid.

"Thank you, my love," she said.

A warm, giddy feeling swam through her body. Isiris was happy. It was not the reaction I'd expected from someone who had come so near to death at the hands of her enemy.

I had been hiding from her all this time, cowering in fear at *the thought of being discovered. Now that she knew I was here—knew I could exert my will over hers—I expected her to be furious. But instead she was ecstatic. She wanted me to watch what she was about to do to Adam. Maybe she'd known I was here the whole time. Perhaps my dream of gaining control of her was just that—a dream. One she'd let me believe because toying with me and the people I loved was just a clever game to her.*

Isiris turned her attention back to Adam, still naked on the bed. He was stirring a little from his narcotic slumber, his long fingers reaching up toward his neck as if feeling some imaginary wound.

Desperation pinned me down. My chance—possibly my only chance—was gone.

Isiris laughed softly, my hopelessness making her buoyant. Adam's left arm was still bent, palm up on the pillow. The coordinates of Isiris's temple were emblazoned on his wrist.

That's where I am right now, *I thought.* I'm not really here. This isn't happening.

Isiris laughed softly again. "Oh yes it is," *she said out loud.*

AFTER:
ST. PETERSBURG, RUSSIA

I startled awake when Parker came back into the room some time later. I'd settled onto a mess of raggedy cushions in front of the fireplace and fallen asleep without even realizing it. Survival was exhausting. Still, every time I opened my eyes and I wasn't inside the temple, it was a gift. Parker walked over and stood next to me as I sat up and rubbed my eyes.

"Hi," I said, yawning. "Sorry. I totally passed out."

Parker looked over her shoulder at Hayes, who was leaning against the doorjamb watching us. She shrugged. "No worries."

I couldn't get a read on how she was feeling—she was being stand-offish, but that was nothing new. She didn't have her headphones on, so that was at least a positive sign.

"So." Parker shifted uncomfortably and shoved her hands in her jacket pockets. "I'm gonna try to get some sleep. Hayes said there's an empty bedroom right down the hall."

"More like a hundred of them. But the one you want is the third on the right," Hayes said in light teasing tone I knew and loved. "Someone will be standing outside keeping watch. You can't miss it."

Parker rolled her eyes a bit, but in a way that seemed more jokey than like genuine irritation. "Right. What he said."

"I'll come with you," I said.

She shook her head. "Nah, I'm a big girl. You go ahead and *talk*."

"Right." I blushed. Maybe I should have protested, but I didn't really have it in me. The idea of being alone with Hayes was something that had sustained me, and it could finally be a reality. Comfort was a commodity.

Parker gave me a thin smile, then shuffled out, dragging her feet across the floor like she was too exhausted to pick them up.

I looked over to Hayes. His smile was much bigger—it lit up the room.

He walked over to me and held out his hand to help me up. My palm slipped into his. I couldn't believe how warm he felt, how the pressure of his hand closing over mine made every nerve-ending in my body spring to life. For a moment we stood still, watching each other in the firelight.

"Come on," he said.

We crossed the parlor to a massive door, where he dropped my hand and stepped back, letting me lead the way into a massive room. I could see his reflection in the shattered mirror that hung from the wall; his eyes followed me as I took it all in. His relaxed demeanor was so purely Hayes.

Always in control. Always confident. Even when everything was in shambles.

The walls were paneled in sumptuous red fabric, interspersed by columns of white marble. Firelight danced off the gold that snaked like vines up the corners and across the ceiling, dripping down like stalactites from above and seeming to writhe in the flickering shadows. There was a collection of regal-backed chairs, covered in fabric that matched the walls, in varying states of disarray—slashed with stuffing torn out, legs hobbled, seat cushions missing—but otherwise intact.

I walked to the center of the room, my footfalls echoing against the parquet floor, and looked around. A second, freestanding mirror the size of a small car tilted precariously in the corner. It too was smashed to smithereens with the pointless spray-paint of hooligan graffiti splashed across it. So this was the heart of the Rebellion. Hayes's inner sanctum, a ravaged relic of something that used to shine so bright.

I approached the fireplace. It was so immense that Hayes could have stood inside it and stretched his considerable arm span without touching either side. There was a pitiful collection of odd debris burning on the hearth, and a pair of curtains, the same hue of red as the paneled walls, lying tangled before it. The curtains must have hung over the windows before they became the only things Hayes had left to wrap himself in at night. I felt myself blush, realizing I was staring at what now passed for Hayes's bed.

"It's not much, but it's home. At least for the moment," he said.

I looked over at him. He pulled the door shut behind him and my heart began to beat double-time.

We were officially alone.

He crossed the room. Finally, he stood in front of me. Everything about him was taut, like a coiled spring set to explode. My mind reached for words, but now that I was here with him, there was no way to verbalize it. I'd imagined this so many times while trapped in the temple, despair seeming to stretch infinitely out in front of me. I'd needed one happy thing to hold on to.

Hayes reached out and touched a lock of my hair, just behind my ear. He tugged on it lightly, and one corner of his mouth turned up into what could almost pass as a smile.

"I can't believe it's really you," he said.

"Believe," I said.

"Is that an order?" he asked.

The air between us crackled with tension.

"I like your new digs," I said. "They're very ... red."

His smile grew. It was like seeing an echo of the old Hayes shining through. I wondered if he felt the same about me.

"I was going for a minimalist vibe," he said, quirking a brow.

"I'd call it more shabby chic, personally," I said.

The light banter felt good, but inadequate. I was filled with so many conflicting feelings. I needed to tell Hayes about Adam—what he planned to do and how I hoped we could prevent it. But what I wanted was for Hayes to take me in his arms and kiss me until my lips were raw. A moment of peace. Escape.

"How did you know it wasn't me that time you came to Twin Falls?" I asked.

He gazed at me. "Remember that day on the beach, when Adam caught us kissing?" he asked.

My face flushed with heat. Of course I remembered.

"Yeah," I said.

"Adam came and found me afterwards. He was pissed, demanded I stay away from you. Said you were under the influence of powerful forces I couldn't understand. It made me think that the things Madam Wang told me about Isiris invading your mind might be true."

Despite Adam's meddling turning out to be my salvation, Hayes's revelation still felt like a slap across the face. I couldn't believe Adam had divulged my secrets so recklessly, not to mention talked about me like I was some kind of possession.

"But you didn't stay away," I said. "When Isiris summoned, you came to Twin Falls."

"Adam's not my master, or yours," Hayes said firmly. "And you're not a piece of property. I'm the leader of the Resistance. If someone's messing with your mind, it's my business too." He scrutinized me. "You know the exact moment when I knew it wasn't you?"

"When?" I asked.

"When I first looked into your eyes. *Her* eyes. I know you don't think it's possible after such a short time, but I know you. And I knew she wasn't you. I was even more sure when she clearly didn't know what had happened between us on the beach."

My heart ached. Hayes, with so little information to go on, had immediately known Isiris was an imposter. And Adam, with all the information in the world, hadn't. Or worse still, he'd refused to see it.

"I knew she was coming for us," Hayes continued. "We fled Bên Trong Mắt right away, had to break up into smaller groups so they'd have difficulty tracking us. At least, tracking all of us." There was anguish in his voice. "That's how we ended up separated from the adults—they were supposed to be the bait, draw Isiris's troops away from the most vulnerable."

"What happened to them?" I asked.

"We haven't seen any of them since we fled the compound. I doubt we ever will." Hayes paused. "The Resistance is a myth—it doesn't exist anymore."

The words were like a shotgun blow to my chest. I had been surviving on the belief that the Resistance would help me set things right, but it was nothing more than a mirage.

"How did you end up here?" I asked.

"We worked our way across the continent—sneaking into the backs of caravan trucks, hitching rides on empty train cars, walking along the edge of endless forest. Our numbers dwindled as people got lost or left behind—one slip of the foot when jumping a particularly fast train, one distraction in a panicked city street, one stroke of bad luck—each was another person gone for good."

"I'm so sorry," was all I could manage.

He continued talking. His confession had taken on an aspect of catharsis, like he was relieved to expunge these terrible secrets from his soul and, in sharing them, be absolved of their burden.

"At least we made the crossing in summer. If it had been winter, we would have either frozen to death or been captured. Isiris and her jackals were setting the virus loose in calculated pockets around the world. Letting vandals run ravage over the remains. Then the Fellowship would come galloping in like a white knight, rounding up the survivors. They were either shipped off to VisionCrest refugee camps or labor camps. By the time we made it to St. Petersburg two months ago, the city was completely ransacked and most of the inhabitants gone underground."

"How did you end up in the Winter Palace? It's not exactly inconspicuous," I said.

"It's supposed to belong to Evil Queen Bitch Harlow Wintergreen. VisionCrest stored corpses here when they were still trying to maintain the illusion that this wasn't a police state. We moved them downstairs—the basement level is basically a graveyard. We packed snow over the bodies, and lucky for us there's no heat to melt it."

"The Watchers don't come here anymore?" I asked.

Hayes shrugged. "Not for a while. We're vigilant, and it's big enough that we have room to maneuver if they do. I think they don't like the idea of facing all that putrefying flesh."

I felt sick. It shouldn't be so easy to decimate a civilization. The threads that hold things together shouldn't be nearly so fragile. But they were. I wasn't sure if anyone could put it back together, least of all me. I was sure as hell going to try, but right now all I wanted was some comfort.

As if he could feel what I was thinking, Hayes reached his hand out and unzipped my jacket. Even though it was freezing in the palace, here in front of the fire it was blazing hot. Or maybe it was just what was happening between me and Hayes that was causing my temperature to rise. He pushed the too-big jacket off my shoulders and ran his hands down my arm, tickling the tender skin on the inside of my wrists as he pulled the jacket the rest of the way off.

He looked at my face, then down the rest of my body as I shivered lightly in my threadbare T-shirt, not from cold but from desire. There was a hunger in his eyes; I knew he would see the same reflected back in mine. It was the hunger that came from feeling desperate and lonely for too long; the hunger that came from knowing that the minutes were dwindling, and every one had to count. It wasn't a feeling the old Hayes-and-Harlow could have ever felt, but it passed between us now, lighting what was kindling into a four-alarm blaze.

"I can't believe you're really here," he said, his voice hoarse.

"Tell me about it," I said.

He made a low moan in the back of his throat and pulled me tight against him. I could feel his heart beating rapidly against his rib cage as he tipped his head down and his mouth found mine. The stubble on his chin scratched against my skin in a satisfying friction and the feel of his lips against mine was like striking a match to tinder. We were set to explode.

His hands slipped to the hem of my shirt as he kissed me urgently, lips crushing against each other, hands reaching. He pulled my shirt over my head and I did the same with his, opening my eyes just long enough to appreciate the now-pale outline of his defined chest and abs.

"I didn't think you could get any more beautiful," he said. "But here you are."

"You're beautiful too. You always were," I said.

Somewhere deep inside, I was thinking about Adam. I felt lightning bolts of longing for my lost love, punctuated by pangs of lust for my current one. But Adam and I could never go back to what we were, and Hayes held the promise of something real. Yet still Adam remained, in every thought and every breath.

Hayes laid us down on the drapes, going expertly down to one knee and tilting me back so the slippery-rough smoothness of silk slid against my bare skin. He hovered over me as my fingernails scratched lightly down his back. He parted my lips and his tongue slipped against mine. It was just like that day on the beach, only amplified a million times over by the depths of my loneliness.

Despite myself, a memory of Isiris and Adam doing this very same thing slipped past my defenses. I hesitated. I knew I shouldn't be doing this. Kissing Hayes. Letting myself believe I could love him. Forgetting, even for a moment, what I was hurtling toward. What I was there to do at any cost.

"Are you sure?" Hayes whispered in my ear.

I bit my lip. For a moment I considered saying no. Stopping this before it started; averting its inevitable conclusion. But right now, I needed this. It was a simple matter of survival. Tonight, Hayes's kiss was my salvation. Tomorrow—well, tomorrow was tomorrow.

"I'm sure," I whispered, pulling his lips back to mine.

I surrendered, and let Hayes heal me in a way that I'd never let anyone heal me before, if only for the night.

When it was over, and I was wrapped in his arms watching the flames of the fire spin and dance, I tried to imagine a way this could all play out to a happy ending. Long after Hayes fell asleep, one strong arm wrapped around me and his breath rhythmic in my ear, I couldn't fathom a way that could possibly be true.

———

I woke up in the thin daylight, shivering and way too nude in front of the dying embers of the fire. I was wrapped in the red drapes from the previous night like some kind of Rated-R burrito. The room, which had felt warm and red last night, was now cast in the cool blue hue of a late winter morning. Hayes was nowhere to be seen. If last night had felt warm with safety, the frigid morning felt more like regret.

Considering he was nowhere to be seen, Hayes likely felt the same. The thought of Adam, and the state he was in the last time I'd seen him, was a sawblade of guilt that cut my memory of the previous night into tiny shreds. There could be no comfort in a time like this. I had temporarily lost control. It wouldn't happen again.

Parker was sitting cross-legged on a settee across the room, popping Fritos in her mouth and crunching loud enough to rouse the ghost of Catherine herself. I clutched the drapes to my chest and looked around for my clothes, a wave of humiliation sweeping over me.

"They're over here." Parker's voice echoed around the room in between obscene *crunch crunch crunches*. She didn't look up from the wrinkled orange bag in her hand. I spotted my clothes lying in a neat pile next to her.

"Well, could you um … bring them to me?" I asked.

She stopped crunching and looked up at me. She smirked. "What did you get up to last night?"

"Clothes," I insisted.

"Doesn't look like much talking happened." She chomped. "Unless it was *naked* talking."

"Please?" I pleaded, embarrassment making even my scalp creep. "This is mortifying enough as it is."

It would be doubly mortifying if Hayes or any of his crew busted in before I could get decent. I was more than a little irritated that Hayes would just leave me here without waking me.

Parker chuckled, little crumbs flying from her mouth. She picked up my clothes in one hand but held tightly to her snack with the other. She held the stack of grungy threads out to me, then held out the bag in her other hand. "Breakfast?"

"No thanks. But do you mind, uh … " I twirled my finger to indicate a need for privacy. The eye roll she gave me then was even bigger than the one she'd had for Hayes the previous night, but she did it.

"So did you and Hayes work everything out?" I asked, wriggling out of my makeshift tortilla and into my smelly clothes. I wished there was something else to wear, but the place looked completely picked over.

"Yup," she said.

I stood up. "Okay, you can turn around."

"Lucky me," she said.

"So do you know where Hayes is? Have you seen him this morning?" I asked. I was annoyed at how my cheeks got warm when I said his name.

"He's out bossing people around. It's a towering strength of his. He asked me to keep an eye on you—make sure nobody woke you up. It was so cute I threw up a little in my mouth."

"Ha ha," I said. But the thought of Hayes watching out for me made my chest swell. I didn't want to want him, but I didn't want him not to want me.

"Yeah, apparently now that her Royal Highness has arrived, we're clearing out of the palace. Irony—gotta love it."

"Hayes mentioned something last night about leaving. Did he say where he plans on going?"

"I'm not exactly his go-to girl for confidential information," Parker grunted. "We haven't even worked our way up to trust falls."

"Right," I said. I wasn't particularly interested in playing Parker's cat-and-mouse game—she was going to tell me what happened with her and Hayes. We couldn't afford to keep secrets. "Speaking of trust, what's the story with you two?"

She was silent, and I moved to the big picture window that ran the length of the room. It was covered in frosted spray paint, but there were pinpricks that let you see out. I peered through one of the holes. We were on the back side of the palace, the raging waters of the Neva River rushing past below. An abandoned ship with a broken sail floated by sideways, amidst chunks of bobbing ice. There were no signs of life anywhere, although I knew the VisionCrest patrols must be out there somewhere. How on earth Hayes planned to get us out of here, and where we were heading, was a total mystery. I wondered if there was anywhere left to go.

"Okay, fine," Parker said. "Remember how I told you about my brother's journal?"

I turned and looked at her. She looked more earnest than I'd ever seen her. The memory of her brother was clearly a wound that was still raw.

"The one you brought to Beijing with you," I said, nodding.

"Well, the police took it from me when they arrested me at the VisionCrest compound in Beijing. When Hayes rescued me, he told me there was no way to retrieve it. The last shred of Aaron's existence in this world, gone for good. Except one day at Bên Trong Mắt, I happened to be perusing Hayes's room when he was away on a trip, and lo and behold, what do I find in his desk drawer but my brother's journal."

"Why were you snooping around in Hayes's room?" I asked.

"I'm naturally curious," she said, without a hint of guile.

"If he lied about it, he probably had a good reason," I said. Lying didn't seem very Hayes-like to me, but maybe that was because I needed him to be pure.

Parker screwed her face up and let out a barking laugh.

"Right—good reason. He came back all in a tizzy over something that happened while he was in Twin Falls."

I knew immediately what that was—his one and only meeting with Isiris.

"I confronted him about the journal, and he said he didn't have time to argue with me, but that my brother was helping the Fellowship experiment on people. I told him he was full of crap. Which he is," Parker said with a defiant tilt of her chin.

"And then what happened?" I asked, feeling ill.

"There was . . . a scuffle," she answered.

"A scuffle," I repeated.

"He tried to get the journal back from me, but I wasn't going to let that happen. He kept ranting about how there were bigger things at stake, which was easy for him to say. It wasn't his brother. So I ran off into the jungle. I wasn't thinking, really—I just needed to protect Aaron's journal. When I came back to the compound, everyone was gone."

"Do you still have the journal?" I asked.

She nodded.

"So what did you two talk about last night?" I asked.

"Hayes still wants me to give him the journal. It has a bunch of names and locations in it, which Hayes says are keys to bringing VisionCrest to its knees."

"Is it true? Do you think it's going to help us track down Isiris?" I asked.

She looked me dead in the eyes. "Hayes is right. There are things in there—things Aaron put in there so that I would find them. Locations of secret bases. Names of who was involved. Knowledge we can use to destroy VisionCrest. It was Aaron's message in a bottle—he knew the Fellowship was going to destroy him, but he did what he could to try and keep it from taking everyone else down with him."

"Did you give Hayes the journal?" I asked.

"No way. But Hayes and I worked out a deal. I'll let him use the journal to help us hit them where it hurts, and he'll let me come along to dole out some whup-ass on the bastards who stole my brother."

"Did he even hint at where he thinks we should go?" I asked, just as Hayes walked through the door.

"Paris," he said.

"Why Paris? Was it in Aaron's journal?" I knew it came off pushy, but I didn't care. This was my operation now.

"No," he said, giving me a guarded look.

"Now that I'm here, we make decisions together," I insisted.

I looked at Parker, who was frowning. Hayes's look was impossible to decode.

"Of course." His tone assumed an air of distant formality. "But I'm pretty sure you'll want to go."

"Oh, really? Why's that?" I challenged him.

"Because someone you love is there," he said.

BEFORE: TRAPPED IN THE TEMPLE, DREAMING OF ISIRIS

"Welcome to the party. I was wondering when you'd arrive."

Isiris's words made me wonder, now, if she thought this was my first time behind her eyes. I decided not to think about it.

Adam turned his head restlessly on the pillow, exposing a length of ink-covered neck to Isiris's hungry gaze. There were more tattoos there—new ones, the skin still raw and angry at the edges. The symbol of the All Seeing Eye, layers of color radiating away from it on all sides. Adam's pulse stuttered beneath the surface, making the image pulse as if it had a life of its own. Isiris leaned over him, kissing the edge of his jaw where the tattoos stopped. I could feel the heat of his skin against her lips, as if they were my lips. Adam's scent—musky, sleepy, the faintest hint of verbena—permeated my senses. If I let myself go, it would be almost as good as if I were right there next to him.

Almost. But the price was too dear. Letting myself go meant losing myself forever. Which was exactly what Isiris wanted.

As if she could feel me defying her, Isiris pulled away from Adam. His eyes rolled, the drugs firmly taken hold. Her mood turned, and she pulsed with determination. She was going to show me who was in control.

Isiris's eyes focused on Adam's hand, lying palm-up against the pillow, his arm flung over his head. She gripped the spine of the razorblade and pressed it into the flesh of his palm, where the trail of ink began. I fought her but nothing happened; nothing other than my own muted suffering. She traced his lifeline, following the snaking trail of a tattoo, splitting the skin down the center to the top of his wrist. Blood sprang red from the gaping seam, beading along its edges. Urgent streams began to form, running in rivulets down the paths that betrayed his fortune. Isiris paused to admire her work. Then she pressed harder.

Bright blue veins criss-crossed beneath the paper-thin skin of Adam's wrist, tattooed numbers swirling over and through them above. If Isiris dragged her blade through that delicate tangle it would kill him. He would bleed out in a matter of minutes.

She leaned down, channeling the weight of her entire body into the blade. Adam's skin bowed beneath it, and she started to drag it—down, down. There was a splitting sound, individual cells tearing away from one another. Warm streams of blood pumped from the break. A wave of nausea crashed over both me and Isiris—mine was revulsion, hers unexplained. I pounded against the mental bars that held me tight, unable to do anything to help him.

She brought his palm to her lips, lapping at the life force that poured from his veins, smearing it across her face.

"Blood is power," she said.

She laid his arm back down, exposed. Her blade returned, tripping lightly over his wrist and the major arteries before sinking into the thicker muscle of his forearm.

I channeled the last of my strength and focused it on Isiris's hand—she wavered. I could feel her struggling against me, the balance of power shifting back and forth between us, hovering on the knife's edge. Crimson blood pumped from Adam's severed veins. Then I felt Isiris weaken, and something broke.

Isiris snatched her fingers away, leaving the blade lodged inside Adam's arm. A phantom ache ran up her own arm as she watched Adam's blood pool. She clutched at it, looking confused. Another wave of nausea swept over her. In her disorientation, I grew stronger. Isiris's fingers twitched, aching to go back to her cutting. But she didn't move—couldn't. I had her bound. Now what?

Adam's blood spilled onto the pillowcase, the circumference of the stain growing wider by the second. He stirred, his eyelids heavy with whatever concoction Isiris had given him to knock him out.

"Harlow?" he said, his voice groggy.

"Shhhh ... " I hushed him. I moved Isiris's hand, brushing a few sweaty tendrils of hair back from his forehead with one hand.

I was doing it—I was controlling Isiris.

I leaned over Adam, his eyes opening and closing as he fought for consciousness. I'd almost forgotten how blue they were. Like sapphires shot with silver. I looked at his lips. They were so red. I wanted so badly to stay here in this moment—to never let it go.

Adam moaned, trying to form a sentence but not quite able to.

"Whaddareyou—" he mumbled, the words jamming up against each other at the tip of his tongue.

Oh, Adam, I thought, my heart breaking. But the words didn't make it out.

My moment of sadness was all the opening Isiris needed to regain the upper hand.

She pushed me down—pinning me so deep I might never rise back up to the surface.

"Consequences," Isiris said.

Adam's brow knit in confusion as Isiris leaned down so her mouth hovered just above his, her arm pinning his even harder. His breath was soft against her. Labored. She closed the gap between them, pressing her lips to his and stealing his breath.

I tried to pull her back. For one glorious moment, it worked. Isiris's body fought against itself, simultaneously pulling back and drawing forward in an invisible tug-of-war. But it only lasted a moment.

In the next instant she surged forward, her lips crushing against his, parting them as her hand moved back to the razor-blade. She kissed him even more deeply, suffocating him, then dislodged the blade from his arm. I could feel the blood, slippery and warm, gushing between her fingers. She continued the kiss as he started to struggle for air beneath her.

Stop, I willed her. I surrender. I'm sorry. Just stop. Stop.

"Stop!" a voice cried out.

It was Dora.

Isiris spun around, taken by surprise. I could only imagine what the gruesome scene must look like through my best friend's eyes. Me, wild-eyed and naked, smeared in blood. Adam, also naked, pinned beneath me. His blood bright, gushing from his arm and soaking into the bed. The thought of Dora having to see this was horrifying.

"What the hell?" she screamed, running across the room and shoving Isiris off of Adam.

Isiris fell backward, taken by surprise and momentarily knocked off-kilter. Then I felt her fury explode in Dora's direction with the force of an atomic bomb. The razorblade was clutched in her hands. She launched herself at Dora like a feral cat, claws and teeth bared, ready to tear her limb from limb. I screamed silently inside her as Isiris swung the blade at Dora and caught her lengthwise across the face, slicing her cheek. Dora reeled backward, putting her arms up to try and stave off the attack.

"What have you done with my friend?" Dora screamed. "What have you done with Harlow?"

Out of nowhere, Stubin came between them, taking Isiris's slashing blows as Dora continued to hurl accusations. Despite the horror of the situation, my heart filled with hope. Dora knew. She knew that Isiris wasn't me. She was going to set things right and they would come to set me free. This ordeal was going to end. It was more than I could have hoped for in a lifetime of wishes.

Watchers rushed into the room, and Isiris dropped her attack. Dora scrambled to Adam's side, pressing the bedsheets onto his wound. Stubin stood like a human shield between them, arms up, protecting my friends. I'd never felt more gratitude for anyone *than I did for Stubin in that moment. He would die to protect Dora.*

Like flipping a switch, Isiris abandoned her frenzy. She drew herself up straight and regal, looking coldly at Stubin and Dora. The razorblade in her hand dropped to the ground as she shifted her gaze pointedly to the Watchers standing in the doorway. She raised her hand and pointed her finger first at Stubin, then at Dora. Her arm still ached. Adam moaned and attempted to sit up but fell back down with a thud, blood still gushing from his wounds.

Isiris's body filled with bitter cold. The feeling burned like a block of dry ice inside her chest, where her heart should have been. Even at a distance, I experienced her emotion as if it were my own. Hatred.

"These two are traitors to the Fellowship," she said to the Watchers. "Try them for treason and send them to the prison camp to await their death."

AFTER:
ST. PETERSBURG

"What do you mean?" I asked Hayes, my heart leaping into my throat. If someone I loved was in Paris, we had to go immediately.

"I have to show you something," he said.

Ever since he'd entered the room, he'd been circling me from an uncomfortable distance, like if he came too close I might faint into his arms and make him say he loved me. Last night's fire was nothing more than a smudgy pile of ash, and an icy draft whistled around us. One of the twenty-foot-tall windows had a crack in it. I shivered and crossed my arms over my chest. It was frightening how quickly things could change.

How quickly people could change. I didn't really need another reminder of that in my life.

"Okay. So show me," I said.

There was an edge of defiance in my voice, and Hayes's

gaze steeled even further. He clearly considered our tryst a mistake. And I wasn't interested in being anyone's mistake.

Extending his arm, he handed me a cell phone with a video queued up on the screen. "We got this today," he said, his voice still scratchy from a night of not much sleep.

Even though the video was grainy, the black-on-gray edges making it hard to decipher one figure from another, I knew instantly that it was of Dora. Hayes had recognized her too, and he barely knew her. It was one of the things I loved most about my best friend—her personality was so big she was impossible to miss. Even when a lot of it had clearly been robbed from her.

The video had been taken surreptitiously. There were objects in the foreground—a shovel maybe, or a pickaxe—that partially obscured the scene, which appeared to be viewed from behind a rusty-barred window. Dora was wearing a tunic the color of Siberian tundra, which hung off her frame. Her once crazy Medusa curls were limp and stringy, and her baby fat was gone. She looked like an upside-down mop wrapped in dishrags.

Yet even in her depleted state, her Dora-ness still shone through. First there were the eyebrows—expressive as ever. There was the way she looked around from behind the shade of her snarled hair to make sure no one was looking before she whispered a word of encouragement to the person beside her. And there were those damn rainbow-striped socks. How she'd managed to hold on to those was beyond imagination, but she loved those silly socks almost as much as she loved me.

The figure beside Dora was stooped, shoulders rounded

in defeat. He was wearing the same gray uniform, only his looked like a pair of hospital scrubs. It was impossible to tell for sure, because his chin never lifted from his chest, but I knew the person next to her was Stubin. It wasn't because he looked anything like the Stubin I knew; it was because when he didn't respond to Dora's verbal nudge, she reached a bony hand out and threaded her fingers through his, pulling his forearm to her side to steady him. My heart broke for them, these faint shadows of my friends.

They were standing in some sort of line. Waiting for something. Or someone. Every prisoner in line looked withered—deprived in all the ways that counted. Of food. Of safety. Of hope.

A figure came into view. Clad in black, thrusting indiscernible implements into the prisoners' hands. A Watcher. I knew those guards well enough, after a lifetime of having them constantly trailing me, to recognize the arrogant gait and uncompromising set of their shoulders.

When the Watcher thrust the small objects into the prisoners' hands, some of them reeled back from the simple force of it. As the Watcher reached Stubin, he paused; Stubin was swaying unsteadily on his feet. Dora had not let go of his hand.

Even though I did not want anything to happen to Stubin, and even though whatever was on this video was already said and done, I was silently urging Dora to let Stubin go. The consequences for helping out a fellow inmate—not to mention the consequences of needing help—were going to be severe. I whimpered, wanting to turn away but needing to bear witness.

The Watcher brought his fist down on Stubin's collarbone. Even with the poor sound quality on the video I could hear the *crack-snap* that could only be his bone breaking. He collapsed to his knees in time with the sound, not even reacting but for the way his left arm seemed to hang loose like a marionette with the string snipped. Dora crouched to help him, totally disregarding the consequences that would surely rain down upon her for doing this. That was D— always watching out for everyone but herself, Patron Saint of Lost Causes. Present company included.

The Watcher reeled his hand back, then slammed it forward across Dora's cheekbone so hard her head snapped back. She lost her balance and sprawled backward as more Watchers rushed into the frame, obscuring the view to what was happening. A sob clawed its way up my throat.

The final seconds of the video showed a knot of Watchers dragging Dora away by her hair, kicking and screaming. Another Watcher had Stubin by his broken arm, dragging him through the dirt on his knees. Stubin didn't even register a protest, even though the pain must have been excruciating. The other prisoners had taken several steps back, standing in a confused semi-circle around Dora and Stubin as the Watchers beat them. When Dora and Stubin were no longer in the frame, the other prisoners fell back in line, vacant-eyed, as if none of it had happened.

Hot tears ran down my face. Anger and revulsion mixed with joy. Back in the temple, when I'd seen Isiris sending

Dora away after the razorblade incident, I didn't think I'd ever see my friend again. The dark corners of Isiris's mind were impossible to penetrate—I feared Dora was dead, or if not, that I would never know enough to save her.

And now here she was. A precious gift in Hayes's extended hand.

The camera panned away so that I could see the cement building that contained them. It looked like a penitentiary, but it must have been some sort of school in its former life. The prisoners were standing in a central courtyard filled with sawdust and gravel, an abandoned merry-go-round, and a toppled metal slide. As the video cut out, I could just make out the top of the Eiffel Tower in the distance, rising like a plume of smoke nearly indistinguishable from the real threads of smoke that snaked across the city's skyline. Paris appeared to be burning. It looked like the end of the world. I guessed it kind of was.

Hayes cleared his throat, still looking at the floor instead of at me.

"Hayes?" I said his name like an entreaty.

Finally, he looked at me. His chocolate-brown eyes were so different from Adam's deep blue ones. What had passed between us the previous night was about raw emotional need; it was a need that was still there when he looked at me now. I realized suddenly that he wasn't staying away from me because he didn't care—he was staying away because he did.

But we couldn't allow our feelings to get in the way of what we needed to accomplish together. Not to mention the shadow that Adam cast over us both.

Dora and Stubin were counting on us. So was Adam, out there somewhere with Isiris, and with any luck he was still hanging on to his last shred of hope. The hope I'd given him the last time I'd inhabited Isiris from inside the temple—when Adam had made clear to me what he planned to do.

I didn't know the location of the palace where he was being held captive, but Dora did. And wherever she said Adam was, Isiris would be too.

The sand in my hourglass had not run out yet.

"We're leaving now," I said.

Hayes nodded his assent.

"Uh, guys? I think we may have one tiny issue with that plan," Parker interjected. She was up on her tiptoes, peering sideways out the window like she was trying to stay hidden from the outside view.

"What is it?" Hayes asked, his body tensing.

"There are Watchers out there—a lot of them. And I don't think they're here to deliver our Girl Scout cookies."

————

Hayes, Parker, Truman, and I were huddled in a sitting room off one of the lesser palace bedchambers.

"A prisoner ferry leaves every day at noon, from the ship-yard just up the way. They round up VisionCrest dissenters, nonbelievers, people who arrive on the train like you did. They shackle them and load them on. Two days later they unload them," Hayes said.

"Where?" I asked.

"We don't know," Hayes said.

"How do you know it doesn't just dump them in the sea?" Parker asked.

Next to me, Truman snorted, his wiry red hair seeming to imitate the poky wires of his braces. "Because I snuck onto the ferry and took a round-trip ride. Done it twice already."

"Why?" Parker asked. She looked like a little girl in her big puffy jacket and cockeyed ponytail.

Truman gave her a sour look. "I was saving people from our group. We don't let our own get taken by thugs, Slim. Unless we're abandoning traitors like you."

"Screw you, you freckled fu—"

"Stop acting like children, both of you," I snapped.

Parker's eyes narrowed, and Truman scowled. In another life, a life without Isiris, the two of them would be avoiding their homework and playing too many video games. We all would. Instead, we were fugitives running for our lives. Of course, for lots of people, this or worse was already their reality, with or without Isiris. The world had always been an awful place for some; Isiris had just evened the score for all.

"So, you have no idea where it docks?" I pressed.

Truman shrugged. "I had to stay hidden in the cargo hold, so I couldn't exactly do any sightseeing. I think it might have been a small island in the Baltic. But wherever it was, it smelled like a glue factory."

"She's imprisoning some, killing others. Purification, they're calling it," Hayes said.

"Extermination," I said.

Purity. Death.

The words Isiris used to whisper to me rattled in my brain. I'd let her get loose in the world, and now she was making good on her promise—treating innocent human beings like cattle shuttled to the slaughterhouse.

"It doesn't matter where the ferry is *supposed* to go. Once it's ours, it goes wherever we want." Hayes drew a crude map on the back of a once-fine piece of art. "That's how we get out."

"Out of St. Petersburg." Parker said it like it was impossible.

Since to get out of St. Petersburg, we had to get out of this palace.

Hayes bent over the paper, his forehead creased in concentration. He traced a squiggly line from where we were, through the Baltic Sea between Croatia and Sweden, and straight on to the northernmost tip of Germany.

"We need to get to Lübeck. There's a port there and a train that goes to Paris, once a day." He ran a hand through his hair, looking up from under his lashes to meet my eye. "At least, there was the last time we had any intelligence to speak of."

I sighed and looked out the one grimy window that allowed us spotty views of the front gates of the palace. At least fifty Watchers were now gathered there. It was impossible to tell exactly what they were doing. They didn't have any corpses with them, so they weren't here to use the palace as a graveyard, and they were heavily armed. It was very likely they were looking for Parker and me. I'd led Isiris's henchmen right to the Resistance's doorstep.

The few remaining members of the Resistance were posted at lookouts around the palace, or hiding in the dressing room waiting for Hayes's orders. Hayes looked like some kind of general or war strategist, and he was. Last night he was all tenderness and vulnerability. Now he was strictly business, looking from me to Parker to Truman and back again.

"So you want us to get on a prisoner boat?" I asked him.

"It's the only way out of here."

"How do we get out of here without the Watchers seeing us?" Parker asked.

"The same way I did it." Truman snorted again. "Very carefully."

"That's not going to work. You were alone, and there were no Watchers," Hayes told him.

Truman's posture slumped. Hayes's approval clearly meant the world to him.

"We can't afford to let ourselves get taken prisoner," I said. "There's no guarantee we could escape, if they even let us live that long."

Hayes looked at me, the uncompromising truth shining in his eyes. "Probably. But it's the only chance we've got."

I thought about my confrontation with the Watchers in the Beijing alleyway. There was another option—it was a gamble, and one that would definitely make its way back to Isiris.

"Not the only chance," I said, trying not to feel like I'd swallowed a gravestone.

They all looked at me.

"Do you know if any of Catherine the Great's clothing

is still here among the artifacts? I need to look like a royal pain in the ass."

———————

An hour later, Hayes and team were tugging open the heavy front door of the palace. Atop the bars of the thin wrought-iron gates that enclosed the expansive front courtyard, the VisionCrest symbol replaced the double-headed eagle of the House of Romanov that had once graced its apex.

I swished through in a ridiculous mink-lined cape made of cornflower silk, lovingly restored by some museum curator who probably didn't think the fate of the world would hang in the balance of her handiwork. There was a hood that I drew up over my head, obscuring my face. A red silk panel hung down the front; Parker had hastily sewn a VisionCrest patch onto the center. Hopefully nobody looked underneath it—my mismatched outfit was a dead giveaway. No pun intended.

"Are you sure about this?" Parker asked before I exited to face the Watcher horde.

"Absolutely," I lied.

She and the others needed me to have no doubt. Hayes was the only one from whom it was impossible to hide the truth.

Truman's gang, Parker included, were all dressed in gray prisoner uniforms pilfered from bodies in the basement. It was the garb that Isiris's troops dressed their captives in before shipping them off. The same ones that Dora and Stubin wore in that awful video. *Nothing like wearing a dead person's clothes to make you feel like a walking curse,* Parker had said. I hoped she was wrong. We needed every four-leaf clover we could get at this point, preferably delivered in person by a leprechaun carrying a pot of gold.

My imposter detainees followed in a grim line, shuffling after me with heads hung low. Knives and lock picks were hidden in the waistbands of their uniforms and taped to their bodies. They were no real match for what was waiting outside, but they played their roles just as surely as I played mine.

As I approached the main gate, my footing swift and sure, my head held regally, a ripple of confusion swept through the Watchers. The one closest to me had his hand on the gate; a massive pair of bolt cutters lay on the snow-dusted threshold and an ice-slick chain coiled on the ground. The Watchers must have locked it when they'd abandoned the palace. Given that I'd ruined this safe harbor for Hayes and his crew, it was up to me to give them a new one.

"Who's there?" the Watcher bellowed. I didn't break stride.

The entire front line drew their weapons and aimed. Just a few more steps and the Watcher would be able to see my face.

"Prepare to fire!" Another voice sounded from somewhere inside the sea of black-polished body armor.

My pace did not let up. A swelling feeling rose inside my chest, the kind of feeling that accompanies great joy and terrible grief. The kind I'd felt that day on the temple steps, when I'd gone through the wrong door and ended up holding the beating heart of an innocent girl. I knew what I had to say to them, and I now knew what the feeling was. Power.

I threw the hood back from my head. "Who authorized this?" I demanded.

The lead Watcher's face was a three-car pile-up of disbelief, incredulity, and fear. His eyes went wide, his limbs a riot of conflicting movement before he finally landed on the correct one and dropped to one knee before me. The rest of the Watchers followed suit, still unsure what exactly was happening but following their leader unquestioningly.

"You aren't supposed to be here," I barked.

The head Watcher lifted his eyes from the ground and regarded me cautiously.

"Matriarch … I … we didn't realize … " He stumbled over the words, a cautious look in his soot-black eyes as he searched my face. The seed of doubt that had already planted itself there was impossible to miss. Although he saw Harlow Wintergreen standing in front of him, the logic of it didn't add up.

"Stop talking," I said. "Rise."

He rose to his feet, his minions following suit. I was keenly aware of the trudging footsteps of Hayes and the others as they stopped short behind me.

"How did you get here?" the Watcher asked. His jaw was like the grill of a semi truck, square and indestructible. Ready to make roadkill of anything in its path.

"I don't recall inviting you to speak freely. I give the orders, you follow them," I said.

His Mack truck jaw worked, considering. His hand

reached for the radio clip at his lapel. I couldn't afford to have him communicating with whatever central command they had set up. There was no way of knowing whether news of the disruption in Beijing had made its way up the ranks, but this Harlow Wintergreen sighting was certainly going to. And that couldn't happen until after we'd set sail.

I glared at him, willing the fiery gleam I'd seen in Isiris's reflection into my own. He hesitated, his hand hovering.

"How I got here is none of your concern. The St. Petersburg unit has proven incompetent time and again, and here you are screwing things up yet again."

The Watcher was silent. His body was tensed. He was on the verge of making a decision I couldn't let him make.

"These prisoners are special. There's going to be a sacrifice to the Inner Eye," I announced. "I am preparing them—purifying them. I should have every one of you added to the group. But since you're here, I'll let you escort us instead. And if you manage not to make a mess of things, I'll let you all live."

The Watcher's hand dropped.

"An escort, ma'am?" he asked. There was a steely edge in his voice that wasn't entirely subservient. He was on notice, but so was I.

"The prisoner transport to Lübeck. We will depart with them. The crew and prisoners on board will be mine, to do with as I please." I raised my hands. "A gift to the Inner Eye. You are welcome to join us if you like."

"I should call this in to my Commander. He will want to know you're here so he can give you a proper welcome."

It was a test. My hand gripped the handle of the bowie knife tucked inside the inner pocket of the cape. I whipped it out and lunged at the closest Watcher, thinking about the dead children nailed to posts around the city as I ran it right into his solar plexus between the seams of his armor.

I pulled it free and he doubled over like a stuck pig, squealing as blood gushed from his abdomen. Hopefully I'd missed any major organs, but there was no guarantee. The horror I felt at my own actions stayed trapped behind my facade. If there was any question that in my quest to stop Isiris I was becoming more like her every day, there could be no doubt now.

The Watcher in charge stared at me, stunned. It's one thing to hear about a ruler's brutality; it's another to see it in the flesh.

"I am your commander. If you—or any of your men—call anyone, I will have you skinned alive. Then I'll have your eyeballs served for dessert at the sacred ceremony. This is a Ministry matter and your very presence here offends. The one way—the only way—you can make it up to me is to obey. Now…shall we?" I asked.

He ground his teeth like he was chewing a cud. Then he made a gruff snorting noise and raised his hand, waving in a circling motion to his men. "Round up these prisoners—we're headed to the transport ship."

"Very good." I nodded. "And one more thing—none of your men lays a hand on these prisoners, or they will find themselves short an appendage. They are pure, and ready for their transition. You lead, we follow."

"Move out, fall in!" he yelled, rallying his troops.

I glanced over my shoulder and briefly met Hayes's eyes. The look on his face told me what I already knew. I had become unrecognizable.

Ruthless. A killer.

And it had saved us.

BEFORE: TRAPPED IN THE TEMPLE

I stood in front of my chosen door, waiting. The Violet Hour was coming; I could feel it like an ache in my bones. My finger tested the edge of the sharp rock inside my fist; the movement reminded me of Isiris and her razorblade. The clock was ticking. This door had to be mine.

I leaned forward, my face inches from the mysterious plane where the temple met the world beyond its gate. A lush expanse of trees glowed green in the deep blue half-light of night's end. Water spilled in needle-thin threads over a tumble of rocks, creating a tiny waterfall. I could almost smell the freshness of the air, the shush of the brook tipping over the stones. I didn't remember the waterfall from before, but I hadn't exactly been in the mental space to appreciate the scenery when I'd first made my way to the temple.

The jungle before me was impenetrable, its secrets hidden. I would just have to take my chances.

A whoosh of air ran through the dark hallway, sending a shiver across back of my neck. The Violet Hour had begun.

I clutched the jagged stone tighter in my fist, gripping it like a knife. I raised it above the palm of my other hand and drew it down with force, dragging it across my flesh. Blood sprang red from the wound, spilling across the creases of my palm the same way it had across Adam's. The same way the water spilled across the smooth stones on the other side of the doorway.

I stepped forward, my hand held out in front of me, dripping blood on the musty floor of the temple. When my hand connected with the plane of the door, it was like I was being sucked into a vacuum. My entire body lurched forward as first my hand, then my arm, were drawn through to the other side.

The temperature dropped, and the humid cling of waterfall spray crawled up the tiny hairs on my arm. *It should be hot, not cold* flickered through my mind. But I pushed the thought away. This had to be the door. I was halfway home.

I closed my eyes and held my breath, as if I were about to dive into water so deep I might never surface, and let the door draw me all the way through.

There was a moment of black nothingness. Then I surfaced, reborn into the last gasp of night, in a world I hoped was my own.

The sky was purple, wet, and crisp. Dew clung to leaves, moisture hung heavy in the air.

The chirrup of a bird was answered by the *snap-swish* rustle of branches and the *twit-twit-twit* of a responsive friend. A mossy smell wafted up from the ground and the chocolate aroma of tree bark swirled around me. I stood perfectly still, waiting for the moment of revelation that would confirm my choice was right. Nothing. Still, the anxiety spinning in my brain was overtaken by another sensation: liberation.

I tilted my head back and lifted my arms to my side, breathing deeply. The intermittent clouds overhead were twinged with burnt orange, the air warming against my skin. I closed my eyes. I'd done it again. I'd escaped the temple.

The temple. I spun around to get a look at where I'd come from and nearly slipped off a rocky ledge into the water. Shimmering, only inches behind me, was a disturbance in the air. There was nothing there but a large, slanted rock and a copse of slim, feathery trees by which to identify it. My heart clawed its way up my throat.

This doorway wasn't the one that led to my world—no hulking temple that rose from the ether as dawn approached. This portal was so unremarkable that it was practically non-existent. And a different portal meant a different world.

Adam wasn't here.

I knew it the same way I knew how to breathe. I just did.

The reality of this fact disconnected my bones from their joints, halted the blood flowing through my veins, ground my hope into dust. I felt desperate, and also selfish. As my bones reconnected and my blood resumed pumping, I thought only one thing. I didn't want to go back into the temple. Ever.

A thump of footfalls sounded from somewhere behind and slightly above me. Instinctively I crouched down, flattening myself against the cool surface of a rock as if it would somehow protect me. The pounding got closer, and as it did, it became accompanied by a rhythmic huffing of breath. A runner.

Not someone who was running from something—the cadence was too even to be frantic—but someone who was running like it was a task. A flash of neon pink came winding through the not-so-darkness and moments later, a woman whizzed by just over my head, the thin cords of her headphones dangling from her headband.

I stood up and peered over the rocky ledge. There was a footpath. Where there was one early morning jogger, there would be an army of others close behind. I looked back at the shimmering air. It was gone. That settled it for now. I was going to have to survive in this world for at least one day. I told myself I would come back, but another part of me wanted to walk away and keep on walking.

I breathed a little easier, though. My first other-world stranger had been a pretty innocent-looking jogger and not some horrible child-sacrificing zombie horde.

A car horn bleated in the distance. I now detected a smoggy undertone in the air that had probably been there all along, lurking beneath what I wanted to perceive. I looked over the tree-tops and in the distance caught a glimpse of a mirrored building, spiraling higher into the sky than any skyscraper I'd ever seen.

I looked down at the mangled, mangy VisionCrest uniform I wore. The emblem of the Inner Eye that was sewn onto the thin gray cardigan had come loose and was dangling halfway off. There were holes and streaks of dirt and blood across the material. The once-white shirt beneath it was on the verge of dissolving completely. My tartan skirt and Mary Janes didn't show their wear, but paired with the rest of the outfit and my nest of snarled hair, they likely made me look deranged—a street urchin masquerading as a schoolgirl.

I wasn't safe huddling here by the little waterfall. This wasn't some remote slice of wilderness; it was an urban jungle. If this place was as normal as it seemed to be, I might get carted off to a mental institution for not fitting in. The irony was not lost on me.

I hoisted myself up and over the rocks. They poked into my knees, branches scratching at my legs. I stood up on the path, brushing the dirt off my skirt. Looking left and right, I memorized my surroundings. I had to find my way back here.

I would come back. I would. I would.

I started walking in the direction of my friend the jogger. Maybe there was a reason I was here, in this specific place. Maybe I would learn something in this world that could help me in my own. Maybe I wouldn't make it back through the doorway.

Maybe was the axis on which my entire existence turned. Maybe.

I followed the paved path through the dense woods, less startled every time someone passed me. First came the runners, their determination written in hard lines across their faces. Although I knew they must see me—it was a little hard to miss a scraggly girl lurching grimly forward like the resurrected dead—they didn't so much as swivel to look. There were probably a lot of creepy things waiting in these woods, and they seemed used to ignoring them.

As the thin morning light became less pink and more yellow, the power-walkers appeared in twos and threes. Less stalwart than their hardcore counterparts, they couldn't resist a side-eye or halted conversation when they saw me coming around the bend. Still, their pace didn't slack. Wherever I was, being unusual must not be that unusual.

I reached a set of stone steps winding down the side of a hill. I could tell by the sounds of car horns honking and buses exhausting that I was close to a transition zone. Down, down, down I went, and finally I emerged from the woods into the full light of day.

There was a road in front of me. Cyclists whizzed purposefully by, heading into the park with their colorful shirts and scandalously tight shorts that made their thighs look like sausages. Apartment buildings of all shapes and sizes loomed on the horizon. I pushed forward. As I reached the entrance to what I now knew must be a park, I saw a sign. This was a place I knew. Or at least, some other version of it.

Central Park. I was in New York City.

––––––––––

Once I realized that this world was like mine, I expected to feel the way I did when our VisionCrest school group had arrived with the Ministry in Tokyo. Like reality, but with the volume turned way up. Instead, I really was walking through a time and place that was a near-exact replica of my own.

I might have even believed it was mine, if it weren't for the conspicuous absence of VisionCrest symbology. No businesses with stickers of the Inner Eye prominently displayed to attract Fellowship customers; no billboards with my larger-than-life face plastered sky-high; no sign of the Inner Eye popping up in street-side graffiti or waving on the red banners that lined the streets of every major city in my world.

The most damning absence of all was what was standing—or not standing—before me now. There was no Vision-Crest temple at Fifth and 59th. In its place was a gleaming cube of glass with a metallic replica of partially eaten fruit plastered to its side. People pushed in and out of the transparent cage, disappearing down a set of stairs in thick streams.

This is where one of VisionCrest's most iconic temples would be, if it were my world. It clearly wasn't.

I sat down on the beveled stone steps in front of the cube, letting the crowds part around me like a boulder in a stream. Everyone here was so focused and industrious, and none of them seemed to really see me. When their eyes found me at all, they slipped right off me again so quickly I doubted if they'd seen me in the first place.

A woman in a strange costume stopped amidst the hustle and flow, looking directly at me. She was wearing a long black dress made of some stiff, unfriendly looking material. Her bell-shaped sleeves, the pointed white collar that rose around her face like a sort of hood, and her rigid black veil made her seem like a character out of some kind of twisted manga. Her mouth turned down in a frown; her gaze didn't falter from mine from behind her heavy-framed glasses. Of all the people to notice me, of course it had to be the scariest one of the bunch. I was a freak magnet.

I drew my knees up to my chest as she moved toward me, throngs of busy people in suits making tight maneuvers to avoid touching her. She must be some kind of witch.

"Are you lost, dear?" she said, drawing her face close to mine.

The beads that were strung around her neck and belted to her side tilted forward. Each had a large metal cross hanging from the end. One of the crosses brushed against my bare leg, making me shrink back even farther.

"No," I said. My voice sounded smaller than I remembered it.

"What are you doing here?" she asked. Not in a demanding way. More in a concerned way. A way that said she knew I didn't belong here. For a weird moment, I actually thought she was going to offer to shepherd me back to the temple, the way I shepherded lost souls out.

"Do you know about the temple?" I asked. The question slipped out before I was aware of it forming.

A quizzical look deepened the wrinkles on her face. "The Buddhist temple?" she asked.

Was that the name of it? I didn't know. But based on her reaction, and the way her eyes slipped down to the Vision-Crest logo on my sweater and then clouded with something like suspicion, this wasn't a conversation I should be engaging in.

"I'd like to be left alone," I said, feeling disoriented by the sudden strangeness of this new New York.

"What's this symbol? Are you trapped in some kind of cult, dear?" the woman asked, putting together my question about the temple with the weird logo. I couldn't tell if I should feel threatened or cared for. Everything felt upside-down.

"No," I said, halfway standing up but falling back again as the step I'd been sitting on hit the back of my knees.

"Why don't you let me take you to the church, dear. We'll take care of you," she said.

"I don't need you to take care of me," I said, unable to keep the trepidation from my voice. Even I wasn't convinced.

"You need to get clean." Her hand found mine and closed around it.

I tugged back, crab-crawling my way back up the steps and away from her.

I had no idea what she meant, *get clean*, but it reminded me of Isiris—always talking about purity. This world was not immune to evil after all.

She stepped forward, her eyebrows falling together in either anger or concern, I couldn't tell which. I found my footing and took off, rushing into a crowd of people. Suddenly everyone seemed to notice me as I barreled through them, running from the witch. I looked over my shoulder once and I could see her standing in the same spot—her arm held out to me, beckoning me back. I turned and ran fast and hard in the opposite direction.

———

As the afternoon shadows slipped across the pavement, I found myself wandering the streets of the East Village. I recognized it from the punk rock documentary Adam once smuggled into the VisionCrest compound for us to watch—lights off, knees touching, hands oh-so-close. The memory made me ache for him, for home.

There were a ton of people my age around here. Dressed in ripped jeans and safety-pins, hoodies and nose rings, every last one of them looked carefully disheveled. They might call a cardboard box home or jump into their Land Rover at the end of the day; who knew. Like human camouflage, they helped me blend in. I was just another off-kilter teenager looking for a cigarette and someone to love me. It was at least half true.

Across the street, I spotted a shop with a red canopy, a massive red sign, and jumbo-sized lettering that screamed *PUNK RECORDS*. There were kids in various states of repose leaning against its poster-plastered windows, each one vying to out-apathy the next. My stomach somersaulted at the sight of a Bad Religion poster. A thousand years ago, I'd heard Adam joke to a friend that his ideal girl would be the perfect trifecta: blond, brainy, and a fan of Bad Religion. At the time, I'd been crushed. I was brainy and I loved Bad Religion, but I was never going to be blond. Thinking back on it now, I wondered if he'd just been trying to get my attention. The reverse psychology of flirting. If I ever found my way back to him, maybe I'd dye my hair blond and shoot for the trifecta.

My eyes raked over the punk menagerie, feeling nostalgic. I gazed at a group of boys squatting on the stoop of a brownstone next door to the record store. Their shoulders were shaking with artfully restrained laughter as they took turns punching each other in the arm. Every one of them had a skateboard underfoot or propped nearby; all but one of them was drinking a tallboy from a crinkled paper bag.

The not-drinking one was the one who caught my eye.

The entire world became devoid of air.

His friends were oblivious, but he looked up, right at me. He was wearing a rumpled blue shirt and tight black jeans. He was long and lanky, and his dark hair spiked up in the front as if he spent half his time anxiously running his fingers through it. His mouth was red and his eyes were blue, and I shouldn't have been able to see either from so far away, but I could. Mainly because I didn't need to see them up close to know whose they were. In this world—or any other—I would know Adam.

My legs suddenly felt like they weren't made for standing. I backed up a few steps, bumping into an oncoming hipster who cursed at me under his breath. I barely noticed. Adam's look was several things all at once. Earnest, intense, questioning. The way you would look at someone you sort of recognize, in that uncertain second before they say your name.

His arms were bare—the skin unblemished by ink, unlike the boys surrounding him. Unlike himself.

One of the other boys jostled his shoulder, then saw where Adam was looking. The boy's face pulled back in something like disgust, and then he gave a derisive little laugh that carried across traffic. He shook Adam's shoulder again, but Adam's eyes didn't leave mine.

He stood up, flipped his board onto the ground, and

skated toward me. I became a still-life rendering of myself, barely real.

The other boys became quiet as they searched the street for whatever it was that had captured their friend's attention. They were suddenly tense and alert, instantly in the mood to see a fight or some other drama go down.

I felt the weight of five pairs of eyes land on me. Scan through me like x-ray vision. They registered various states of confusion. Then heads and shoulders resumed shaking, punches resumed being thrown. Although they couldn't understand what their boy wanted with such an obvious hot mess, far be it from them to swerve his game.

"Hey," he said, stopping just in front of me. One foot on the ground, one still on his board. "I know you from somewhere, right? You go to Dwight?"

I shook my head. The capacity for speech escaped me.

His eyes flickered down to the VisionCrest patch hanging by a thread from my cardigan. They were the same deep blue as the eyes of the Adam I loved.

"I guess not. What school is that?" he asked, gesturing at the patch and breaking into a crooked smile. "One without a very strict dress code, huh?"

"It's not around here," I managed to say, smiling despite myself.

The desire to take his hand overwhelmed me. I realized I could just stay in this world and start again.

"Seriously, though—did I meet you at Chim-Chim's party last week or something? I was kind of messed up that night, and if I didn't get your number I was even more wasted than I thought."

This was all wrong. A crass, ordinary-boy kind of thing to say. Weirdly charming, yet totally off-putting. Not at all the type of thing my Adam would say. My serious, brooding, sensitive Adam. This boy wasn't him. He wasn't mine.

"I wish I'd met you there," I said, and I meant it. Tears threatened to overtake me.

A look of puzzlement crossed his face. I could tell part of him wanted to leave, and at the same time something unknowable forced him to stay. Like he too was answering some forgotten call from across the quilted universe.

He moved closer. His hand rose and wiped a tear from the corner of my eye.

"I wish you wouldn't cry," he said, the corner of his mouth turning up in a smile.

I couldn't help but smile. I ducked my head, my face nestling into the crook of his neck. I could feel the gentle thrum of his heartbeat, the pulse of blood underneath his warm skin. Just for a moment, I wanted to pretend.

"No, I know you. Definitely. Your name is ... it's ... Har—no, that's not quite ... " His hand snaked around the small of my back.

I held my breath, my heart hammering in my chest. I looked up. Our lips were nearly touching.

"Harper?" he whispered, vaguely triumphant.

Just like everything in this world, it was almost right. But not quite. This Adam wasn't my Adam. The blood pumping through his veins held no power over me. We had no bond.

"Oh my god," I said.

His eyes lit up. "Was I right?"

That was it.

A blood bond.

When I'd forced the razorblade to Isiris's neck and it bit into her skin—Adam had cried out. When Isiris ran the razorblade over the tender skin of Adam's forearm—she'd felt his nausea and pain. Adam and Isiris were bonded by blood. That was what the tattoos she'd given him were all about.

Blood is power, Isiris had said.

But she hadn't foreseen that the power went both ways. What hurt him, also hurt her.

Blood wasn't merely the secret to getting out of the temple. It was the key to bringing Isiris to her knees.

Not *my* blood—the injuries I'd sustained in the temple had no effect on her. But Adam's . . . his wounds were hers, and vice versa.

It was as terrible as it was revelatory. To destroy Isiris was to destroy the boy I loved.

"I'm sorry, Adam. I've got to go."

"It's Aidan—and how did you know?" he asked, seeming like a sleepwalker just coming awake.

He backed away from me, confused. Afraid.

"I'm sorry," I said.

I turned and ran.

As night fell, I found myself huddled back against the rock by the babbling brook in Central Park, counting the hours until the Violet Hour. I wondered if I was making the wrong choice, going back. Maybe I would never make it back to my world. Maybe there was nothing left to save there. But as I shivered in the darkness, I knew that an almost-happiness was no happiness at all. I wanted my own life back, or I wanted no life at all.

AFTER:
GULF OF FINLAND

The Watchers stood still and silent on the dock, chess pieces on a board, the truck-jawed leader their king. His midnight eyes followed the ferry as it made its way out of the harbor, not a muscle out of place in his body save the one in his cheek, which I swear I could still see twitching as we rounded a spit of land and broke free into the gulf.

The smell of the sea coated my skin, flecks of salt crystallizing on my lips. The arctic air cut right to the bone, despite the ornamental noonday sun. Driven by the urge not to show weakness in front of the Watchers, I let my cape flutter around me as if I were unhindered by cold.

Their leader had known something wasn't right, but he couldn't put his finger on it. I knew that, despite his promises, he was very quickly going to weigh the options. Should he keep the silence he'd sworn to me, or should he conclude that something was wrong with this picture: Harlow Wintergreen appearing like a phantom from inside the Winter Palace and demanding to board a prisoner ship with no crew save the captain and sailing off into the Gulf of Finland with the key to the prisoners' chains in her pocket. This time, would Isiris know it was me—that I had escaped the temple and was coming for her?

As the last few wedding-cake houses faded in the distance, I knew the Watchers were radioing their superiors.

The gauntlet was laid down.

The captain was at the helm; Hayes and the Resistance, along with the actual prisoners, were shackled below deck. It was time to take care of that. I strode across the bow, giving the captain—the lone Watcher who remained onboard— a piercing look as he glanced over his shoulder at me. He couldn't hear me over the grind of the motor, but my eyes spoke volumes. A little shudder went through him—fear.

A rush of warmth rolled through my body, and for a moment I felt more than human. There was a lot of communication and GPS equipment at the captain's disposal, and until we could dispose of him, it represented a threat. I needed him to keep his hands at the wheel until we got him tied up below and Hayes took his place. Still, I didn't like how practiced I was getting at embodying Isiris. It felt too much like I was stepping into a skin that fit me better than my own.

I walked below deck, the boat cresting up and chopping down each swell like a guillotine stuck on repeat. Steadying myself on the railing, I descended into the near total darkness. The groaning of the ship as it battled the waves in the gulf was nearly overshadowed by the rattles and moans of the human cargo it carried. The stench of sweat mingled with something sharper. I knew it the way you know the scent of rain before a storm, because I'd smelled it before in Sacristan Wang's horrible basement laboratory. It was despair.

This is what power created. Misery. Heartbreak. Death and destruction. Isiris's skin wasn't mine. I couldn't let it feel right.

It took a moment for my eyes to adjust to the darkness. Huddled together in groups were prisoners wearing the same drab gray uniforms our ragtag group had donned. Like Dora, they were hunched and shriveled—spring flowers pummeled by an unforeseen hailstorm. They looked up at me with full-moon eyes filled with fear, stunned and terrified to see Harlow Wintergreen descend into their midst. In their faces I saw echoes of the train passengers who'd ridden into St. Petersburg with Parker and me only a few days before. A cruel paradox. Moments ago they were living normal lives, with normal triumphs and normal heartaches. Yet they had been prisoners for a lifetime.

One small girl with ragged cornsilk braids stared me directly in the eye. Her wrists were bound behind her back, and her mother tried to herd her away from me, panic and terror warring on her face. But the girl was too young to know better.

"Are you a princess?" she squeaked.

"Not really. Well, kind of," I answered, kneeling down.

"Are you here to save us from the bad people?" she asked.

"Yeah, Harlow. Let's get the heroics rolling here," Parker said from somewhere inside the black hole.

I squinted into the darkness. I saw Parker lift her wrists a few inches behind her back and rattle the chains that held them. Hayes, Truman, and the others stood behind her, looking grim.

I reached into my pocket and withdrew the master key. It would be so easy to lie to this girl, to pretend that everything would be okay now. But it didn't seem fair.

The key turned in the lock, and the chains biting into the little girl's wrists fell free.

"I'm not sure if I can save you. But I'm here to set you free," I told her.

Her gap-toothed smile brightened the darkness with hope. Others fell to their knees, crying with relief.

I tried to ignore the thrill that ran through me, the mean little voice that whispered *worship me*.

I wasn't the same as Isiris. I wasn't. I could stop.

It didn't take long for Hayes and team to tie up the captain, set course for Lübeck, and destroy all the GPS and satellite equipment they could find. In the meantime, Parker and I set about freeing the rest of the prisoners. Now Parker, Truman, Hayes, and I were up at the helm while the others passed out some of the food and water rations we'd found below deck; apparently, the crew of Watchers planned to eat like kings while their captives starved. I wondered if a world without humanity was even worth saving.

"What happens when we get to Lübeck?" Parker asked Hayes.

I didn't feel I had to assert who was in charge anymore; that had been put to rest outside the gates of the Winter Palace. But it was nice to have partners. Hayes was strong, kind, and infinitely capable in ways that made me better. Parker was scrappy and intelligent. Even fearless Truman was starting to grow on me.

"We have to jump ship in the bay. Swim the last mile or so into shore," Hayes said.

"Are you kidding me? It's the middle of winter—we'll die of hypothermia!" Parker looked accusatorially at me, as if this plan was one that I'd hatched.

"You won't die right away," Truman offered with a sly smile. "If you swim to shore fast enough, you'll probably make it."

Parker's face went white.

I quirked a brow at Hayes. "Probably?"

"It's the only way. We'll pull in as close as we can—maybe half a mile out—in the middle of the night. Then we hope for the best. For them and for us," he said, motioning below deck.

"And what happens to people who stay onboard? They sail off into the sunset?" I asked.

"They double back to the Gulf," he said. "Head in the direction of Scandinavia. The more remote, the better."

"They can't manage this ship on their own," Parker said, her voice barely a whisper. Her hands were trembling.

"They won't be on their own. Truman's the captain now.

He stays with the prisoners, and so does everyone besides me and Harlow," Hayes said.

"What? No way—" Truman started to argue, but Hayes's stare silenced him. Truman's face shuffled through a deck of emotions, from indignance to defeat to grim acceptance. It didn't have to be said that he would probably never see the rest of us again.

Parker's whole body was shaking now. "No. No, no, no. You can't leave me. I won't let you." Her eyes were fixed on me, tears forming at their corners and slipping in steady streams down the sides of her face.

I looked from Parker to Hayes. There was no way I could leave Parker behind, not now. Besides, she was resourceful. She was the reason I'd gotten this far; leaving her behind now would be a mistake.

"Parker stays with me. I need her."

For some reason this seemed to make Parker shake even harder.

"It's for the greater good," Hayes said. "The fewer people we have with us, the better our chance of success."

"What makes you so sure I'm the greater good?" I asked without looking up. It was speaking aloud one of my greatest fears—that I would be no better than Isiris, if time and opportunity were ever on my side.

"Because I know you," he said.

"Parker stays with me," I said.

"Okay, fine," Hayes said, his voice softening. "She stays with *us*."

He reached his hand out to me and pulled me into an embrace. I let my head fall on his shoulder, for a single moment allowing my doubt and fear and self-loathing to fall away.

"It's a plan, then," I said wearily.

"One thing, though," Parker said, her voice so small I could have trapped it in a jar.

"What's that?" I sighed.

"I kind of can't swim."

The boat's engine pulled back and we slowed to a choppy crawl, then cut the motor altogether. Waves buffeted us as Truman made his way over to where Hayes, Parker, and I sat stock-still, huddled on the deck. He made a swirling "it's go-time" motion with his hand before getting nearly knocked off his feet by a particularly vicious wave. A tarp that covered some random barrels snapped in the vicious wind. We had arrived in the Bay of Lübeck, and it was time to swim for our lives.

Earlier in the evening, a baby had been delivered stillborn to one of the prisoners. The mother sobbed as the newborn was folded in a blanket and laid in its watery grave. The other prisoners said that in the past weeks, a rumor had been circulating—every baby had been stillborn. Not just on the ships, and not just in St. Petersburg—*every* baby, everywhere.

The words chilled me to the bone, a shock of ghoulish certainty radiating through me. The timing of this supposed phenomenon aligned perfectly with my escape from the temple. It couldn't be a coincidence.

As we prepared to jump ship, Parker's eyes went wild with fear. She clung to Hayes's sleeve as he extricated her arm from around his. To his credit, when Parker had revealed that she couldn't swim, he didn't try to re-argue his case that she should stay aboard with Truman and the others. He simply said, *Then I guess I'll have to carry her to shore. All those summers lifeguarding might as well count for something.*

Parker wasn't the only one who was petrified of getting in that water, and I knew how to swim. As I looked at the frothing white caps of the pitch-black waves, I couldn't even imagine the terror she must be feeling.

Truman handed me a waterproof sack he'd found in the captain's quarters. It held a change of clothes for each of us, along with stolen treasure from the bunkroom. We gave our heavy-duty jackets to the prisoners and stuffed what we could into our tiny bags—thin windbreakers, scarves and hats, flimsy shoes. We needed more, but everything else was too heavy to lug to shore. Survival was job one. The rest could be figured out later.

Hayes and Truman exchanged an urgent glance. The land was a dim outline. It looked about a thousand miles away. One murky light pulsed somewhere on a shore otherwise drenched in darkness. The sea lapped hungrily at the boat, and the air around us had the crisp white smell of ice.

I measured my breaths, trying not to hyperventilate. It was time to go. Truman looked warily from side to side, scanning the horizon. Then he turned back and gave the thumbs-up, moving aside to let us pass.

Hayes went first, his upper body and then his legs disappearing over the side. Parker turned and gave me a fierce hug that caught me totally off guard. There were tears in her eyes.

"Everything's gonna be okay," I whispered as Truman tugged her arm, even though I wasn't sure it was true.

She climbed up on the lip of the boat and sat there, trembling.

"I can't do it," she rasped.

Hating myself for having to do it, I gave her a push from behind. Truman looked at me wide-eyed for a moment, then jerked his head and signaled for me to go. We exchanged a look that I hoped expressed my gratitude for what he'd done, and still would do. Then I took a deep breath and tipped myself over the side.

The first sensation I had was a symphony of icicles boring into my skin, stopping my heart thudding in my chest and making me gasp so furiously that I took on about a gallon of brackish water. I coughed and sputtered violently, unable to get my bearings as the water pulled me left, right, up, and down all at once. I got a split-second view of Truman watching from the ferry. Then he turned and ran toward the upper deck to gun the engines and get out of there before anyone discovered them.

I finally pulled it together enough to tread water, and Hayes swam up. His arm was crooked around Parker's chest, his hand tucked under her armpit. She was floating on her back, eyes closed and face turned up to the sky, probably pretending she was anywhere on earth other than here.

I tried to say something to him—tell him something, maybe how grateful I was or how much he meant to me—but my mind was foggy and a gulp of seawater sent me sputtering again.

"Swim," Hayes said, jutting his chin toward shore, "and don't look back."

I knew we didn't have much time before hypothermia would set in and paralyze us, dragging us to an icy tomb. So I willed my legs to kick and my arms to pinwheel. And with my eyes on the shoreline, I did what Hayes said and didn't look back.

BEFORE:
TRAPPED IN THE TEMPLE,
DREAMING OF ISIRIS

Isiris's eyes fluttered open and her head lolled against the crushed velvet of the wingback chair. A grandfather clock tick-tocked gently from some corner of the cavernous room. Book-cases and oil paintings and Persian rugs surrounded me in three dimensions. One of those odd crystalline replicas of the Inner Eye logo perched atop the fireplace mantle. Across the room, an enormous picture window festooned with lush green curtains looked out over a gunmetal sky. Although I couldn't see it, I knew there was a wide, bleak river out there, sucking inexorably toward the sea. I tried to unearth the name of the city I was in, but once again nothing came.

A horrible agony pulsed through the muscles of Isiris's left arm. Even in my untethered state, the pain throbbed across my synapses like I had a phantom limb. Her head lifted, eyes drifting down to examine the milky white skin of her bare forearm, which stretched gingerly across her lap. There was nothing there. No injury to explain the all-consuming ache radiating through her flesh, so deep that it settled in the roots of her teeth.

I was so overcome by the fiery throb of it that for a moment I didn't notice the absence of thought pollution inside my mind. Isiris's head snapped up, but it wasn't her movement—it was mine.

Isiris wasn't here right now, I realized.

I used to have episodes like this—losing consciousness while Isiris asserted full agency over my body, like the time Adam found me in Yoyogi Park after she'd taken over my mind with an elaborate murder fantasy involving a Harajuku girl.

Isiris had been weakened, and now I knew why. What hurt Adam, hurt Isiris. And Isiris had hurt Adam a lot.

There was no time to waste. I had to find him.

I stood up, Isiris's legs swaying underneath me like the building was moored on stilts. I steadied myself against the chair as a lightning storm of pain branched its way up my arm. Isiris's knees went weak, her legs nearly giving out and sending me collapsing back into the chair. Her center of gravity felt off—oddly front-heavy. There was an odd flutter in her tummy, like a flock of butterflies set loose from their net. It must be my lack of experience commandeering her body.

My frustration conjured hot tears to Isiris's eyes—tears she would disdain. This wouldn't last. I had minutes, maybe seconds, before Isiris would resurface and my chance to find Adam would be lost. This might be my one chance to talk to him as Harlow—possibly ever.

"Adam," I croaked, Isiris's voice sounding cracked and pathetic.

"I'm right here." His voice was low and broken. "I'm always right here."

It was the voice of a prisoner without hope. There was resignation, but also something more. A kind of acceptance. As if he were learning to love the bonds that held him.

Adam was used to Isiris summoning him. What was different was that he no longer seemed to be fighting it.

It took me a moment to spot him stretched out across a plush red settee—T-shirt clad, his left arm bandaged to the elbow. Brilliant dots of blood soaked their way to the surface of the bandage, as if mocking the gravity of his injury. He cradled his arm across his body the way Isiris had cradled her own. The pain in her arm still pulsed with sympathetic hurt. He had been so still and silent, I hadn't even noticed he was there. His eyes were closed, his brow creased.

"Adam. Adam, it's me," I said. "It's Harlow."

The crease in his brow didn't diminish. He didn't even react.

"Adam," I pleaded.

His eyes opened, but they were dull and disbelieving, the deep blue gone nearly black.

"You should just kill me. No matter how much you claim to be Harlow, I will always know the truth."

My heart swelled with love for him. Love that I'd thought dead with his betrayal. The tears that had started as frustration now spilled over into sadness.

Something flickered in Adam's eyes, and he was suddenly a

shade closer to his normal self. He struggled to sit, unable to use his injured arm.

"It's really me this time." I repeated. "Not blond, but still brainy and still loving Bad Religion."

"Harlow?" he said, his voice breaking a little.

"I have Isiris's mind to myself right now, but she'll be back soon. There isn't much time."

Even though he was visibly weak, he managed to stand and cross the room to where I was sitting. He winced in pain as he knelt in front of me. His good hand rested on my leg. I leaned forward and our foreheads tipped together. For the space of a heartbeat, we were silent. His breath was warm against my cheek. I remembered the warm summer day he leaned me up against the carriage house behind my father's mansion; I remembered the kiss we shared in the Fairy Tower on the Great Wall of China. Despite the time and distance that had separated us, I felt closer to him now than I had any of those times before. I wanted to preserve this moment—hold it sacred in my memory and let it nourish me during the long, lonely days in the temple. It was all I had, but I had to let it go.

"I can feel the pain. The pain in your arm. I can feel it in her body," I said.

Adam nodded, a small sigh escaping his lips. "She's been acting strange since . . . since she hurt me," he said.

I considered telling Adam what I knew about the blood bond, but he was so broken down and desperate I worried what he might do with the information. I wasn't even sure what I was going to do with it—the only way I knew to hurt Isiris was to hurt Adam, and I didn't want to do that.

"I know how to get out of the temple," I said.

He snapped to attention, leaning back so he could look into my eyes. His gaze burned with need.

"You do?" he asked, a desperate edge in his voice.

"Yes, but I need your help," I said.

"Anything. Just tell me, I'll do it," he said.

"I can't find our door—the one that leads back to our world. You have to tell me how to find it."

He shook his head, closing his eyes for a moment. When he re-opened them, they were filled with anguish.

"I don't know where it is. Everything was in a panic when we left. All I remember is following you—I mean, her," he said.

I clasped my other hand over his and looked intently at him. I steadied my voice, trying to project calm. We weren't going to be alone much longer—it couldn't last.

"You have to tell me anything you remember. Other door-ways. Turns you made. Anything you remember that stands out. Please," I said.

His jaw flexed. He was trying not to cry.

"The doors were all closed. We made so many turns. It was dark. I remember wondering how it was you knew your way, because it definitely wasn't how we came in. I should have questioned it. I should have, but I didn't. And now you're trapped and the world is going to hell and I can't remember shit and all of it is my fault," he said.

Questioning him was futile. I could see that now. No matter how much I wished he would hand over the Rosetta stone that would spring me from Isiris's trap at last.

"Shhh... it's okay. This is Isiris's fault. What you need to do is stay strong," I said, pulling him close to me.

He burrowed into my neck. My lips grazed his ear as I moved my hand to the back of his neck.

"This will all be over soon, I promise," I whispered.

"No, it won't. It's never going to be over. This is all we have," he said.

His chin tilted up toward mine. He leaned in and placed a hungry kiss on my lips. As much as I wanted to reciprocate, I couldn't forget that these were Isiris's lips and not mine. I didn't kiss him back. He pulled away, crestfallen.

"I'm sorry. I shouldn't have—" he started.

"Adam, I... it's just... there's been so much—"

"Shhh... it's okay. I know. Listen, you have to promise me something." His hand found mine, squeezing it so hard that it hurt a little.

"What is it?" I asked.

"Don't try to find me. Don't come here to confront her. If something happened to you, I couldn't—" He swallowed, on the edge of a breakdown and unable to go on.

Profound sadness knotted in my chest. It was torture seeing him like this—utterly devoid of hope.

The shuffling of feet interrupted us. There was a small, surprised sound, swallowed down by the interloper before it could escape her lips.

Adam and I both stood up, turning to face the doorway.

It was Mercy. My childhood friend and one-time enemy. With her came a rush of feeling—a nostalgia for home and everything we'd collectively lost.

The tea service balanced in her hand rattled ever so slightly. She was worse off than last time I'd seen her. Both her eyes were missing now, her flesh necrotizing and flaking away where it had been burned with acid.

"Tea, madam?" she asked. There was a quiver in her voice that echoed Adam's.

"Mercy," I whispered.

"Madam?" she asked, clearly afraid. Her daily life must be a series of impossible tests and horrifying punishments. The tenderness in my voice could only seem like another trick.

"I tried to help her get out. That's what Isiris did in response," Adam said.

My friends were trapped in a hell worse than the one I was in, and I was powerless to help them.

"Mercy, I'm so sorry," I said.

Rage and sadness roiled inside me, and it was an invitation too tempting to resist. Before I could do anything to hold her back, Isiris rose up and took control.

"Harlow?" Mercy asked. The tray dropped from her hands.

Isiris stalked toward her. Adam stayed where he was, oblivious to the fact that Isiris had returned to subjugate me once again. Just before she reached Mercy, she leaned down to pick up a shard of ceramic from the shattered teapot on the floor.

"Yes, Mercy. It's me." Isiris's voice was dripping with false sweetness.

Her fist closed over the shard. Mercy let out a little yell and a sigh, opening her arms and leaning toward the sound of Isiris's voice. I tried to scream No. Tried to stop her. Tried to do anything but what Isiris was about to do.

She raised the weapon in her fist and brought it down hard into the side of Mercy's neck, burying it to the hilt. She caught Mercy as the girl slumped into her arms, a fountain of blood pumping from the side of her neck. Adam was yelling somewhere in the background, his feet pounding uneven across the floor.

"Why?" Mercy's piteous voice exhaled her last word, her last breath.

"Because I can," Isiris said.

As Adam's arms closed around Isiris, wrenching her away from Mercy's limp body, I slipped away into oblivion.

AFTER:
PARIS, FRANCE

The streets of Paris looked even more eerily abandoned in the pre-dawn light. After jumping ship we'd stowed away on the cargo train from Lübeck, too sluggish and cold to be properly afraid. Human Popsicles don't have the capacity for fear, another life lesson courtesy of Isiris the Terrible. But every time I felt sorry for myself I thought of the ferry full of defeated people we had rescued, which was hopefully on its way to relative safety in Scandinavia, and of all the other prisoners, before and since, that we hadn't. It spurred me on.

We'd wound our way through the darkened streets of Paris since arriving in the train yard just before sunset. After our run-in with the Watchers in St. Petersburg and the hijacking of the prisoner ferry, there was no doubt in my mind that Isiris knew I was free. What I didn't know yet was what she would do about it.

There were no working streetlights in this city, and every

office building, residence, and shopfront was pitch dark, with a few chilling exceptions. Three times during the night we'd passed by heavily guarded fortresses—former hospitals, schools, and offices—with floodlights and guard towers. This was where they were keeping, and possibly killing, high value prisoners like Dora. The scent of burning rubber mingled with an unidentified sickly-sweet stench outside every one we passed by. I didn't want to guess what it was, but it made me desperate to get to the school where I prayed Dora was still being kept. Isiris couldn't know that I knew where Dora was being held, but still, I feared my friend was still in mortal danger. Isiris took twisted satisfaction in hurting anyone I loved, even if I had no way of knowing about it.

Snow crunched under my feet and our breath made foggy clouds on the crisp night air. Every now and then, a mongrel dog would come padding by on some inscrutable mission, not one of them so much as pausing to sniff the wind in our direction. We hid among the carcasses of broken-down cars and the shadows of shattered-glass shopfronts.

Even more than in St. Petersburg, Paris appeared to have been drained of life. Unlike St. Petersburg, where it seemed that every living thing was hidden underground like the telltale heart, here it was as if every last beating heart had been exported, exsanguinated, or eradicated. An occasional dash of brilliant blood marred the pavement. It was like a movie set from the apocalypse, waiting for extras to populate it. Paris was a picture-perfect postcard, torn to shreds and tossed to the wind.

"We're almost there," Hayes said, clutching the city map

we'd unearthed from an abandoned bookstore. "According to this, the school is right on the next block."

He looked more attractive than ever in his newly pilfered bomber jacket and army surplus cargos, clutching his pistol across his chest. Adversity agreed with him, it seemed.

I needed to stop thinking of Hayes that way, but I wasn't having much success.

Parker and I hadn't fared quite as well in the clothing department as Hayes had. I was wearing a pair of mouthwash-colored hospital scrubs, cinched at the waist with a plastic belt. Parker was drowning in an oversized sweatshirt with a picture of a wolf on it and polka-dotted stretch pants. Neither of us was happy about it. Paris would be pleased to know that even at the end of the world, fashion was still a going concern.

The three of us were crouched behind an overturned produce cart discarded at the side of the street. We'd been in this same place for almost an hour. The half-built Tour Montparnasse skyscraper towered overhead, its scaffolding reaching toward the sky, which purpled behind it. The former government of France had halted construction, and the building had stood half-finished for the better part of a decade; now it probably would never be completed.

"Let's review the plan one more time," I said.

Parker looked at me and raised an eyebrow. "The plan is: we don't have a plan."

"Sure we do. The plan is, we look for an opportunity to present itself," I said.

"Whoever thought that plan up should know it's not a very good plan," Hayes added.

"Whoever thought that plan up should be fired," Parker agreed.

"You can't fire me. I'm a figurehead," I said.

They both rolled their eyes. It occurred to me that there was no one else I'd rather take the longest long shot in all of human history with than these two.

"Seriously, though. Let's go scope out the school. I'll think of something," I said.

"Not if I think of something first," Hayes said playfully.

"While you two are flirting, I'll be the one coming up with a stroke of genius," Parker said.

Hayes cleared his throat and the vibe got very uncomfortable. He looked at me for a second, then conveniently became a tornado of action.

"Let's move. Everybody stay low." He motioned with his gun in the direction we'd been heading.

We scuttled diagonally across the street, exposed and in full view of the surrounding buildings for one painful minute as we made our way to the next street. Any second I expected to hear the staccato thunder of sniper fire, or a shout of alarm from a vigilant Watcher. But there was nothing except the electric hum of anticipation flowing between the three of us as we rounded the corner and ducked behind another line of cars. The low-slung building from the grainy video came into view.

Hayes held his hand up, signaling us to stop. I peered through the smashed-in rear windows of the red Fiat in front of me. The building was much bigger than it looked on video: four stories of butter-yellow stone with row-upon-row of barred window. A VisionCrest flag waved from a post in its center; pale phantom lettering from its former incarnation as a school, *Lycée Technique*, floated like a shadow underneath the VisionCrest symbol. And the place was crawling with Watchers. Two pairs of them patrolled back and forth along the sidewalk in front, toting machine guns that were little more than dark smudges in the Violet Hour light.

The sight of it knocked the wind out of me. My best friend was in that building. Not just that, but she was the only one who could help guide me to Isiris.

I was going to get Dora out or die trying.

"Psssst—over here." Parker's voice sounded behind us.

She'd climbed through the broken double doors of an apartment building right behind us and was standing in the shadows of the cavernous lobby. She pointed up, her ponytail swishing insistently, and gave us a big, toothy smile. "There's stairs!"

Hayes and I exchanged a look. It was a good idea—once the sun was fully up, we might be able to see down into the courtyard. Maybe even figure out what area of the building Dora was being held in.

"Well, if there's stairs ... " Hayes said, flashing me the half-smile again.

As he moved to follow Parker, I put my hand on his arm. "Wait until they head back the other way."

The two Watchers stopped at the corner of the building and scanned the block. Both Hayes and I ducked down.

After a minute he peeked back up. "It's clear. Let's go."

He grabbed my hand, and we ran inside the building after Parker.

We waited all morning, pilfering canned food from the abandoned apartment and watching. We finally spotted Dora at mid-day. She was shuffling across the courtyard, the crown jewel of a waifish chain-gang. I pressed my face and hands up to the window, not caring that someone might spot me. I felt simultaneously flooded with gratitude and paralyzed by outrage.

Dora hung her head, dispirited in a way that didn't match with the person I adored. I vowed that once we rescued her and she told us the location of the elaborate palace I'd dreamed of, I was going to feed Isiris her own liver after I'd ripped it out.

Then I remembered the blood bond. If I ever found Isiris, I wouldn't be able to exact revenge on her, much less stop her. Not without doing the same to Adam in the bargain.

Hayes put a hand on my shoulder as we looked out over the courtyard. "We're going to get her back. Don't worry."

"I'm not worried," I said, looking at him. "I'm pissed."

He pulled me closer. I wanted to cry, but I wouldn't give Isiris the satisfaction of my tears.

———

Parker opened the back door to the Range Rover. She'd hot-wired it in the parking garage under the apartment building and it was now idling outside the doors to the Lycée. I took a deep breath, conjuring the memory of being in Isiris's skin. Mainlining her malice.

There was no way I'd admit it to Parker or Hayes, but I was so terrified I thought I might lose my lunch all over the car's polished-leather bench seat. Pretending to be Isiris pretending to be me was a tricky business, and my best friend's life hung in the balance. Plus a whole lot more. But it wasn't just that. I feared that one of these days, I might crawl into Isiris's skin and never come back out.

I didn't like the way I liked her power.

The garage for the apartment building opened to the back of the school, so the Watchers stationed in front of the school hadn't seen us emerge. For all they knew, when we'd rounded the corner we'd just arrived from the airport or the local VisionCrest headquarters. I was wearing large, dark sunglasses and a slinky black pencil skirt and white silk blouse we'd found in some rich lady's closet. I looked disconcertingly like the leader of a relentless corporate religion.

But looks can be deceiving. The cliché seemed like the understatement of the century after what I'd been through.

I'd managed to chew my thumbnail to the quick in the time it took us to circle the block. The sting of it gave me a strange sort of relief from my anxiety that Isiris might anticipate this move. I couldn't help but notice how my hand was shaking, just a little. Enough for someone who was looking for it to notice.

As we'd pulled up, two Watchers had drawn their guns and trained them on Parker as she exited the SUV. "Freeze!" one of them yelled.

I bit down on my fingernail to dampen the pain—the tinny taste of blood sparked on my tongue.

Parker calmly held her hand out to me. The Watchers were flummoxed—they probably didn't get a lot of visitors of the non-prisoner-of-war variety.

Hayes turned around in the front seat and tilted his head down to look at me over the aviator glasses he'd lifted from the rich lady's once-significant other. He tossed me a little vial filled with a yellow liquid.

"What's this?" I asked.

"I found it when I was foraging. I think it's perfume. But doesn't it look a little bit like a virus?"

"I'm going to threaten them with perfume?" I asked.

"Eau de toilette. And only if deadly force is necessary," he said, that halfway-smirk I loved so much playing at his lips.

I smirked back.

He nodded—a silent message telling me that I could do this. He was right. *I* was the freaking Matriarch of the most powerful organization this world had ever seen. *I* was. Not Isiris. Like it or not, it was time to start owning it.

I slipped the vial into my pocket and a sense of calm and composure came over me. There was no turning back now. I looked toward Parker, still holding her hand out to me. Her cheek twitched.

I put on the self-satisfied smile I'd seen in Isiris's reflection, eschewed Parker's offer of assistance just as Isiris would, and climbed out of the Range Rover. I whipped my sunglasses off and surveyed the building disdainfully, my final measure of disgust settling on the Watchers themselves.

Four pairs of stern eyebrows shot toward the sky, immediate recognition dawning on their faces. From these first glances, I knew they wouldn't question me. They believed I was Isiris—or rather, they believed I was her twisted version of Harlow Wintergreen. If this situation got any more meta, we might open a wormhole in the fabric of space-time, and currently I had all I could handle for this particular Monday, thank you very much.

I narrowed my eyes, giving my best possible scathing look at first one Watcher, then the other. "Let me inside. I want to speak to whoever's in charge."

The bigger Watcher visibly gulped at this—whether he was swallowing fear that this spelled disaster for all of them or relief that he could pass me off to one of his superiors, I couldn't tell. What I could tell is that they took the bait.

I strode toward the gated door like I owned the place, tossing my sunglasses at Parker, who scrambled behind me also doing her best to look authoritative. Both Watchers knelt as I reached the door. The second pair of Watchers were hovering in the background, slack-jawed, radios squawking. From the fearful looks in their eyes, they weren't necessarily expecting to survive my visit. Isiris's reputation preceded her.

"From your Inner Eye," they said in unison. A current of fear was audible in their voices.

How did brutes so tough and mean when pointing a machine gun at innocent people turn into such quivering babies when confronted with an unarmed teenaged girl? If I'd ever doubted that fear was about the perception of power, I never would again.

"Get up," I spat, not finishing the customary Vision-Crest greeting as they'd expect. "And let me in the building before I tear out your fingernails and have them made into a necklace."

They leaped to their feet, one of them fumbling with the locks while the other murmured for him to go faster. The metal grate swung wide, revealing a set of creamy marble steps and a pair of polished wooden doors. This had been one posh school in its former life, but the dissonance of the luxe surroundings and what was occurring within these four walls gave it an air of intense creepiness now. Like all things Isiris, it felt like a taunt meant to make the mental blows hurt even worse than the physical ones.

Parker stood at my side as the door swung wide, controlled by some unseen mechanism. I was expecting to be greeted by a cadre of senior Watchers who were less Cowardly Lionish than their perimeter-patrolling counterparts, and I wasn't disappointed. Flanking either side of the long hallway were two columns of Watchers, in their woolen gray suits and deceptively jaunty berets. And at the very far end was their massively tall, grim-faced leader.

Even from a distance I could see the hardness in his gray eyes that belied a tempered core of cruelty. It felt like those x-ray eyes could see right through me.

My confidence faltered and I hesitated. Parker pinched my elbow to remind me who I was supposed to be. Nobody scared Isiris, and Isiris was me. Ergo, by the virtues of the transitive property, nobody scared me.

Except this guy did. But there was no turning back now.

AFTER: PARIS, FRANCE

I breezed down the hall and every Watcher snapped to attention, stiff as boards, saluting me with their hands across their brows. My stilettos clicked along the slick and over-buffed floor and I silently prayed my balance wouldn't betray me. Even though I felt like a little girl playing dress-up, I had to exude an air of unflagging confidence.

The gray-eyed man regarded me with a steely countenance. Not a muscle twitch out of place. He looked like someone who had spent most of his life screaming at others to do unspeakable things.

I closed the final distance and was face-to-face with him. Well, face-to-chest. He stared down at me. I stared back up. It was a silent game of chicken, but I wasn't sure if it was the winner or the loser who would speak the first word. There was a clock on the wall behind him that tick-tick-ticked the seconds as we stood there silently, daring the other to make the opening salvo. I tried to imagine that each click of the second-hand was a drop of water as I melted this icy man with the intensity of my stare, until he was nothing more than a puddle I would step over.

Finally, after a series of minutes that felt more like eternity, he got down on one knee. His head hung; his gaze was fixed on the patent leather peek-a-boo toe of my shoe. The columns of Watchers behind us did the same.

"Matriarch," he said, his voice like a mouthful of gravel.

Not knowing what possessed me, I extended my shoe out and shoved it up against the bottom of his chin, forcing him to look up at me. Then I kicked him swiftly in the chest, knocking him backward.

Parker sucked back a gasp. The rest of the hallway was so silent you could hear a spider spinning its web.

The gray-eyed man got up on all fours, then stood up. His face was impassive as he saluted me the way the other men had done.

"I've come for a prisoner," I said. "I expected you to kill her by now, but I see that I will have to do it myself."

There was no momentary cloud of confusion in his eyes like I'd expected. Instead his hands went down to his sides, smoothing out his uniform.

"I received your orders. We were making preparations to have her execution broadcast just before sunset," he said.

My stomach leaped into my throat. Isiris had sent the order to have Dora killed, and she'd planned to do it for all the world to see. For me to see.

"No broadcast. Kill her now so I can watch," I said.

A flicker of something crossed his eyes. Doubt. Suspicion. "Better yet, why don't you drop the blade?" he said. "That guillotine there in the courtyard—I had it restored. The blade's so sharp it cuts flesh like butter. It will treat her like a queen."

He motioned with his stare to a small, grimy window. Through it, I could see the courtyard I'd seen in the video. There were no prisoners out there now, but through the low fog hovering just above the ground I could see the old-fashioned execution device clear as day. Slashes of red painted the ground. Bile threatened to rise up my throat, but I willed it back down. I knew then that I couldn't just "save" Dora— the gray-eyed man was making a blood sport of this post.

"I prefer to squeeze the life out of her with my own two hands," I said, looking back to him.

The gray-eyed man stared back, unflinching.

"Bring us Sister Elber," Parker said.

The gray-eyed man gave no indication he was aware of Parker's existence.

I stared at him. He stared back.

"Very well," he said. "Wait here just a moment and I'll go collect her."

"Do that," I said.

Mr. Gray-eyes did a tight military turn on his heel and began clicking down the marble hallway. One step, two. I exhaled in relief. This was far easier than I'd imagined. I could hardly believe we'd pulled it off. Three steps. Four.

Then he halted and turned back around.

"You told me that a day might come when someone

came to collect Sister Elber in person. A day that you might even arrive to collect her," he said, standing about twenty feet from me.

"And that day is today," I agreed.

This was all wrong.

The corner of his mouth twitched up. He was enjoying this, the way a tomcat might enjoy the feint and parry of cornering a helpless mouse.

"Do you remember what you told me I should do, in the event that occurred?" he asked.

He took three steps back toward me, closing the distance between us.

My stomach dropped out from under me. Was it a code? A trick?

Out of the corner of my eye, I saw Parker stiffen. Her hand twitched, moving for the gun.

The answer came to me all at once. It wasn't that I'd been inside Isiris's head enough to make an educated guess about what she would do. It was that I knew what *I* would do if the tables were turned and it was me trying to prevent Isiris from impersonating me to get something that she wanted. The thought that our motivations could be so aligned made my stomach turn.

Three more steps and there he was, right in front of me once again. He seemed taller than before.

"I said you should kill that person, even if it was me," I replied, the surety of my voice faltering ever so slightly.

His eyes narrowed almost imperceptibly. My instincts were right. But how could I get him to doubt his convictions?

"So now the question is—will you pass my test?" I asked.

"Test?" he asked.

I nodded. Staring, staring.

"Bring me the girl," I commanded. "And all the rest of the prisoners."

His eyes flashed, and in a split second his gun was out and pointed right between my eyes.

Parker scrambled for hers, but I grabbed her arm and said, "Stop."

For a moment, it seemed that no one so much as breathed. The gray-eyed man pulled the safety back, its soft *click* echoing down the hallway. I pulled the perfume vial out of my pocket, willing my hand not to tremble. Slowly, I raised it up so the gray-eyed man could see it.

"This—" I said, "is the virus. The faintest whiff will cause its victims to hemorrhage internally. Vomit blood. Liquefy from the inside out. Convulse on the ground like sad little fishies robbed of water. I am immune. But you are not."

As I spoke, the gray-eyed man's gaze flitted nervously from me to the vial.

Like everyone else, this Watcher had surely seen his fair share of death, although from a position of safety like all VisionCrest loyalists. Paris, abandoned as it was, must have been hit hard by Isiris's targeted virus attacks. Anyone not sent to prison camps to die a slow death had invariably been doomed by the virus to a quick one.

"You mean to kill us, then?" he asked. His tone was cruel. Nonchalant. He was an even better liar than I was.

"I mean to kill the prisoners. At least, I mean to kill all but the one I am saving for my private audience."

The gun dropped to his side.

I sent a silently thank you out to Hayes. If it weren't for the perfume vial, I would have been sporting a bullet to the brain.

"Round the prisoners up into the yard. Then take your men and leave—march to Bordeaux and wait there for your next assignment," I said, pulling the name of another French city and the rest of the made-up instructions out of thin air.

He looked nonplussed. "Bordeaux? That's over six hundred kilometers from here. We have no supplies and it's the middle of winter."

It was scary how fast my hand shot out and slapped him hard across the face. The gray-eyed man's head snapped viciously to the side. I no longer needed an internal mantra of WWID, What Would Isiris Do? I knew exactly what she would do, and that terrified me. The gray-eyed man slowly turned his head back, the outline of my fingers an angry silhouette on his cheek.

"Disobedient. Perhaps I should kill you right here and now, as it seems you are incapable of following simple instructions."

His eyes flashed—a steely, hardened look—and his jaw flexed. For a moment I thought I'd gone too far, thought I saw a flicker of doubt in his murky eyes.

"Gather the prisoners in the yard!" he bellowed.

The battalion snapped to attention and shouted, "Sir,

yes sir!" behind me. The sound of fifty pairs of boots clomp-clomping down hallways and up stairs filled the air.

"Bring me the girl," I said.

The gray-eyed man nodded, then turned to go.

I exhaled, flooded with profound relief.

The clipped staccato of his footsteps halted. Parker grabbed my arm, as if bracing for something. The gray-eyed man's head turned slightly, halfway looking over his shoulder like he was about to turn back around. Like he'd forgotten or remembered something that had been niggling at the back of his mind.

My stomach plummeted to the floor.

But he didn't turn around. He shook his head and resumed walking, as if deciding that whatever his doubts were, it wasn't worth the price of being wrong. His feet disappeared up a sweeping central staircase and out of view. Parker's grip on my arm eased up.

"Will Dora know it's you when she sees you?" Parker whispered.

"Yes," I said. I was sure of it—my best friend would know me anywhere, just like I knew her.

"Will she know how to act?" Parker asked.

"She's the smartest girl I know, and the gutsiest. She'll know what to do."

Her mouth turned down at the corners. She wasn't as good at hiding her hurt as she thought she was.

"She's a lot like you," I added.

A little light returned to Parker's eyes, and an almost-smile turned up the corner of her lips.

Through the windows, I could see prisoners being herded into the courtyard. The Watchers were poking them in the ribs with the nose of their assault rifles, getting in their last digs. I told myself it was okay—the Watchers would get what was coming to them on their long winter walk.

A few tense minutes later, the click of the gray-eyed man's heels returned and his feet came into view on the stairs. A pair of bare, grubby feet attempted to keep pace next to him. I bit back tears; I would know those chicken legs anywhere, even if they'd finally been robbed of their rainbow-striped socks. Dora had lost a ton of weight, her hair had been chopped haphazardly and was snarled into almost-dread locks, and her face was obscured by a layer of grime an inch thick. But none of that could keep the Dora I knew from shining through.

When she saw my face, she recoiled. She tugged back against the Watcher, who had her arm in an iron grip, dragging her along beside him. But then I saw recognition light in her eyes, and I knew that she saw the real me.

I trained my gaze on the gray-eyed man. Looking at Dora was threatening to overwhelm me with emotion, and we'd come too far to have the ruse fall apart over tears of joy. Finally, he and Dora were standing in front of us. Dora was out of breath. It struck me how frail she was. How fragile. It made me want to strangle the man with my bare hands, just like I'd promised him I'd strangle Dora.

He yanked hard on her arm and she fell to her knees in front of me. She hung her head, but not before I caught the hint of a smile on her face. She did her best to huddle in an approximation of fear and dejection.

"Matriarch, your property," he said.

"Take your men and leave," I commanded.

The gray-eyed man considered me for a moment, then let out a piercing whistle. Watchers streamed back through the doors from the courtyard, re-assembling into their lines behind us. When they were all in place, he raised a sharp arm and saluted me. I raised my hand and made Isiris's three-fingered symbol. There was, again, the flicker of something in his eyes.

I wondered how far he would make it before word got back to Isiris that someone pretending to be her had freed her most prized possession. Well, second-most prized. She still had Adam.

Then he suddenly kicked a huddled Dora hard in the ribs. I only barely managed to contain my reaction as she yelped in pain and fell over, coughing and sputtering. The Watcher sidestepped us and walked briskly down the corridor created by his men, and they fell into step behind him as he passed.

I waited until I heard the front doors fall shut, the slam echoing down the hallway. None of us moved. It felt too good to be true. Impossible that we'd actually pulled it off.

Finally, Parker turned around. "They're gone."

Dora turned her face up to mine. She was beaten, but she still managed a half-smile. "What took you so long?"

I fell to my knees, wrapping her in an embrace. "I had stuff to do," I half-laughed, half-cried into her hair, which had the unfortunate smell of weeks-old garbage.

"Uh, guys—I'm all for touching reunions, but don't you think we should get the hell out of here?" Parker asked.

"Dora, meet Parker. Parker, Dora. You guys are going to get along swimmingly. Hayes Cantor will be our chauffeur."

Dora's eyebrows rose a hair as I helped her to her unsteady feet. She knew my history with Hayes.

"Parker's going to help you to the car," I said. "She's right—we have to jam before Isiris gets wind of this."

Dora gave Parker a wink and a wry smile. "She's always been this bossy, in case you're wondering."

I could see Parker's stand-offishness melting despite herself. She wouldn't see Dora as a threat for long. She held her arm out to her.

"Stubin?" I asked.

Dora shook her head, a tight *no* that said it all. My chest clenched. Then she jerked her chin toward the courtyard. "We can't leave them here."

"I never would. Go to the car and I'll meet you there."

I waited until the hobbling Dora and Parker reached the front doors. They had to be safely inside the car before I set the others free—even though the prisoners were free to go, they would probably be desperate to flee. I couldn't chance them injuring Dora in their hurry to escape. I kicked off my high heels, preparing to run like hell.

I went to the door to the courtyard, opened it, and yelled out, "You're free now! Get out of Paris whatever way you can and try to take care of each other!"

Heads turned in confusion, trying to discover the source. Trying to discern if it was some kind of evil trick. Then a ripple went through the crowd—the first stirrings of defiance. They would make it out.

I closed the door and sprinted as fast as I could down the hallway to the front door.

I heard the courtyard door open behind me as I ran. Bursting through the double doors and into the street, I wanted to scream with joy. It was the best feeling in the world.

The Range Rover idled, the back door open and waiting. I jumped in and yelled, "Go go go!" just as a mob of desperate prisoners spilled into the street behind me.

Tires squealed against pavement as we lurched forward. Out the back window, I could see the disoriented prisoners looking after us, some already breaking off to run down the street. Free.

I turned to see Dora smiling at me. "Harlow Wintergreen is a total drama queen."

I pulled her into another hug. In this moment, life was pretty freaking beautiful. "Why take down your evil twin if you can't do it with style?" I asked.

Dora's smile wilted a little at the mention of Isiris. "Stubin's dead."

The pain on her face made my heart ache. I wished I had something that would take it away. Some measure of comfort to soothe her.

"Mercy is too," I told her.

We shared a pained look. There was no room for words.

"She took my brother from me," Parker chimed in, putting a comforting hand on Dora's shoulder. "And we're going to make her pay for every single one of them."

We both looked at Parker. I felt a solidarity with the people in this car that I'd never felt before in my life.

"So where to, ladies?" Hayes met my eye in the rear-view mirror. We were sailing down the empty streets of Paris, headed toward the outskirts.

I looked to Dora. "D. I'll explain later, but the palace you were living in with Isiris and Adam when she sent you away—where was it? That's where we have to go."

Dora shivered. "That place put me off the Clash forever."

"'London Calling'?" Parker asked. If I didn't know better, I'd say she was hoping to impress Dora.

London. Hayes's home turf. At least we had that going for us.

Dora nodded. "The Palace of Westminster. She took it over and turned it into her evil lair."

So that was it. Westminster was the castle I'd seen in my dreams.

"Perfect," Hayes said with a wry smile. "London. Just a hop, skip, and an English Channel away."

"No swimming," Parker said.

Everyone was silent for a moment. We'd ridden across a continent, busted out of a Russian palace, stowed away on a ship, swum icy waters, hopped trains, stolen cars, and impersonated killers to get to this point.

And even though it seemed unreasonable to demand more from luck and fate, we still had to cross that narrow strait. I was completely out of ideas.

"No swimming," Hayes agreed. "I know a way."

BEFORE:
TRAPPED IN THE TEMPLE

I bolted upright, gasping for air as I surfaced from the vision. The image of Mercy, dead, was seared into my mind.

Sobs crested through my body like a tidal wave, lodging in the narrow passage of my throat. I couldn't see the temple around me—all I saw was Mercy's limp and blood-soaked body crumpling to the floor as Adam wrenched Isiris from the death-grip she had on her.

I'd once considered Mercy my nemesis. Thinking about that now, I realized how stupid and meaningless it all was. Thinking of Mercy as threat? Treating her like an enemy? What a waste of precious time, for both of us, on something so inconsequential.

I buried my face in my hands as grief racked my body. My entire world was going to shit and I was helpless to stop it. I was never going to get out of here. It would take a thousand lifetimes of wandering these halls to paint the right door crimson with my blood. By then it would be too late. Everything would be destroyed, remade in Isiris's image just like she wanted it to be.

I scratched my nails across my face, trying to find a way to let the pain trapped beneath my skin out.

I was so overcome that at first I didn't hear the sound of beating wings. Doors flying open. The Violet Hour.

A shadow crossed above me, dampening the glare of the dazzling light overhead. I looked up.

It was a wraith. But instead of the usual wispy purple, this one was gravestone gray and swirled like a tempest. I'd seen spirits like this before—they were tormented, fighting the truth of their departure from their prior life. I knew on some primal level what made them this way—some great injustice had caused their life to end and they were unable to accept it. Souls like this were difficult to guide through their door. I wasn't always successful, and some of them were doomed to watch me mournfully from the shadows as their spirit became dust and their bodies became the hollow flesh that Isiris had once commanded as an army.

Usually these gray wraiths flitted listlessly, bouncing off walls and rushing swiftly away from me. While others welcomed my touch, these restless few were terrified of moving on—they weren't ready.

But this thundercloud of a spirit wasn't running. It was surrounding me, zipping around in frantic circles, tighter and tighter every second.

I jumped to my feet as it wrapped itself around me, turning circles in a futile attempt at escape. Despite the soul's lack of substance, it constricted around me, holding me so close it began to force the air from my lungs.

But instead of becoming more afraid, I experienced a strange sensation of familiarity. As the wraith wrapped itself tighter and tighter, I became more and more serene. It was like curling up with a well-worn blanket and worrying its fray between sleepy fingertips. This soul knew me, and I knew it.

Then it hit me—the shard of ceramic buried inches-deep in white skin, the spray of blood like a dancing fountain, the look of disbelief and horror.

"Mercy?" I whispered.

She released her hold, spinning around me and then materializing like a plume of smoke in front of me. The faint outline of her face shimmered, the gauzy threads of her formlessness shifting and changing, and yet so purely Mercy that I didn't know how I'd failed to recognize her immediately.

"I'm so sorry," I said.

Mercy turned, swirling away from me.

I chased after her, needing to make amends in some small way. But she only fled faster.

"Please don't run away," I called, tears choking my voice. "Mercy, I'm so, so sorry."

She stopped, gathering density as her misty tendrils recombined. I slowed down, approaching her cautiously, the way you would a skittish colt. Unexpectedly, a little trail of dishwater mist reached out and wound its way around my hand. The shapeless mass that was now Mercy moved away with purpose.

Suddenly I realized what was happening. She wasn't running—she wanted me to follow her.

My heart leaped into my throat. There was only one place I could think of that Mercy would be leading me.

I picked up speed as she raced toward one of the numerous dark, anonymous hallways that lined the heart of the temple. I'd been down every one of them so many times I was probably anemic from the loss of blood that marked my return path, and this one was no exception. My heart was pumping double-time and my pace matched it as Mercy raced ahead. The Violet Hour was nearly over—the doors would be closing soon. Was it possible that this was the moment? I ran harder, memorizing the turns as we went instead of my usual process of dotting each turn with a smear of scarlet from my fingertip.

We twisted and turned, Mercy growing luminescent in the dark, lighting the way to salvation. A sucking rush of wind pulled us over the slippery stones and I felt a magnetic tug inside me that I recognized in my bones. Home.

Mercy was taking me back to the gateway from which she came, hoping for something that would set things right. For justice, if such a thing existed. I ran harder, every breath a brilliant dagger through my lungs, toward the door at the end of the tunnel. It was the only dead end I'd ever seen in the temple, and I wondered, not for the first time, if this place changed based on the wishes and whims of some unseen hand. Mercy and I were just feet from the door, then inches. I could see the luminous green of the Cambodian jungle illuminated in the violet-soaked light.

And then we were there. Standing right in front of it.

I turned to look at Mercy. She was no longer a formless soul, but rather an almost-real approximation of her physical body. Only the barest hint of transparency—the rustic stones of the temple shining through her chest—gave her away for what she was now. A spirit. A wraith. A captive in this temple, just like me.

Mercy nodded urgently toward the door, urging me forward before time ran out and the Violet Hour was over.

Tears of gratitude were sliding down my cheeks. Mercy had saved me. And there was nothing I could do to make the outcome different for her.

My head shook no. I didn't cross through.

The door slammed closed. I put my palm against its solid nothingness and leaned into it.

There was nothing I wanted more than to return to my world. But that could wait. Two more Violet Hours—one for Mercy's escape, and one for mine.

I didn't know if that meant a week or a month or a year outside, and I didn't care. There was no guarantee I could rescue any of my friends on the other side—but I could rescue my friend on this one.

I wouldn't leave her trapped here like I had been. Mercy had brought me to my doorway, and I wasn't going to leave until I guided her to hers.

And after that, I was going to get the hell out of here and go kick some doppelgänging ass.

AFTER:
MONTREUIL SUR MER, FRANCE

We navigated our way through back roads toward Calais, where the underground tunnel linked France to England. It would be our passage to salvation or ruin, and we hoped the tunnel would make us hard to detect. Parker guided us with a crumpled map we'd found in the Range Rover's glove box.

Isiris knew I was out, and she knew generally where she could find me. I didn't know exactly how she would do it—"Look sharp, my evil twin's on the loose"?—but I had no doubt she was hunting us.

We passed through hamlet after hamlet, all of them like a still-life replica, devoid of motion. Houses stood stoic. Shopfronts hung open, inviting commerce. Streets wound empty. Green hills rolled. Unlike St. Petersburg, there were no children nailed to VisionCrest iconography. Unlike Paris, there were no suspicious trails of pungent smoke curling from prison camp furnaces. There was no air of disrepair or civility undone—but I feared what lurked behind those closed doors.

"I'm starving," Parker announced as we drove up a steep hill, passing a sign that said *Montreuil Sur Mer*. I looked in the rearview mirror at her and Dora sitting together; they seemed to have formed an instant bond. I could tell that Parker was really speaking for Dora, who looked like she literally was starving.

The smooth brown walls of a medieval rampart enclosed the village at the top of the hill. I wished we could hunker down behind its rounded corners and high walls and hide forever.

"We're close. Calais is a few hundred kilometers from here," Hayes said.

"I only speak miles," Parker replied.

Hayes raised an eyebrow at her in the rearview mirror.

"We should stop and find some food and water," I said. As much as I dreaded doing it, we had a lot in front of us and although she'd never say it, Dora was in a fragile state.

Hayes nodded, then put his hand briefly on my leg. He knew I was thinking of Dora.

Nobody said a word as we rolled to a stop in the tiny main square. The village looked like something out of a picture book—squat brick buildings faded to a crumbling, pasty cream by the passage of centuries; curlicue lamps arching from their corners; trellises full of wilting red-bloomed flowers and overflowing vines; ornate-lettered signs boasting *Hostellerie* or *Restaurant* jumbled along the sides of a bold, peak-roofed building. It looked like a place where nothing bad could happen.

The sound of our car doors shutting echoed off the buildings, amplified in the silence. The rolling green hills in the background projected false tranquility, the smell of the sea in the air a devil's peace. The sun shone down as if it hadn't gotten the memo about the end of the world.

Cookie-cutter houses with white walls and red roofs dotted the road. They were shabby and spare but charming, with pie-crust windows that invited visitors. There was a sign in one of them that read: *What is happening to our babies?*

We walked in silence down the smooth cobblestone center of the lane. There was a low din coming from an open shopfront down the street. Like moths to a flame, it drew us in. It was a bakery, the pastries lined up in the case visible through the front window. I could see the flashing reflection of a television in the glass case. As we approached, the static din coalesced. The voice coming through it was a twisted version of my own. Isiris.

"I'll go in," I said.

"I'm coming with you," Hayes said, a steely glint of determination flashing in his eyes.

"We'll wait here," Parker said. She grabbed ahold of Dora's hand. Dora looked off into the distance—I knew she recognized the voice, too.

Hayes and I crossed the threshold. A bell tinged above our heads.

There, suspended from the ceiling in the corner of the shop, was a television projecting the image of Isiris. The

VisionCrest symbol was super-imposed over her face, then faded as the message embarked again on its repeating loop. I looked for signs of weakness, but it was impossible to discern Isiris's physical state.

Everything in the broadcast looked produced, enhanced. There were flowers in Isiris's hair and her eyes glowed green. She was sitting in an elaborate, throne-like chair. The Vision-Crest symbol loomed above her.

"Citizens. There are enemies at our gate. They give me no choice. The time for the purification is upon us."

The image cut away to a huddled mass of prisoners in gray uniforms. Right at the front there was a shock of red hair, a glint of braces, that I immediately recognized.

"Truman," Hayes breathed.

Tears sprang to my eyes as I noticed other familiar faces— the prisoners from the ferry. They hadn't made it, and Isiris wanted to be sure I knew it. This was a message meant for me. This blood was on my hands.

Whimpering and crying, people fell to their knees one by one, choked by some invisible source. Tears of blood leaked from their eyes, boils erupted from beneath their skin. I had seen this before, in the visions Isiris used to send me. It was the virus. She knew I was free, and she was commencing her planned apocalypse. Time was up.

"Today, we start the world anew."

The camera panned wider, and now I saw Adam sitting at her side, the two of them seated behind some elaborate altar inlaid with a jeweled replica of the Inner Eye. His face was drawn, his eyes vacant and hollow. He looked made up—

computer-enhanced. It was impossible to discern his physical state.

"From your Inner Eye," Isiris said.

"Inner Peace," Adam finished. The low timbre of his voice sent a familiar wave of emotion through me, like the twisting of a knife.

The image of the VisionCrest symbol reappeared on-screen, the background fading to black. Then it re-started again.

Hayes re-animated, stalking toward the counter and vaulting over it. He grabbed the pastries from the case and bottles of water from the refrigerator and shoved them in his bag, slinging the haul angrily over his shoulder.

I imagined all the people, from this and other towns, watching this message over and over.

That was when I saw them, through a crack in the door at the back of the shop.

"Hayes," I whispered, my voice strangled with horror.

My feet were rooted to the spot; I was no longer paying attention to the television as people I thought we'd saved died all over again. Wedged in the crack of the door was a plain brown shoe, attached to a man's leg. The shoelaces were untied. It was the shop owner. Through the crack, I could see the rest of his family, huddled together. There was a mom, the tendrils of her copper hair forming a protective curtain, her arms curled around a little boy and a little girl, no older than five or six. There was a faded pink bunny clutched between the two little ones, its ears drooping. Each of them wore the VisionCrest symbol around their necks, as if they hoped it was a talisman that would save them. The father was reaching for them, his fingertips not quite grazing the tangle of arms and legs that was his family's final moments. All four of them had threads of blood seeping from their open, unseeing eyes. It dripped on the floor next to an ice cooler.

On the floor lay the shattered remnants of a crystalline VisionCrest logo—the ones that Isiris had sent out for people to prove they were faithful members of the Fellowship. The red liquid had evaporated. I suddenly knew what the purpose of those strange icons was. They contained the virus.

There was no saving anyone. Believer or nonbeliever, Isiris would not discriminate. It was the beginning of the end.

Hayes tugged at my arm. I moved as if sleepwalking. I heard a rumbling outside.

The bell on the cafe door dinged again as Parker and Dora slipped inside. Their eyes were wide with fear.

"It's the Watchers," Dora said, her voice verging on panic. "They're here."

I ran to the window, staying low. Down the street, a military-style caravan idled. Watchers poured from the vehicles, strange artillery strapped to their backs that looked like fire extinguishers. They weren't.

"Oh shit," Hayes said. "Shit, shit, shit."

They were flame-throwers. This was the clean-up crew.

Fountains of flame poured forth from the artillery, setting the buildings of the town on fire. It would only be minutes before they reached us. If we waited, we burned. If we ran, they would see us.

"Out the back," I said. "Maybe there's a door."

I led the way, stepping over the man's body and saying a silent prayer for him and his family as we passed. Holding my breath, I threaded through the leaning towers of produce boxes and pastry racks. There had to be a door. There had to be.

The sound of the flame-throwers grew close. I felt the temperature rising. The building next door was on fire. It was coming.

I saw a door. There was no way of knowing what was on the other side, but it was our only hope. The wall next to us began to darken, then melt away. Flames licked through from the other side.

"Hop on my back," Hayes said to Dora. She linked her arms around him. The four of us looked at one another, wondering if it was our last moment.

"Ready?" I asked.

Three pairs of owl-eyes blinked back.

I turned the knob and opened the door. And we ran for our lives.

————

"Do you want to talk about what happened to Stubin?" I asked Dora.

We were by ourselves, picking our way across the tracks of the tunnel in the near-total dark. We'd barely made it out of Montreuil. The back of the cafe had opened onto an alley, which connected to another and then another. After vaulting over fence after fence, we came to an open pasture, where we huddled behind a hay bale and watched from a distance as the city burned and the Watchers moved on. The car was back in the village, so we walked for three full days—plenty of time to fill Dora in on my history with Isiris, which I'd withheld from her for so long. She was hurt I hadn't told her sooner, but understanding. It was in the past now, and if we were going to survive, we couldn't linger there. It did take a while for her to get her head around my explanations about the temple and how it all worked.

We stayed one step behind the Watchers as they burned, pillaged, and camped their way to Calais before going on to wreak destruction who-knew-where. Hopefully none of them were waiting on the other side of the tunnel. The next place I hoped to see them was in hell.

I'd peered into a few windows during our journey, only to see the same tableau repeated over and over. Groups of people gathered around still-flickering televisions, shattered crystal strewn on the floor, Isiris and Adam presiding over the funeral of the faithful. The icons must have had some kind of remote-activated explosive inside them. Luckily, none of us was sick, at least not yet. Immunity might be protecting Dora and me, but the same couldn't be said for Parker or Hayes. Maybe the virus was just too swift-acting to be contagious for long, or else it hadn't mutated yet. Either way, I was grateful.

Every hundred yards or so, the tunnel's emergency lighting system cast a bright gray spotlight on a thin section of the tracks, the dim chemical glow the only thing saving us from total blackout. Sometimes there were bodies—people who had tried to outrun the virus. Hayes had ripped up his

T-shirt and we all had pieces of it wrapped around our faces, as if that might offer some protection. The virus killed fast, and it wouldn't survive long outside a dead host. It was our only advantage, if you could call it that.

I wondered if we were too late—if everyone was already gone. Maybe there was no one left to save.

Adam. Perhaps he could still be saved.

Hayes and Parker had gone so far ahead of us that I could no longer make out their silhouettes on the horizon. I was grateful for the space—they knew I needed to be alone with my best friend right now. Not just for my mental health. It was time we talked about Stubin. And that was just scratching the surface. We'd both gone through so much, and for the first time we hadn't gone through it together.

Dora sighed. "I was with him until the very end. They dragged him right out of my arms. I watched through the tiny grate in my room as they hung him in the courtyard."

Her voice had this detached quality. Like she was recounting the plot of a movie she'd once seen. I reached for her hand and held tight. "Oh, Dora. I'm so sorry."

"He looked right at me, in that last second. Saw me watching through that tiny grate. He was right there, looking at me. I'm so grateful for that moment. The next moment, he was just a puppet dangling from a string."

"He deserved a witness. Everyone does. You gave him that," I said.

It was the only thing I could think of to say, other than how sorry I was.

"Yeah. I gave him that," she said bitterly.

I didn't know what to say. We tramped on in silence for a while. Occasionally one of us would yelp in surprise as our feet thudded against a body, and one time Dora fell down. It was weird, but we sort of didn't acknowledge it; like if we didn't talk about it, we weren't really dodging dead people like land mines.

"So what about you?" she asked, her voice a little brighter. "How did you spend *your* summer vacation? Let me guess ... tropical hideaway? Room with a view?"

"Room with a million views, more like it. I would have sent you a postcard but I couldn't seem to find a stamp."

She laughed. I laughed. Both seemed forced.

"When I was in the temple all that time, I imagined you were there with me. You were the only thing keeping me sane," I said.

Dora guffawed, the sound reverberating off the tunnel walls. "I think we need a new definition for sanity in that case, cuz the old one's past its expiration date." She got quiet for a second. "I'm really sorry Adam left you there, Harlow. In that temple. And I should have known sooner that she wasn't you. How could I not know?"

I stopped walking, our hands still connected. "It's okay."

In a way it was, and in a way it wasn't. If Dora was willing to leave the past behind, then I should be too. It was time to forgive ... mostly, to forgive Adam. Isiris was a master of deception, and she had fooled them both. That was all. I just wished it didn't hurt so much.

Dora made a soft hiccuping noise. She was crying, which

was something she almost never did. I pulled her into a hug and we clung to each other in the darkness.

"I can't help but think of all the things that would have been different if I'd only realized sooner," she whispered through soft, gasping sobs. "The virus. All the people in those horrible prison camps. The friends we've lost."

My own silent tears ran down my cheeks and onto my best friend's shoulder. The mention of our friends cut deep.

"I saw her in the temple," I whispered into Dora's shoulder.

She sniffled and stopped crying, pulling back. "Saw who?"

"Mercy—she's the one who showed me the door that led back to our world."

The moment I said it, I instantly regretted it. There was only one logical place Dora's mind could go next.

"You saw Stubin too, right? Made sure he got through one of those door thingies okay?" Her voice was manic with hurt and hope.

I shook my head. "I'm sorry," I said. I could barely make out Dora's eyes, shining with tears in the dark.

"Do you know about the babies?" she asked, sniffling.

My stomach dropped. "The stillborn ones," I said. It was a statement, not a question.

"Do you think that has something to do with what happens in the temple?" she asked.

It had been in the back of my mind ever since the baby was stillborn on the ferry. "I think it's because nobody's there to send souls through the doors," I said.

"If we kill her ... " Dora let the sentence trail off.

"Yeah," I said softly.

She didn't have to finish that sentence. *Adam dies*, was one way to complete it. *You have to return to the temple or mankind does too* was another.

"I don't know if I can do it," Dora said.

I knew what she meant. She meant all of it. Facing Isiris, and what came after.

"You won't have to do it," I said. "I'm strong enough for the both of us that way. But I'm going to need you to do something for me."

"Eeny meeny miny moe, anything for my girl Lo," Dora said softly. This was the same rhyme her apparition had used in the temple. A glimpse of the old Dora shone through, though I knew she might never fully return. If I failed, she wouldn't even have the chance.

"All right. When the time comes, I'll tell you. But right now," I said, "let's keep walking."

She put her hand on my arm, stopping me for a moment. "I'm afraid, Harlow. About what's going to happen to us."

"I know. I am too," I said.

Her hand found mine again, and we soldiered on.

BEFORE:
TRAPPED IN THE TEMPLE,
DREAMING OF ISIRIS

Isiris's eyes opened—once, twice. Too heavy. The world was horizontal, a tangle of arms and sheets and slumber. Three times. I had to keep her eyes open for her. Will them open. She was very, very tired. Tired in her bones. Too tired to stir at my presence. Buried deep, far below. Something was wrong. Very, very, very wrong.

Adam came into view. Hovering above, shimmering in and out of focus like a desert mirage. Isiris's hands felt like they were encased in ice. The mattress tilted as he straddled Isiris, one knee on either side of her. His eyes were drowsy with desire. No. Not this. I couldn't bear to be a witness to their intimacy anymore. To feel the boy I love surrender his secrets.

A ghost of a smile graced Adam's face. Foreboding loomed like a shadow.

His fingers closed around Isiris's throat, each finger an icy dagger burning into her skin. His grip was weak, but strong enough. Her head felt like an over-filled balloon, straining to pop. I could feel her heartbeat in her temple. Her eyes strained, her ears popped, everything above Adam's grip pushing out, out, out.

"Stop." I struggled to form the words. Isiris's lips were numb, her tongue would barely move. The word was a jumble of sounds bumping into each other, none of them able to escape.

Adam's fingers faltered, his breathing shallow and rasping. A greedy lungful of air seared Isiris's lungs and tears slipped from her eyes. Adam moaned, a low, guttural sound belonging to an animal.

He flexed his fingers, trying to grip her neck again but unable to make his fingers cooperate. He blinked, slow and heavy like he was fighting to stay conscious. Despite the electric fear sparking through Isiris's central nervous system, despite the fact that I desperately wanted her to die, I was rooting against Adam. If my insight about the blood bond was right, Isiris's death would mean Adam's too. I feared perhaps it didn't go the other way—while Isiris would be weakened by Adam's demise, it might not kill her.

There had to be another way. I had to find it.

Adam placed his palms flat against Isiris's jugular veins and leaned in. Even the diminished weight of his body was leverage enough to cut off her blood supply once again.

I hoped my eyes conveyed a warning. I managed to shake Isiris's head.

No. No. No.

More tears slipped from the corner of Isiris's eyes, but this time they belonged to me. This was the end. One way or another, it *was all over. Pinprick stars swam in Isiris's vision. The familiar dissolving of a film reel, which used to mean the onset of one of my visions, now signaled the final moments of Isiris's presence in the world.*

"Please." The word slipped from my consciousness, exhaled from Isiris's lips.

Adam let out a strangled cry. He crumpled onto the bed beside to her.

"I can't. I can't do it," he cried.

His skeletal frame was racked with sob. Tears ran down his face while his body shuddered. His hair looked blacker, his lips redder, his eyes more sapphire against the stark white of the pillow than ever before. I could see Isiris reflected in an antique hand mirror perched on the nightstand. She was also blacker and redder and more emerald than either she, or I, had ever been. Whatever transformation Adam and Isiris were undergoing, it was a beautiful undoing.

I wanted to reach out and touch him. I wanted to cry until there was no such thing as tears. But Isiris's body would not cooperate.

His sobs subsided, his body too frail to sustain them.

I blinked at him. Turned the corner of Isiris's mouth up into the barest of smiles.

"It's you, isn't it, Harlow?" he rasped.

I nodded, unable to summon another word.

The light in his eyes faded.

"Isiris is going to purify the world. Mass genocide. I'm not strong enough to stop her," he said.

You are, Adam. But you can't.

The injustice of silence was a cold ache within me.

"I think when I get hurt it affects Isiris, too. If I weaken her, maybe…"

So Adam suspected what I knew already—that he was bonded to Isiris. To some unknown extent, his pain was her pain too. I feared what he planned to do with this knowledge.

I coughed, too feeble to react any other way. Adam made a shushing sound and reached his arm up to brush away something on Isiris's face. I felt his touch, just beneath Isiris's nose, as if from a thousand leagues underwater. His hand came away smeared with blood.

"Rat poison. Works pretty good, heh." His laugh was nothing more than a puff of air. "I've been eating a little bit every day, and she's finally losing strength."

I blinked again, hoping it signaled my displeasure.

"Buddha said, 'Holding a grudge is like drinking poison and waiting for the other person to die.' I thought in my case it might actually work. I thought I could do it, but I can't. When I look at her, I still see you. There's only one way to end it now. Maybe that will be enough."

His words chilled me. I knew exactly what kind of end he had in mind—the fevered shine of self-destruction glinted in his eyes.

I couldn't bear it.

The shock of Adam's statement knocked something loose inside my subconscious, and Isiris awoke. She unfurled inside me, rising up like smoke and twining herself around me.

I had no way of knowing if she'd heard Adam's revelation. Or if maybe she already knew.

"No," I said, something bubbling at my lips. The triumph of the spoken word was brief. I couldn't summon any more.

A tiny dot of blood dropped, scarlet against the sheet. I had so much I needed to tell him. That I'd found the door out. That he needed to wait for me. That Isiris was too strong to be beaten that way. But if he could keep her weak, I might find the strength finish her. We could end this together and have the life, the love, that we were meant to have. The way it was supposed to be.

"She's so strong. It might already be too late. But I have to try," Adam said.

His eyes closed. He was drifting away, visibly weakened from talking.

Stay, I whispered in my mind, but the sound was nonexistent. No more substantial than the whistle of the wind through branches in a world far beyond ours. I summoned the strength to push Isiris down. To try and convey one last message to my love.

I found the door, I cried silently in my mind. Please wait for me. I'm coming. I found the door out of the temple.

"Door." My voice was paper thin, but it was there.

Adam's eyes fluttered but did not open.

It was impossible to tell if he'd heard what I'd said. But from the swirl of rage I felt surround me as I slipped away, I was certain that Isiris did. I only hoped she didn't know that I'd also discovered the key to passing through it.

Hold on, Adam, I thought. I don't know how I will save you, but please just hold on.

BEFORE / AFTER

Before. After. Before. After.

Before: trapped in the temple. After: escaped from the temple.

Me, the real Harlow Wintergreen, precariously balanced on the razor's edge between before and after.

I ran. Sprinted away from the temple and the doorway marked with my blood into the outstretched arms of the jungle. Red-fire fear burning in my belly. Teeth aching in time with the *pound-pound-pound* of unsteady feet on unsteady bones. Through the barbed-wire brambles and sticky-hot certainty of what was coming if I didn't, I ran.

It wasn't what I expected freedom to feel like.

I had no idea how much time had passed on the outside since I first became trapped inside the temple. Just as my eyes had once been Isiris's windows to the world, her eyes had shown me many things, those days and nights in my prison. But not everything. Not enough.

The jungle remained unchanged, the eerie purple-green glow of it just the same as it was during that Violet Hour when Adam and I first entered Isiris's nightmare.

Adam. The boy I'd always loved. The boy I still loved. The boy who'd betrayed me, once upon a time. The thought of him propelled my body and mind forward relentlessly. I felt my way by instinct, hoping that I was rushing toward redemption and not oblivion. Hoping that it wasn't too late for him. Or me.

I ran.

AFTER:
LONDON, ENGLAND

"Don't let anything bad happen to you, Missy-moo," Dora said, kissing my cheek. Parker stood awkwardly behind her, watching with a mixture of envy and trepidation. "I'll literally kill you if you do. *Literally.*"

We were standing at a retaining wall on the Thames, where we'd found a tethered motorboat untended. We were about a mile upstream from the Palace of Westminster— where Isiris was holding court and Adam was captive.

I untangled myself from Dora's arms and beckoned to Parker. "You're not getting off that easily. Give me a hug for good luck."

She grimaced a little and swallowed hard, but then she threw her bony bird arms around me like her life depended on it.

"I'll literally kill you too. I would kill you right now if

I thought it would do any good," she whispered, her voice hitching like she might cry, if such a thing were possible.

"I'll look out for her," Hayes said. Waves on the river lapped against the sides of the motorboat. He was standing inside it, waiting for me to finish my goodbyes.

"I'll look out for *myself*. And for him." I jerked my thumb toward Hayes.

"And we'll take care of each other," Dora said, throwing her arm around Parker's shoulders.

The thing I'd made Dora promise to do for me was to take care of Parker, and I secretly made Parker promise to do the same for Dora—she was too weak to take on Isiris, and too vulnerable to navigate London alone. This arrangement seemed to satisfy both of them, filled as they were with a sense of purpose. It was reassuring to know they were looking out for one another, and if I wasn't mistaken, something more was blossoming between them. The idea that even if this suicide mission wasn't successful, love might survive in this world, filled me with hope.

Hayes had made them a map of how to get to the Resistance's London enclave. There was no guarantee anyone would still be there, but hopefully supplies would be. On the surface, life in London was proceeding at a freakishly normal clip, with none of the death and destruction that had been visited on the rest of the world. People buzzed around the streets with purpose, heading to jobs and homes and television programs.

I'd expected us to be apprehended the moment we'd emerged from the tunnel in Dover, but Hayes had hot-wired a car in the parking lot and we'd driven into London, the traffic thin at first but picking up as we reached the city center. You wouldn't know from looking around that on the other side of that completely empty tunnel, there were bleeding bodies lining the roads of Calais and an all-but-abandonned Paris. The legitimate world news media had been obliterated, replaced with VisionCrest's talking heads. The only sign of the apocalypse in London was a woman, rabid in rags, ranting on the corner about stillborn babies. She was carried off by Watchers while we peered on from a darkened alley.

Even though the Internet was down, and lines of communication decimated, London carried on as if the rest of the world weren't crumbling. It was the same way the first world had always operated. Willful ignorance. If they were at all aware that the downfall of civilization was coming for them too, they never let it rise into their collective consciousness. Yet they must have known, on some level, that the Vision-Crest-imposed "quarantine" meant to keep them safe from a mysterious virus ravaging the outside world was a grave sign.

"Go on," Dora said. "Get the H-E-double hockey sticks out of here." She held her hand out to steady me and I reluctantly climbed into the boat.

I was going to rescue Adam. Tonight. Right now. If he was still alive to be rescued.

Hayes pulled back on the engine and it sputtered to life. Dora blew a kiss to me. Parker gave me a reluctant smile.

We lurched into the night. I sat down on the bench seat and watched Dora and Parker recede on the shoreline, tears slipping from my eyes. It felt like I might never see them again. I hoped I was wrong.

When they were nothing more than watery smudges reflected in the river twilight, I looked back at Hayes. He was squinting up-river, which was completely empty but for a few stray buoys. A chill breeze ruffled his hair. I wondered where all the other boats were. It was another subtle symptom of the hateful new reality that was eating away at this city like a cancer.

I looked at the mole beneath Hayes's lip, the strong tilt of his muscular shoulders, the confident way in which he navigated us toward a danger he could have just as easily ignored. After a moment he felt my eyes on him, and turned to meet my stare.

He gave me a sad smile, like he knew this was probably the end of the small something between us instead of the beginning. Whether Adam was alive or dead, it likely wouldn't matter much—what was between me and Hayes was unlikely to survive either outcome. If we survived at all.

The hum of the motor was too loud for us to say this in words, but we didn't need to. The look that passed between us was enough.

———————

My stomach bobbed up and down, up and down, in time with the sickening rhythm of our boat. The hulking shadow of Westminster rose from the Thames, its sandstone spires twisting toward the blue-green, near-night sky. It was like a paper doll cutout. At its back right corner, the massive clock tower, Big Ben, began to chime. If it weren't so terrifying, it would be magical.

I examined the intermittently lit stained-glass windows of the vast complex, wondering which one I'd looked out of when I'd invaded Isiris's mind. The Palace of Westminster was like a Russian nesting doll, each layer paradoxically rising from and folding in upon itself at the same time. Each turret and tower seeming to loom and collapse all at once against the choppy black-white backdrop of the raging river.

"Harlow," Hayes said.

I turned to look at him, my eyes adjusting to the sight of him as if to a stranger. It seemed to me now—here with him, yet moments from Adam and Isiris—that I barely recognized him. Had I really been in his arms? Kissed his lips? It seemed like a dream. The only thing that felt real was Adam's heart, imprisoned within those close-by walls.

But if that was true, why did my traitorous pulse speed up when I looked at Hayes? Maybe I loved him. But I couldn't think about that now. Not when Adam's life depended on my loyalty. On my love.

"We're almost there." The simplicity of his words belied the depth of what was happening behind his golden-brown eyes. He gave me a wry half-smile.

I thought about the last time I'd seen Adam. The deep blue of his eyes. The way his black lashes brushed his cheeks. The way his cold fingers had curled around my neck. The way he'd shuddered and cried like he was broken.

I wondered if we would ever be normal again.

Probably not. Then again, we'd never been normal in the first place.

Finally, the palace loomed above us. I imagined Isiris somewhere within those turrets. Thought about my own fingers curling around her neck. Squeezing till her eyes really did pop from their sockets. What would happen to Adam if I did? What would happen to me?

Hayes killed the engine and we drifted toward the cement blockade that prevented the palace from crumbling into the Thames. The river was very low this year, so we had a long way to climb.

"I expected there to be Watchers. Or someone," Hayes said.

"I've barely seen any Watchers the entire time we've been here. It's weird," I agreed. "Then again, maybe she's just that sure of herself."

"I was kind of hoping to watch you command your way into another building—it's pretty hot."

"You're twisted," I said.

"Isiris is an idiot to underestimate you like this," he said.

"She's not an idiot. She wants us to find her."

A silence fell between us, my words like stones.

"Hold this," he said finally, hefting a length of yellow nylon cord my direction.

The unexpected weight of a grappling hook at the cord's end made me bend over. "Where the hell did you get this?" I asked.

"What? Were you expecting Rapunzel to let her hair down? I brought it in my backpack," Hayes said.

The insolent smile I loved, but pretended I didn't, graced his face. Even with the likelihood of probable death facing us, Hayes still had a sense of humor. That was often a great quality in a boyfriend in some twisted world. Maybe in this one.

I looked up at the retaining wall. Unlit lampposts lined the balustrade at the top, dotted at short intervals along what must be some sort of promenade in front of the palace. Ideally I could toss the hook up and over the railing, but getting it onto one of the iron lampposts would probably do as well. I threw the hook as hard as I could. It sailed over the railing on the first try, and I tugged it firmly into place. The most gratifying moment of the evening thus far was watching Hayes's eyebrows raise in appreciation as the hook found its mark just over the lip of the barrier. I hid my surprise and tried to look smug instead.

"Thank whoever's in charge of this crazy universe for small miracles," I said.

"I'm a big fan of small miracles," he said, his lips quirking into his signature smile.

"Of all the times to be flirting, this is an interesting choice," I said.

"Who's flirting?" Hayes held his hands up in surrender.

A somber quiet fell between us. We knew that was likely to be our last moment of levity.

I turned and looked up at the rope. It was the last obstacle between me and rescuing Adam; the last barrier that lay between me and confronting Isiris. I gave Hayes one last glance over my shoulder, wrapped my hands around the slippery, silky rope, and hoisted myself up. The burn in my arm muscles was an oddly satisfying reminder that, at least for now, I was alive.

Halfway up the two-story climb, that burn wasn't so satisfying anymore. A freezing wind had been blowing steadily, making my ears ache and biting the skin of my fingers, which were so cramped that everything in me screamed to let go, just for a second. Right, and plummet to my death. No big deal.

Hayes was dangling not far below me. I knew I was holding him back. Given the ease with which he pulled himself higher every time I finally made a few feet of progress, he could have shimmied up this rope in a few minutes.

"You got this, Harlow," he whisper-yelled.

I nodded and gave him a smile, this one far weaker than the last.

"I got this," I said to myself. My arm muscles felt as if searing-hot pokers were being driven through them. My quads were like two slabs of stone as I tried desperately to keep them locked together. I had only about twenty feet to go, but it felt like two hundred. I didn't think I had anything left in me.

And then I saw her. In the highest bank of windows, smack in the center of the palace facade. She was backlit by some kind of soft glow, her face close to the glass and one arm leaning against the frame to brace herself.

Isiris.

Her skin was pale, and her lips tinged blue. Her hair hung in limp strands. She leaned forward and rested a cheek against the cool pane of glass. She looked tired but satisfied.

Like she hadn't a care in the world. Like she'd already won. All she had to do was cast her eyes down and she would see Hayes and me attempting to breach the palace walls. Then she really would have won.

Our fate was balancing on the razor's edge of one small movement, one tiny choice that was Isiris's to make or not. And it filled me with fury.

It couldn't happen. I willed her to leave.

She receded back into the shadows, and I began to breathe once more.

I memorized the window—five floors up, ten windows in from the right. That was where I was headed. My arms sprang to life, and I recruited every muscle in my body to inchworm the last precious feet.

"Gah!" With one final gasp, I pushed myself up and over the side of the wall and collapsed on the solid ground.

A minute later, Hayes's leg swung over the side. In an instant he was on the ground next to me, heaving away. We stayed like that for a moment, gulping freezing-cold air.

"Ready for some heroics?" he asked quietly, still breathing heavy.

"Sure, why not. I've got nothing else to do."

The sound of footsteps on flagstone echoed from around the left-hand corner of the building. Hayes sat up like a shot and pulled me by the arm to follow, tossing the grappling hook off the ledge. We took off running, down the promenade in the opposite direction. The hook hitting the water making a dramatic splash that drew a battalion of Watchers from around the corner. Hayes and I plastered ourselves against the palace facade, where the promenade dead-ended in the right-hand turret of the palace. There was no getting around the side of the building without inching along a ledge above the water. Apparently this place wasn't entirely without protection after all.

As the Watchers peered anxiously over the lip of the wall, murmuring to one another in alarm and confusion as they spotted our abandoned boat lingering below, Hayes motioned to me silently. We climbed up onto the ledge, shuffling as lightly as we could across the cement and hiding in the shadow of the building. The wind on my chapped cheeks felt like a warning—one serious gust and I'd be blown off this ledge and into the freezing Thames. One glance from a Watcher and we would be shot dead on sight.

Hayes never let go of my hand, just kept me shuffling slowly, slowly, to the side. At last we slipped around the right-hand corner and Hayes jumped down onto a darkened side lawn. Big Ben loomed above us, the ghoulish green glow of the lights shining up on it from below making it seem threatening. Hayes held his hand up to me and I jumped down. He caught me in his arms. He was solid, just like always.

Up ahead was a wrought-iron gate fifteen feet high, spiked crowns dotting its top. My stomach plummeted. We didn't have long. Maybe only minutes.

Please take care of Hayes, and let Adam be okay. I wasn't sure if I believed in a higher power, but the mantra made me feel better all the same.

"Check it out," I whispered.

By some twist of fate, or maybe even an answer to my

prayer, the little door cut into the iron gate was ajar. We could see more lawn on the other side of it, and the circular front drive that lay beyond Big Ben. We were one step closer.

I moved toward it, and Hayes grabbed my hand.

"Wait," he said.

Turning, I ran right into his solid chest. He put his hand under my chin and tilted my face up to him.

"What is it?" I asked, even though I could see in his eyes exactly what it was.

"Don't you know by now?" he asked, his voice rough with emotion.

I didn't want him to say it. My own emotions were too elusive.

I nodded. "I know."

Hayes tilted his face down to mine. The press of his lips flooded me with an emotion that might have been joy but could just as easily have been grief. Both emotions made my heart ache with longing. It was getting harder and harder to tell them apart.

Hayes pulled away, his hand squeezing mine.

One way or another, this was the end.

AFTER:
THE PALACE OF WESTMINSTER,
LONDON

If I didn't fear that Isiris was expecting us, the fact that the many doors along the front of the building were unlocked and unguarded would have seemed like an unbelievable stroke of luck. But there was no such thing as luck. This was a trap that had to be sprung.

We slipped through a door without anyone noticing us save a silent security camera, which tracked our motion on its smooth metal hinge. We tried to dodge out of its path, but it followed our every move. I hoped that whoever was on the other end of that camera was asleep on the job.

The corridor we'd entered was narrow, with unremarkable ceilings and dim lighting, and adorned with oil paintings that looked like they'd been conceived by the same painter along one side. The opposite side of the hallway was lined with windows that looked out on a darkened court-yard where naked trees with whisper-fine branches twisted in on each other, like from the curse on Sleeping Beauty's castle. I led the way, and Hayes hustled along behind me. The only sound was our labored breathing as we ran.

I didn't know exactly where I was going, but I'd tapped into some primal source of memory inside me—the part of myself that visited Isiris as I lay dreaming in the temple. The part of myself that I wanted to deny, but which was undeni-ably a part of her.

We came to a fork—left or right? Both were blocked by dark wooden doors in the shape of a bishop's hat.

"Which way?" Hayes asked, keeping his voice low. I had the creeping feeling these walls had ears.

I nodded toward the one in front of me, because some-how I knew the one on the left would be locked.

He opened the door and poked his head in. I got on my tiptoes to look over his shoulder.

All the lights were blazing in the cavernous, wood-paneled room. Tiers of green leather bench seats, arranged stadium style, rose on each side. Boom mikes hung from the ceiling. There was a green, throne-like chair with a wooden overhang presiding at the far end, in the middle of the floor. The VisionCrest symbol hung above it, a gleaming, gold, upside-down triangle with a ruby-irised eye in the center.

This was where Isiris had filmed that message we'd seen in Montreuil Sur Mer.

"The House of Commons," Hayes said. "Before Isiris took over, it used to be the seat of government."

Even on the off-chance we were able to stop Isiris, things would never be the same, given the virus and the anarchy she'd released. There would be no government, at least not like there once was.

"We've got to keep going. You can't see it, but there's a door behind that chair," I said.

"I won't ask you how you know that."

"Perfect, because I don't know," I said as I ducked into the room. We scurried across the floor of the toppled House of Commons.

The next doorway spit us out in a cavernous, square room with dizzying ceilings and arched doors on every side. The only thing I could make out in the darkness were pedestals from which stone-faced statues of leaders lorded their secrets over us from beyond the grave. It looked like it was constructed entirely of white marble and nefarious intentions.

There was one statue, at ground level. And as my eyes adjusted to the darkness, I saw it move.

I jumped, stifling a startled yelp.

Hayes whipped around frantically. "What? What is it?" He followed my eyes.

A Watcher stood there, looking directly at us except for the fact that he had no eyes. As my gaze swept the room, I saw they were everywhere, lined up against the wall like tin soldiers.

"They know we're here, but they're not trying to stop us," Hayes whispered, mystified.

"Either they don't want to or they're following orders," I said grimly.

"She knows we're here," he murmured.

"Like I said."

"So what now?" he asked.

Tip. Tap. Tip. Tap.

The sound of footsteps echoed around the chamber. It was impossible to tell which direction they were coming from. Passageways branched off in all directions.

Tip. Tap. Tip. Tap.

A chill ran through me. Hayes put his hand on my shoulder. Both of us looked around, frantic to find the source. I didn't need the once-familiar buzzing in my brain to tell me who it was.

I looked at the arched double doors directly across the lobby. They were ajar, and a needle of light stretched through the crack.

Tip. Tap. Tip. Tap.

"It's her," I whispered, so quietly it was barely more than a puff of air.

"How do you know?"

"I know."

Hayes drew his handgun out of his pocket. I thought about Adam and Isiris's blood bond.

"No," I said, pushing the nose of the gun down. "Not until I know if Adam's still alive."

Hayes gave me a conflicted look but reluctantly put the gun back in his pocket. His hand, however, remained clutched around the weapon. If Isiris threatened us, there was no guarantee he wouldn't pull the trigger.

We slowly crept toward the barely open doors. The

eyeless sentinels pivoted as we progressed; always facing us, never letting us forget that they were there.

The footsteps began to fade.

Tip … Tap … Tip … Tap.

I rushed to close the distance to the door, pushing against it just in time to see the sweep of a robe disappear through yet another doorway, partially hidden behind yet another marble statue.

It was the lure. After the lure came the hook. But the hook was what I'd come for.

I raced across yet another cavernous rotunda, this one with a five-pointed star embedded in the marble floor. It reminded me of the temple with its symbol of the Inner Eye. I could see why Isiris would feel at home in this house of a thousand doorways, a terrestrial temple for her to haunt.

That was when I heard it, echoing through the bowels of the ancient building. A horrible harbinger.

Someone wailed.

An infinite suffering was contained in that one syllable, and it seemed to come from everywhere at once.

"Adam," I said.

He was alive. Adam was alive, and he was in excruciating, unfathomable, unending pain.

A breeze blew lightly through the rotunda, and the door through which Isiris had disappeared banged lightly on its hinges.

"Nooooo … " Adam moan-wailed again, the sound growing louder and sharper.

"We could leave now. Start over somewhere, far away,"

Hayes said. He put his hand on my arm. He wanted me to make a choice—stay or go, Adam or him—but there'd never really been a choice.

"I can't. I'm sorry," I whispered. "You don't have to come with me."

He didn't respond. He didn't need to; I knew he would never let me go it alone. Hayes was following me to almost-certain death, to help save his rival, because he cared for me. It made me want to wrap myself in him and never leave. But for now there was only one thing left to say.

"Thank you."

I darted toward the almost-hidden door. As I approached, it blew open, a strong gust of icy wind rushing down the staircase just beyond it. On that wind, another wail carried. Whatever Adam was enduring, he couldn't handle it much longer.

I took one last look over my shoulder. "Give me your gun," I said to Hayes.

He hesitated, then flipped it around and gave it to me handle-first.

"Please … please … please … "

Adam's screams crescendoed and I was driven forward. If this was a choice, it didn't feel like one. This was the end, and there was no going back. There never was.

———

The stairs seemed to go on forever. Needles of pain shot through my legs, and a trail of fire blazed through my lungs. At every landing I wanted desperately to collapse, but Adam's screams kept urging me upward, closer all the time. The freezing wind grew stronger and stronger until finally I curved around a landing and looked up to see the top of the stairs.

There were no lights on in the room above me, but still I recognized it from my dreams of Isiris. The sound of the crushed velvet drapes whispering in the winter wind was achingly familiar. The way the moonlight slanted across the gilded walls. The echo of mirrors whose reflections clashed against one another, infinitely.

"Aggghhhhhhhhhh! Agggghhhhhhhhh!!! Aggggg-hhhhhha!"

Adam's anguished cries, no longer human but something more elemental, drove me up the final ascent. I crested the staircase and took in the scene.

He was tied to a regal, wing-backed chair fit for Henry VIII himself. The soft white light of the night sky washed over his bare chest, the vivid tattoos on his pale skin shimmering in the darkness. A thick leather band kept him immobile. The massive picture window behind him was thrown open, the source of the frigid wind blowing in off the Thames. It ruffled his dark hair. His wrists were bound, as were his ankles, and a strap ran between them—if he were able to rise to standing, he would be hunched over, hobbled by the connection between the two.

In the thin light, his eyes were wild. He was covered in fresh blood, but I couldn't identify the wound.

My heart constricted.

I ran to him, my eyes searching the shadowed corners of the room for Isiris. This was her trap, and she was here somewhere. Waiting for me to spring it. Hayes hung back, scanning the room. Waiting for Isiris to emerge from the shadows.

But that didn't matter. What mattered was that the boy I'd loved so hopelessly and desperately was now hopeless and desperate himself. In my peripheral vision I could see the rumpled bed where Adam and I had last spoken. Where I had told him to hold on. Well, here he was. Holding on. And what had it bought him?

I wasn't anyone's savior. I realized that now. Now that it was too late.

I knelt before him. He was skittish and wild. Unfocused. He flinched back from the light touch of my palms on his thighs.

"Adam, it's me. It's Harlow."

I strained to keep my voice from cracking, the tears from breaking free.

His rough breathing halted. Up close I could see nothing wrong with him. No source of the blood splattered across his chest.

"Harlow?" he whispered. "You came."

I nodded, and this time the tears slipped out. They might never stop.

"Yes. Adam, where are you hurt?"

"It's not me," he sobbed. "It's not me, it's not me, it's not me."

He was virtually hysterical.

"What do you mean?" I asked, my hands working furiously at his wrist bindings.

"She knew you would come. She wanted you to see," Adam said.

"See what?" I asked, not stopping.

"Here, use this." Hayes held out the knife that he kept in his boot.

I tucked the gun in the back of my waistband and held out my hand. He tossed me the knife and I went to work.

"All of it," Adam said. "Me. Dora. Other ... things."

I froze.

"What?" I looked up at him. "What about Dora?"

"This is her blood. Isiris carved her up. Her and the other girl."

I dropped the knife and it clattered to the floor. Adam began wailing again.

"No. No, no, no," I repeated over and over. It felt like the world had frozen on its axis.

Hayes picked the knife up off the floor. He sawed at Adam's bindings, freeing his arms while I just repeated the same word, over and over.

"Which way did they go?" Hayes asked Adam.

Adam's chest racked with sobs. "Harlow, you have to forgive me."

Hayes grabbed him by the shoulders.

I heard a muffled scream from somewhere in the building. It sounded both near and far away. It was Dora.

"Which way?" Hayes yelled.

"You know what you have to do, Harlow," Adam said, ignoring Hayes.

More excruciating screams—this time in symphony.

Parker and Dora were somewhere nearby, being taken apart piece by piece by my enemy.

I knew what Adam meant. Knew what I had to do to stop Isiris.

I pulled Hayes's gun out of the waistband of my pants. I swung it around, the weight of it like finality in my hands.

Click. The safety pulled back, driven by fingers that felt disconnected from my body.

Adam went very still. His jaw set. There was no more fear on his face—only resolve.

"You have to finish it," he said. "She doesn't think you can."

"What the hell, Harlow?" Hayes asked, panicking. I remembered he didn't know about the blood bond.

Adam held his arms out to me, embracing the bullet that would end his life. "I didn't mean for it to happen, Harlow. Do you forgive me?"

"Don't, Harlow," Hayes whispered. "This isn't you."

"There are things you don't know," I said to Hayes, my voice tight.

"It doesn't matter," he said.

The gun was aimed squarely at the VisionCrest symbol tattooed over Adam's heart. It was so close, the shot would make it explode on contact. Painless. Quick.

"Do it. Please," Adam begged.

I dropped my aim.

Hayes was right. I wasn't a killer. No matter what else happened, that line separated me from Isiris. From becoming what she was.

"AHHHHHHHH!!!" Another scream echoed down the hall.

Adam's eyes cast feebly in the direction of one of several elaborate mahogany doors circling the room. He pointed with his chin. "Go that way."

Hayes handed Adam the knife. "Save yourself and don't look back. You're pretty good at that."

Adam's head hung down, his dark hair obscuring his downcast eyes. "I need you to forgive me," he whispered once more, looking at the floor.

I forgive you. My lips moved, but the words would not come.

Adam didn't look up.

"Come on, Harlow," Hayes said, tugging at my arm. "Let's go get Dora and Parker."

I nodded, coming out of my daze.

I wasn't sure there was any point. I had no bargaining chips left on the table. Still, I had to try.

AFTER:
THE PALACE OF WESTMINSTER,
LONDON

Isiris was waiting for us just down the hall. Candles lit the way as we passed the tall, unseeing sentinels of her Watcher army.

The double doors were cast wide. Inside the chamber, Isiris sat on a backlit dais with two VisionCrest symbols hanging on the wall behind her, on either side. Something was pinned to each of them, squirming ever so slightly. Moonlight flowed in through the window, flickering shadows dancing against the walls. It was a grander, darker, more elaborate version of what we'd found in the House of Commons. And more gruesome.

"Let me handle her, Harlow," Hayes said, trying to move around me.

"No," I said. "This battle is mine."

Hayes hesitated, then acquiesced. "I'll be right behind you the whole time."

We moved farther into the room, and the horrifying tableau Isiris had laid out for us emerged from the shadows.

Hung upside down, their bodies pinned in triangle poses to the VisionCrest icons, were Dora and Parker. Dora to Isiris's left, Parker to her right. Their clothes hung in tatters, soaked through with the blood that poured in rivulets from their bodies and pooled on the floor beneath them. Dora had gashes all over her body, each one in the shape of the Vision-Crest symbol. Some of them were deep, the layers of fat and muscle sparkling as they sluiced blood. Parker was in even worse shape, one of her eyes sliced to ribbons, fleshy whites hanging in flaps, tears running red.

Isiris clutched knives in her fists, dripping scarlet. It was a threat, a promise of more. With one swift move, she could drive the dagger into either of them and send their souls onward, to the unguarded temple.

Dora stared at me, her lips trembling. Parker was disoriented, unable to see clearly through the river of blood pouring from her injured eye.

I was so transfixed by the horror of it that I almost missed the most terrifying thing of all.

"Welcome to the end of your world," Isiris said, standing.

Her belly was round.

My knees went weak. Isiris was pregnant.

With Adam's baby.

There was no way that I could kill her now, no way I

would even try. She was evil, but her baby—Adam's baby—was innocent.

This was what Adam had meant when he said Isiris wanted me to see "other things." This was why he was begging my forgiveness.

"You're..." I said.

"About to be a mother, yes. It's Adam's, of course." She smiled beatifically, like some virgin saint.

"A m-mother?" I stuttered.

Isiris moved toward Parker, ignoring me. Her white dress and pregnant belly were outlined in the moonlight. She wrapped one hand possessively around Parker's bird-like wrist, then twisted it until it crunched. Parker howled.

Her other hand rose up. The blade glinted, beautiful and bright. She drove it through the palm of Parker's hand, pinning her to the Inner Eye, and then ripped it back out. Small shreds of tendon and flesh were visible through the gaping wound.

Parker cried out.

"I think I might pull them both limb from limb like little voodoo dolls. There will be a point at which one of them will be able to withstand no more, and I wonder who will be first. Care to make a wager on it? If you guess right, I won't do the same to your little boyfriend here." She jutted her chin toward Hayes.

Parker's good eye watched me, her mouth set in a grim line as she battled against the pain.

"It's not them you want. You want me," I said.

"You should have stayed where you belong," Isiris said.

"This is what you *made me* do. To your world. To the ones you love. And when it's all over, you will go back to the temple anyway."

I looked from Parker to Dora, Dora to Parker. Outrage boiled inside me. Isiris might think she was a goddess, but I was no deity and I'd bested her at every turn. I might have been entirely ill-equipped to take her on, but she had another Achilles heel and I knew how to exploit it.

"Tie them up and tear them apart all you want. They'll always be mine," I said.

The smug look on Isiris's face didn't falter. "The virus is loose in London now," she said. "You and your friends die tonight. By tomorrow morning, the world will be pure. Ready to start anew." She caressed the curve of her stomach.

"It's so sad you couldn't make Adam love you," I said. "You tried so hard, but still, I'm the one he loves."

Isiris's smile fell. "My baby will love me," she said.

"Your baby will be born dead."

Isiris roared, slashing the knife across Dora's face. The wound gaped, but Dora did little more than whimper.

"My baby is a god."

"As long as we're both out of the temple, no baby will live. Is that a chance you want to take?" I asked.

"You're going back there," she said. "I will put you there myself."

"Oh, but you can't. You thought you knew the secret to escaping the temple, but you were wrong. You thought another Guardian needed to be put in place in order for you to leave, but that's not it. You got lucky. I know the real way to get out."

"I'm not interested in how to get out. I will hobble you and make sure you can never escape," she threatened. But she didn't sound so confident anymore.

Then Isiris turned and drove a blade into Parker's thigh. It made a horrible sucking sound when she withdrew the knife, blood spurting out from the wound. Parker only moaned, her energy flagging. They couldn't take much more. Neither could I.

"Don't pretend that you have the upper hand," Isiris said.

The tick of the grandfather clock in the corner, the one I'd heard so many times in my dreams, counted off the seconds that Dora and Parker and Hayes remained alive. Every one of them counted.

"I'll go back to the temple," I said.

"What?" Hayes whispered, behind me. "Harlow, no."

"But my friends will come with me," I added.

Giving Isiris what she wanted was the only way to stop her short of killing her. And that was something I wouldn't do. I would send Dora, Parker, and Hayes on to that other New York I'd found. And I would stay to guard the gate. To ensure that in some other world, they and their children would survive.

"What about Adam?" Isiris asked.

"He will stay here, where he belongs," I said.

"You know about our bond, right? I know you do."

"Yes. What hurts him, hurts you."

Hayes drew a sharp breath behind me.

"But you were too weak to kill him. I knew you would be," she said.

She turned to Dora, tracing the cold tip of the blade up Dora's side, over her ribs. Dora gasped in fear, but Isiris didn't drive it in.

I felt Hayes snatch the gun out of my waistband. I grabbed his hand, fumbling with the cold, heavy lump of metal, slipping over its rounded ridges looking for purchase. Isiris crouched into a defensive stance, holding the sharp-edged blade against a pale, vulnerable patch of Dora's throat.

"Screw this. I'll kill her myself," Hayes rasped.

I touched his wrist, staying his hand. "No. We're not murderers," I said.

"That's very touching," Isiris said. She dragged the blade across Dora's throat, deep enough to draw blood but not enough to kill. "You're just not strong enough kill me, even to save the people you love," she mocked.

She drove the blade into Dora's shoulder, then out again. She plunged it into her arm, then out again. Dora couldn't take much more. Isiris was killing her. I had to stop it.

I lifted the gun, pointing it at her. My whole body began to shake. Tears ran down my face.

"Without a guardian in the temple, your baby will be born dead. And you and Adam will be alone in your new, godforsaken world," I said.

"You won't do it," she said, smiling.

She plunged the knife in again, this time to Dora's leg. Dora didn't scream. Her eyes fluttered closed.

"No!" I let loose an animalistic scream. I ran up to the

dais, still pointing the gun at her. "I'm not as weak as you think I am."

My finger hesitated at the trigger.

In the smudgy shadows behind her, I saw the glint of moonlight off a blade. The knife. We had left it with Adam, and now it was here. In his hand, lurking in the shadows.

Isiris didn't know Adam was behind her. Maybe he was going to try and cut Dora and Parker free, but I knew she would never let that happen. She would kill them first.

I looked Isiris in the eyes. My own eyes, and yet so much colder and emptier for what was not behind them. Once, I'd worried that being of Isiris made me like Isiris. Now I could see it wasn't true. What made me Harlow were the choices I made. Isiris was where I'd started, but I was everything after that.

I'm not like you, I thought.

As I took my finger off the trigger, she smiled.

She was going to win.

There was a flicker of movement behind her. Adam. He had the knife clutched in his hand and he was looking at me. Suddenly, I knew exactly what he planned to do.

"Adam, no!" I yelled.

Isiris spun around, a moment too late. Adam plunged the blade into the tender flesh of his biceps, hitting the brachial artery that was pulsing fiercely behind the tangled tattoo jungle. He would be dead in seconds.

A fountain of blood splurged from his arm in pulsing beats—one, two, three. He staggered, then fell to his knees, knocking into Isiris as he crumpled to the floor.

Isiris faltered as the deathblow hit her too, the weight of her belly throwing her off-balance as her knees gave way beneath her. She fell to the floor. Her Watchers crumpled to the floor—marionettes with their strings cut, her mind control interrupted.

Blood pulsed from Adam's wound, a lake of blood forming around him. Isiris lay motionless beside him.

Hayes ran up to the dais and pulled me to my feet. "Are you okay?" he asked, holding me up by my shoulders.

I wrenched free and went to Adam. He took a feeble, shuddering breath. A thick lake of blood pooled around him.

It was over. Almost.

I grabbed Adam's hand. His fingers curled around my palm.

"Adam," I said, tears dripping off my face.

"Forgive me," he whispered.

"I forgive you, I do. I'm sorry I didn't say it sooner. I'm so sorry."

Adam's breath was shallow and fast. "I love you. I always did," he said.

For one moment, his vision cleared and his eyes locked onto me. I got one last glimpse of his sapphire eyes, shot through with silver like doves in flight. Then they closed for the final time.

I hung my head over his chest and broke down into sobs. The boy I'd idolized, the one I'd thought existed only in my heart, was in there all along. He wasn't perfect. But in the end, he was the boy I'd always wanted him to be.

Hayes felt for Adam's pulse, then shook his head. Adam was gone.

I caught a movement out of the corner of my eye.

Isiris.

There was a rippling across her belly. The outline of a foot appeared, kicking, kicking. I stared at it, transfixed.

Slowly, like a zombie arising from its grave, Isiris squirmed to life. Her hand moved to her stomach. Her eyes fluttered open. She was weak but alive.

"I knew you would protect me. Our bond is stronger than any other," she whispered.

It was the baby. The life force inside her was what had saved her.

For a moment, I imagined plunging the knife into her abdomen. Ending it all. For good. But I wasn't that person. I wasn't a monster like Isiris.

"Hayes, tie her up!" I yelled. "I'll get Dora and Parker down."

Hayes sprang into action, tearing a length of braided rope from the dais and immobilizing Isiris's hands and feet as I set about freeing Dora and Parker.

"It's gonna be okay," I said, smoothing Dora's hair. She and Parker were in bad shape, but they weren't going to die. I wasn't going to let them.

"I knew you'd come," Dora wheezed, a faint smile gracing her blue lips.

Parker stayed silent, but her breathing was steady.

I glanced over at Isiris, who was unconscious and hogtied on the ground.

"You're going to be okay," I said. "We all are. I promise."

Hayes knelt down next to me, putting a comforting arm around my shoulders.

"Are you sure you don't want to kill her?" he asked.

"No. She goes back in the temple where she belongs."

I thought of my bloody handprint—how I'd marked the gate to our world with crimson. How blood was the key that had allowed Isiris, and then me, to escape the temple. When we went back, I would wash that handprint away. Isiris would never learn the secret.

"You wouldn't have to kill her yourself. I'd do it for you. I'd do anything for you," Hayes said.

I met his eyes. The love I saw there healed the first of the million tiny wounds inside my battered soul.

"We can't become like her. We have to be worthy of starting over," I said.

He nodded.

"Get the video room ready. Before we take her back there, we have a message to film."

AFTER:
TWIN FALLS, IDAHO.
FORMER VISIONCREST
HEADQUARTERS

There's this picture of Adam and me on the desk that used to belong to my father once upon a time, when VisionCrest still existed, when Isiris was still just an echo in my head. We're both dressed in these ridiculous white robes, the ones we sometimes wore as pre-initiates. Dora snapped a picture of us with her cell phone; we were goofing off like we weren't supposed to, both of us open-mouthed and glitter-eyed. Adam's telling some kind of joke, and I'm looking at him in obvious adoration. I always thought I was so on the down-low; I wonder if he knew all along that I loved him, or if he was as oblivious as I always thought he was.

It doesn't matter now. He's gone from this world, and I'll

never really know the answer. I think maybe he's out there in a million other worlds, living incredible lives. I'll never know that either. But there's a lot that I do know.

"Am I interrupting something?" Hayes asks, poking first his head into the room and then his whole body. His brown hair is mussed and his gray T-shirt sweaty from a recently-finished basketball game. He's always playing with the kids who lived here, now that we've turned the former VisionCrest headquarters into a community for the precious few who managed to survive Isiris's apocalypse.

My heart swells at the sight of him. I already have more good fortune in this life than anyone has a right to, and there are still miles to go before I sleep. At least, I hope there are.

I shake my head and smile. "No. I was just thinking."

"That's been known to be hazardous to your health," he says, leaning in to kiss me on the forehead. I know he knows I've been looking at the photograph again. That's the good thing about Hayes—he doesn't push. He knows my gradual yet complete loss of Adam is still death by a thousand cuts, each memory, each thought, each reminder another shallow slice across my heart. He tries his best to heal them, each and every one. And he does a pretty damn good job. Maybe one day it will be just me and Hayes, and the memory of Adam will be just that—a memory. A sweet one, I hope.

"I have a telecast in an hour," I say.

There are now outposts of survivors on three continents—bands of people intent on repopulating the world. Beginning it anew.

He nods. "Need some company?"

His brown eyes are warmer than ever, the flecks of gold seeming to swim with emotion. Hayes loves me more deeply than I ever could have hoped.

After we'd broadcast our message from the palace, it hadn't been hard for us to sell what was left of the world a story about my long-lost twin sister, who'd kidnapped me and then held me hostage while she ravaged the world and usurped the VisionCrest throne. The craziest lies are the closest to reality, I guess. To be honest, the virus had already done its damage. With the exception of a few survivalists, isolationists, and a lucky few who had natural immunity, the world as we knew it was gone. Isiris's crystal Inner Eye trinkets had made their way into enough homes on the planet—due to the fear that not having one would result in deportation or worse—that the virus had made very efficient work of modern civilization. She'd even lived up to her promise to wipe out London; by the morning after Adam sacrificed himself to defeat her, most of its citizens were gone.

Together, Hayes and I tore VisionCrest down and built something else—something stronger and better. Not a religion, but an organization to help people who needed it. It was Dora's suggestion, actually. She and Parker help us run our new organization, which we call Mercy's Hope. Mercy's Hope is for all the people ravaged by Isiris, whose future is now an empty and sometimes bleak canvas. It's for the new world we're creating, together, now that the old one is just a memory.

Dora and Parker got married one month A.I., *After Isiris*. They were young, yes. But it's not the same now as it once was. Dora was still in a wheelchair from the injuries she'd sustained at the hands of Isiris, and Parker wore an eye patch adorned with leather and lace, but luckily none of the blows had struck anything life-threatening. They adopted a baby—the first one that was born after we put Isiris back in the temple. Its mother was one of the survivors of the virus, but she was too weak to withstand the labor. She lived long enough to hear her baby boy's first cries. The beginning of a new world.

Dora and Parker named him Adam.

Together, we've accomplished more helping the world rebuild than my father and Isiris ever did destroying it. Sometimes doing something small can be bigger than the whole wide world. At least, that's the story that helps me sleep at night. And despite the fact that it seems completely crazy for people to look to me for guidance after all they've gone through at the hands of my so-called twin, they do it all the same. I'm their leader, for better or worse. It makes me wonder if my father would be proud of me, but it also makes me feel powerful.

And feeling powerful makes me feel afraid.

Because try as I might to deny it, people believe in me. The more good I do, the greater their faith in me. The greater my success, the closer they come to worshiping me. I don't want this; it just happens. At least, I tell myself I don't want it. And I'm not sure if I could stop it. Or if *I* could stop.

Whenever these thoughts plague me, I worry that maybe it's Isiris—invading my mind, influencing me from afar. Starting the cycle once again. But the truth is, I'm the only person I ever find inside my mind. Maybe I'm too strong for her now.

Maybe after everything that happened, it isn't possible for her to trespass against me. Maybe she's ceased to exist. Maybe.

Hayes smiles at me, though his eyes flicker just for an instant to the picture of me and Adam.

"Company?" he asks again.

"I'd love some," I say, taking a breath and standing up. Trying to pretend I'm entirely here with Hayes, not existing in my memories of Adam.

His hand slides down my back and he burrows his face into my neck. He smells like salt and sun. Like the sea. He is handsome. Brave. Loving and thoughtful and kind. In this life, for all it is and is not, I am so lucky.

"Come on, it's showtime," I say. And take his hand.

All my fears about Isiris vanish. We put her back where she belongs. Babies are being born now, and the world turns and turns. What happens from here is anyone's guess.

EPILOGUE

Isiris woke up, her arms aching in a human way. An entirely foreign sensation, and yet one that, having been free in the world, she recognized implicitly. They were twisted behind her, bound. Her feet were, too. She was blindfolded. Something writhed in her belly.

Memory was impossible.

There was a gun. There was a knife.

There was screaming. There was blood. There was nothing. There was now.

The nerves of her shoulders pinched and her hands felt like a million icicle pinpricks. A violent spasm took hold of her middle.

Her baby. It was coming.

Out of the darkness, a tiny sliver of light invaded like a surreptitious crescent-moon behind the blind. Beating wings. A press of wind. The Violet Hour, once again.

No. No no no no no.

Gun. Knife. Screaming. Blood. Nothing. Now. Baby. No.

Over and over the sequence raced, her fingers squirming to be free, the tiniest give beginning in the bindings that held her.

This was colossal in its unfairness. It simply could not be. Hot flames of rage consumed her; her body wrung itself inside out.

She was not here. This was not real.

She pushed, even though she did not want to.

She would go to sleep and wake from this nightmare.

Gun. Knife. Screaming. Blood. Nothing. Now. Baby. No.

It came anyway.

———————

It took her a hundred Violet Hours to break free from her bindings. Another fifty to regain her strength. Ten determined days to clear what souls she could and banish the rest to the bowels of the temple. Five days to teach the little beast that toddled after her what must be done in her absence. One to find what she was looking for.

A smear of blood. Another.

A signal.

A sign.

Faded, as if someone had tried to erase its existence.

A crimson gate.

The portal was just as she'd remembered it—verdant and lush. Full of a glowy, leafy, greenness. Everything beyond it was obscured.

At first, the blood had puzzled her. Trails of it wound their way throughout the temple.

But when she saw the ghost of it on the door, she knew. She *knew*.

How that stupid man had made it out with Harlow when she was a baby, so long ago. How she herself had made it out in Harlow's place. How Harlow had escaped to find her and thwart her and tie her up and bring her back here.

Blood was power.

They all thought she was stupid. She wasn't stupid.

All along, she'd thought that one of them needed to be present in the temple. That this was the secret, the rule. But it wasn't the rule. The rule was: no guardian, no babies.

But the *secret* was blood. Just like her bond with Adam. It was blood that held them in and let them out. Blood was power.

A flash of fury ignited inside her once again, but this time she quickly turned the flames to smoldering ash. It was time for action. Vengeance could come later.

She looked around, evaluating. Found a suitably jagged edge. Turned to her daughter.

"You are the guardian," she said.

The girl raised a chubby hand in answer. "Mama."

"Be a good girl now."

The Violet Hour came. She slashed her hand and pressed forward through the door.

And just like that, she was through. Back into Harlow's world.

Vengeance. It was time.

She blinked in the near-dawn light. It wasn't what she'd expected. There were trees and there was green, but there were also paths. There was concrete and life.

The dub-thrub of a jogger's shoes along the footpath beat a rhythm above her head. This was no Cambodian jungle. It was some kind of park. She had gone through the wrong door.

Isiris craned her neck.

Thought of going back. Trying again.

Then thought the better of it. There was havoc to be wrought.

She wandered on. Over a path, down a set of stairs. She saw a sign. It read, *Central Park*.

This world would do as well as any.

Maybe it was time to try again.

Acknowledgments

To every reader. Thank you. You are my favorites.

Hugs and kisses to my family. Thank you for the limitless love and support.

Agent extraordinaire, Jennifer Laughran. Thank you, you are a gem.

Not to mention … Brian, Sandy, Mallory, and the entire Flux team! Thank you.

Kid Lit bloggers. Thanks for helping my books find more readers. Extra love to Jean BookNerd!

YA, That's Why! Martha, Ingrid, Heidi, and Veronica. Thanks for helping me shine.

One Four Sisters. Best ever.

Unparalleled. Unending. Unbelievable. Thank you to my one and only, Reid.

Photo by Kate Davis

About the Author

Whitney A. Miller lives in San Francisco with her husband and a struggling houseplant. She's summited Mt. Kilimanjaro, ridden the Trans-Siberian rails, bicycled through Vietnam, done the splits on the Great Wall of China, and evaded the boat police in Venice. Still, her best international adventures take place on the page. Visit her online at WhitneyAMiller.com.